FROM GOVERNESS TO COUNTESS

Marguerite Kaye

This book is produced from independently certified FSC™ paper to ensure responsible forest management.

For more information visit www.harpercollins.co.uk/green.

Printed and bound in Spain by CPI, Barcelona

MILLS & BOON

Published in Great Britain 2018
by Mills & Boon, an imprint of HarperCollins*Publishers*
1 London Bridge Street, London, SE1 9GF

© 2018 Marguerite Kaye

ISBN: 978-0-263-93269-0

Th ... per

Marguerite ... ...es from her home in cold and draughty ~~~~ Scotland, featuring Regency rakes, Highlanders and sheikhs. She has published almost fifty books and novellas. When she's not writing she enjoys walking, cycling—but only on the level—gardening—but only what she can eat—and cooking. She also likes to knit and occasionally drink Martinis—though not at the same time. Find out more on her website: margueritekaye.com.

For my cousin Allison Rankin,
who requested that her namesake be a feisty heroine
with red hair. Be careful what you wish for!

This is also for Alison Lyndsay and Alison Lodge,
heroines in their own right. A huge thank-you for your
generosity and support, in terms of research and book
recommendations, and most of all for your friendship.

Prologue

⧼⧽

Hampstead, near London—summer 1815

The village of Hampstead enjoyed an enviable location on the fringes of the capital. Though its popularity as a spa retreat had declined somewhat, the fresh, clean air and its proximity to London had encouraged a number of well-heeled new residents to settle there. Passing through fruit farms and dairies on her journey from the city, the woman known only by her enigmatic epithet The Procurer had enjoyed the rustic charm and tranquil atmosphere of her surroundings, a stark contrast to the hustle and bustle of London where she plied her clandestine trade. Reining in her greys, she brought her phaeton to a halt before summoning a small boy standing idly nearby. She handed him the reins and proffered a sixpence. 'I am looking for a Miss Galbraith.'

The child's eyes widened, though he accepted both the reins and the coin. 'Me mam says she's one as don't want to be found,' he answered in a hushed voice. 'She don't answer the door to no one.'

The Procurer's face tightened at this tangible evidence of the woman's fall from grace. If it was at all possible, she was determined to provide this most deserving of cases with the means to redeem herself. No one deserved to be vilified by the gutter press in the manner she had been. Provided, of course, Miss Galbraith was a satisfactory match for her client's requirements. The Procurer approved of altruism but drew the line at charity. 'Then it is as well that I am someone,' she said crisply to the boy. 'Rest assured, she will answer the door to me. Now, point me in the direction of her abode, and no more of your lip.'

The cottage was located at the end of a row on the far edge of the village. It had a sunny, south-facing garden, but it was sadly neglected and overgrown with weeds. Though the street appeared deserted, The Procurer had the distinct impression that behind the curtained windows of the other cottages, the occupants were watching intently. As she picked her way up the little path to the front door, the contented buzzing of bees collecting pollen from the thicket of wild roses filled the air.

The cottage looked for all the world as if it was uninhabited. The windows were tightly shuttered. The shape of the door knocker was outlined by the bleached paint, but the mechanism itself had been removed. The Procurer rapped sharply with her knuckles.

'Please go away, I do not receive or welcome visitors,' a voice from behind the door urged.

'That is disappointing to hear, since I have travelled from London to discuss a matter of great import with you.'

'Then I'm afraid you have had a wasted journey. Whoever you are, and whatever it is you want, I cannot help you.'

'You mistake my purpose. It is I who have come to help you. But I cannot do that if I am to be left standing on your doorstep. Will you not invite me in and at least hear me out? I am acquainted with your recent history and understand your natural suspiciousness, Miss Galbraith, but I bear you no ill will, I assure you.'

There was no immediate response but The

Procurer's patience was rewarded about thirty seconds later when the door opened just enough for her to slip inside before it slammed shut again.

The woman who stared back at her in confusion bore a clear resemblance to her many newspaper caricatures, though her expression was wary, rather than evil. Her distinctive bright copper hair was tied in a simple chignon, not tumbling wantonly over her shoulders as it was customarily depicted in the press. Her chin was determined, but her mouth was soft and full. Of petite stature, she looked to The Procurer to be twenty-five or six, though she had, according to the gutter press, turned thirty. There were shadows under her big hazel eyes flecked with gold, her skin had the dull, lacklustre look of someone who had been hiding from plain view, skulking in the shadows. 'Do not look so afraid, Miss Galbraith,' she said, 'I truly have come here to help you.'

'I am sure you mean well, but you are mistaken. No one can help me.'

'Not if you are determined to let Dr Anthony Merchmont and his medical cronies destroy not only your reputation as London's pre-eminent herbalist, but your entire life.'

Allison Galbraith's eyes flashed with anger at this barb. An encouraging sign, The Procurer decided.

'As you have pointed out, my reputation is already in tatters.'

'Very true,' The Procurer conceded. 'However, six months have elapsed,' she continued briskly. 'Time to embrace a new challenge. I can offer you rehabilitation.'

'Impossible.' Miss Galbraith's voice was resigned. 'Look, I have no idea who you are, but…'

'I am known, rather fancifully in my opinion, as The Procurer. You may have heard mention of me.'

The revelation was met by a surprised widening of the eyes, a mouth curved into the faintest of smiles. 'All of London has heard tell of The Procurer, though few have ever encountered you in the flesh. I was not aware you were a fellow Scot. I certainly did not expect—' Miss Galbraith broke off, blushing. 'You are so young and nothing like…'

'The person my reputation would suggest? Then we have that much in common, do we not?'

A dejected little laugh greeted this remark.

'We might, if I still had a reputation. Your position in society is quite unassailable, while I...'

'You are a social pariah.'

A harsher laugh greeted this remark. 'You certainly do not mince your words.'

'In my business, straight talking is essential.'

'Then I will reply in a similar vein, madam. I cannot for the life of me comprehend why you should wish to help me.'

'I know what it is like, Miss Galbraith, to be a woman in a man's world. To succeed as you did—and as I have—requires an uncommon level of determination and ambition. The sacrifices you have made, the hurdles you have overcome, would have defeated a lesser character.'

'But not you?'

The remark was intended to be flattering, but provoked a different reaction. 'I have succeeded on my own terms, but at considerable cost,' The Procurer said, as much a reminder to herself as a boast. She would not permit herself to wonder whether the sacrifices had been worth it. 'It is not simply a matter of character, Miss Galbraith. I am in control of my own destiny and answerable to no one, that is true, but it was not always so.'

'In that sense we differ greatly, madam,'

Miss Galbraith replied wryly, 'for even at the height of my success, I was beholden to society.'

'And society chose to condemn you. Now you are choosing to abide by that judgement. Do you agree with it, Miss Galbraith? Or do you think you deserve a second chance?'

'Is that what you are offering?'

'I am offering you the opportunity to fashion a second chance for yourself. What you make of it is very much up to you.'

'Why me?'

The Procurer smiled faintly. 'We are kindred spirits in more ways than you can know. You are also, as you pointed out, a fellow country-woman and we Scots must stick together.'

'Forgive me, but since we are speaking plainly, you do not know me. I cannot believe your motives are entirely philanthropic.'

The Procurer nodded with satisfaction. 'There, you see, we do understand one another. We are both, in our way, hard-headed business-women. As such, you will not be offended, I am sure, if I tell you that I have carried out exten-sive diligence on you to my satisfaction. I have a business proposition for you, Miss Galbraith, which will be mutually beneficial, as all the best contracts are. Now, shall we make ourselves more comfortable, and I will explain all.'

Allison spooned camomile leaves into the china teapot and set it down on the table beside the cups and saucers before taking her seat opposite her unexpected and uninvited guest.

'You were exceedingly difficult to track down,' The Procurer said, looking perfectly at home, 'though I can understand your desire to avoid the unwelcome glare of publicity.'

'Notoriety would be a more apt description. In another few months I will be old news, and the world will find a new scandal, another cause célèbre to salivate over.'

'Is that what you are hoping for?'

Resentment flared as Allison met her visitor's challenging look. What could this elegant, haughtily beautiful woman with her flawless complexion, her black-as-night hair and her tall willowy frame, clad in the kind of understated carriage dress that screamed affluence, truly know about shattered dreams, about ravening guilt, about endless, sleepless nights going over and over and over those vital hours and asking, *What if? Could I have done something differ-*

ent? Should I have done something different? Would it have made any difference if I had?

'If you mean, do I think I will be able to re-establish myself, then the answer is no.'

'So what, precisely, are your aspirations? To avenge yourself on the man who has engineered your spectacular fall from grace, perhaps?'

Allison took her time pouring the tea. There was something about The Procurer's clear, steady gaze, that made her feel as if the woman could read her innermost thoughts. Even those she didn't choose to admit to herself. 'I have no aspirations at all,' she said, 'save to be left in peace.'

If she expected compassion, she was destined to be disappointed. 'If you really mean that,' The Procurer answered, 'then I am wasting my time.'

'As I have already informed you.'

'But you don't mean it, do you?' The Procurer took a sip of the fragrant tea. 'You are angry, and with just cause, for you have been made a scapegoat, your livelihood stolen, your reputation left in tatters. You have been the subject of lurid headlines, both libellous and slanderous and, I hasten to add, patently false. That is punishment out of all proportion to your alleged crime, if indeed you are culpable?'

Allison's hands curled into fists, but she could not stop the tears from welling. 'I committed no crime,' she said tightly. 'But to speak in the plain terms you prefer, I will tell you that I cannot be certain I was entirely blameless.'

She was trembling now. The memory of that night, her role in the events that unfolded, however significant or not that role might have been, threatened to overwhelm her. She screwed her eyes shut, opening them only on feeling the fleeting, comforting touch of The Procurer's hand on hers. 'How can I not blame myself?' Allison demanded wretchedly, for the first time, and to this complete stranger, allowing herself to utter the words. 'I did not believe, did not question—until *he* did. And now I will never be certain that I was not culpable in some way.'

'No, but you can ask yourself, Miss Galbraith, what are the odds? Have you ever before miscalculated so badly or made such a catastrophic mistake?'

'Never! Nature has defeated me on occasion, but I have never precipitated such a tragic outcome.'

'And yet you meekly accepted the verdict and the punishment as if you had.'

'Yes, I did, and now it is far too late to contradict it, even if I wanted to.' Allison thumped her fist on the table, making the teacups shake in their saucers. 'The medical profession in our country...'

'...is a cabal of exclusively male-vested interests, whether it be doctors, surgeons, or apothecaries. There are midwives, granted, but even the most skilled do not carry any real authority. You, on the other hand, had gained a real foothold in society as a gifted herbalist. You were a successful woman, Miss Galbraith, a real alternative to accepted medical practice and as such, a threat to the old guard, as the systematic defamation of your character has demonstrated.'

'Yet no one, not a single one of my former patients, has spoken out in my defence.'

'They too must accept the rules of society, the world they inhabit. Has it occurred to you, Miss Galbraith, that your refusal to practise once that tragic event became public confirmed your guilt?'

'It certainly confirmed what I should never have lost sight of,' Allison said bitterly. 'I am an outsider. Despite all my efforts to conform to their standards, they had no hesitation in stabbing me in the back. I am not, and never will be one of them. They would have found another excuse to point the finger at me sooner or later.'

'So you have chosen to surrender, to grant them their victory?'

Under The Procurer's steady gaze, Allison bit back her instinctive denial, and contented herself with a shrug.

'Guilty, innocent or plain negligent, you have spent the last six months in hiding, sitting on your hands,' The Procurer continued. 'It is not Anthony Merchmont who is preventing you treating patients, is it, Miss Galbraith? Do you not miss your vocation?'

'More than I could ever have imagined,' Allison replied instantly. 'It means everything to me, to heal pain, to help...' She stopped short, fighting for control. 'Do you know the worst thing, madam? They destroyed more than my reputation, they destroyed my confidence.'

'Doubting yourself is a perfectly natural consequence of what you have been through, but I speak from experience when I counsel you to overcome that fear, lest it destroy you.' A shadow clouded The Procurer's eyes, though it was quickly banished. 'If I were to provide you with an opportunity to utilise your specialist knowledge and experience, would you grasp it?'

'It is not possible,' Allison said automatically, though she was already wondering if it was, for The Procurer's calm, matter-of-fact logic had roused her crushed spirit to push aside its suffocating blanket of bitterness and regret.

'My reputation, Miss Galbraith, has been forged by making the impossible possible. Whether you give me the opportunity to prove that to be well founded is entirely dependent on you.'

'But I can't. You said it yourself, I am a social pariah. No one in London…'

'The position I require to be filled is not based in London.'

'Oh.' Oddly, it had not occurred to her to consider a change of location from the city in which she had worked so hard to establish herself. But it made sense, if she was considering emerging from her hibernation. And that was an apt word. She felt as if she had been sleeping, or living through a nightmare. Was it over?

'Where, then?' Allison asked.

The woman smiled very faintly in acknowledgement of this progress. 'All in good time.

You must understand, this is no ordinary contract of employment that I offer you.'

Extraordinary. Allison's grandmother had always told her that was what she should aspire to be. Ordinary, Seanmhair always said, was for life's passengers. Would her grandmother expect her to grasp at this straw? The answer was a resounding yes, but did she possess the courage to do so? The answer to that was suddenly both clear and unambiguous.

'I flatter myself,' Allison said, 'that I have demonstrated myself capable of the extraordinary. As you pointed out, I have succeeded against the odds.'

'I take it then, that you are willing to consider my proposal?'

It took Allison a few moments to recognise the fluttering in her belly. Not fear, but anticipation. She had not dared allow herself to hope, but suddenly here was hope, and—oh, good heavens—she wanted it so much.

'Well?' The Procurer raised one perfectly arched brow.

'Yes.' The relief was almost overwhelming. 'Yes,' Allison repeated more firmly. 'Just tell me what it is you require me to do.'

But for several long agonising moments The

Procurer said nothing, studying her closely through heavy-lidded eyes, as if she were a specimen in a laboratory. Allison held the woman's gaze, clasping her hands tightly in her lap to stop herself squirming. The woman's smile was slow to dawn, but when it came, it would be no exaggeration, Allison thought, to liken it to the sun coming out.

'A very wise decision on your part and on mine too, I believe. You will do very well for the vacancy I have been asked to fulfil. Now, to business,' The Procurer said briskly. 'Before I disclose the nature of your appointment, I must apprise you of a few non-negotiable ground rules. I will guarantee you complete anonymity. My client has no right to know your personal history other than that which is pertinent to the assignment or which you choose yourself to divulge. In return, you will give him your complete loyalty. We will discuss your terms shortly, but you must know that you will be paid only upon successful completion of your assignment. Half-measures will not be tolerated. If you leave before the task is completed, you will return to England without remuneration.'

'Return to England?' Allison repeated, somewhat dazed. 'You require me to travel abroad?'

'All in good time. Do you understand me, Miss Galbraith? This conversation, the details which I am about to unveil, are given in complete confidence. Unless I can guarantee my discretion to my clients—'

'I understand you very well, madam,' Allison interrupted. 'Discretion is—was—intrinsic to my calling too.'

'Another trait we have in common, then. Do I have your word?'

Allison startled the pair of them with a peal of laughter. 'Madam, you have ignited the flame of hope I thought was quite extinguished. You have my word of honour, and you can have it signed in blood if you wish it. Now please, tell me, where is it I am to go, and who is this mysterious client of yours?'

Chapter One

⧼◦◦◦◦◦⧽

St Petersburg—six weeks later

The voyage across the North Sea to the Baltic coast had been both speedy and surprisingly comfortable. Standing on the deck of the ship as they docked at the port on the delta of the Neva River, Allison wondered if The Procurer had, amongst other things, arranged for the winds to consistently blow in the most advantageous direction, and instructed the sun to welcome her arrival. It beamed down from the cobalt-blue sky, making the majestic buildings which fronted the river glitter as if studded with jewels.

Allison had been prepared, by several enthusiastic fellow travellers, for the grandeur of St Petersburg, but the city known as the Venice of the North by dint of having been constructed from thirty-three islands, was, in reality, infinitely more beautiful than she could have envisioned. She gazed around her, quite dazzled by grand frontages in pastel colours, huge pillars supporting imposing porticoes, golden domes soaring into the sky, and as the Neva River wended its way into the heart of the city, a vista of bridge after bridge spanning its banks.

A flotilla of small boats bobbed on the azure-blue waters. Stevedores called to each other in what she assumed was Russian, the words like no others she had ever heard, and Allison began to panic. The Procurer had assured her that French and English were the languages used by the aristocracy and their entourages with whom she would be mingling, but what if The Procurer was mistaken? What if this was an elaborate trap? What if The Procurer was in actual fact a procuress? What if she had been brought here under false pretences, to serve not as a…

'Miss Galbraith?' The man made a bow. Just in time, she noticed he wore a royal blue-and-gold livery, and spared herself the embarrassment of addressing him as her new employer.

'I am come to escort you to the Derevenko Palace,' the servant said, speaking just as The

Procurer had promised, in perfect, if heavily accented, English. 'I have a carriage waiting to take you there.'

Allison picked up her travelling herb chest by the brass handles, staggering under its weight, but waving the servant away when he made to take it from her. 'No, I prefer to keep this with me, the contents are extremely precious. The rest of my baggage…'

'All necessary arrangements have been made. The journey is a brief one. If you will follow me?'

She did as he bid, swaying a little as her feet adjusted to the solid ground beneath, coming to an abrupt, awed halt in front of the transport which awaited her. The carriage was duck-egg blue elaborately trimmed with gold, a coat of arms emblazoned on the doors. Another servant in the same livery sat on the boxed seat, holding the reins of two perfectly matched white horses. Inside, the plush squabs were the same royal-blue velvet as the groom's livery, the floor covered in furs.

Peering through the large window as they trundled into motion, Allison observed that they turned immediately inland, following a road alongside a canal. The waters sparkled.

The grand houses glittered. The sun shone. Everything looked so very perfect, so very beautiful, so very, very foreign and strange. A bridge spanned a small river not straight enough to be a canal, and the carriage followed the embankment for a short distance, passing ever more majestic mansions, before slowly drawing to a halt.

The groom opened the door and folded down the step. 'Welcome to the Derevenko Palace, Miss Galbraith.'

It was indeed a palace. The edifice faced out over the river, on the other side of which was a vast expanse of open ground where what looked like a cathedral was under construction. Her first impression of the Derevenko Palace was that it reminded her of Somerset House on the Strand, neo-classical in style, three storeys high, with two wings stretching from the central portico, terminating in two smaller pedimented wings set at right angles, the shallow roof partially hidden by a carved balustrade. Above the central section, which was constructed almost like a square tower, a massive eagle-like stone bird was perched, gazing imperiously down its vicious curved beak at the shallow, sweeping staircase, and on Allison, who stood in trepidation on the bottom step. She shivered, thoroughly intimidated and battling the urge to turn tail and flee.

And where did she think she would go? Back on to the ship, back to the reclusive life she had been so delighted to leave behind?

Absolutely not! This was her second chance. She would not fail the woman who had presented her with it. More importantly, she would not fail herself. Not this time. Reluctantly handing her herb chest over to the groom, Allison straightened her shoulders, gathered up the folds of her travelling cloak and followed the manservant inside.

The interior made the façade of Derevenko Palace seem almost plain. A long strip of rich blue-and-gold carpet covered a floor of silver-and-pink stone laid in a herringbone pattern, which glittered under the glow of a magnificent chandelier. The carpet continued straight through a small entrance hall into another, bigger reception hall where two huge bronze lamps lit with a halo of candles flanked a sweep of enclosed stairs. Allison had a fleeting impression of immensely high and ornately corniced ceilings, before she was led up three flights of stairs to a half-landing, which then opened out into two stairways with elaborate bronze-gilt balustrades which in turn led to a massive atrium lit from above by light pouring through a central glass dome.

The servant paused in front of a set of double doors elaborately inlaid with ivory, mother of pearl and copper. He straightened his already perfectly straight jacket, and knocked softly before throwing the doors open. 'Miss Galbraith, Your Illustrious Highness,' he declared, waiting only until Allison edged her way into the room before exiting.

Your Illustrious Highness? Allison was expecting to meet a minor member of the aristocracy. She must surely be in the wrong room. Sinking into a low curtsy, she saw her own surprise reflected in the man's demeanour. He had turned as the servant announced her, but took only one step towards her before coming to an abrupt halt. From her position, on legs still adjusting to being back on land, precariously close to toppling over, he looked ridiculously tall. Black leather boots, highly polished, stopped just above the knee, where a pair of dark-blue pantaloons clung to a pair of long, muscular legs. Which began to move towards her.

'Surely there is some mistake?' the imposing figure said. His voice had a low timbre, his English accent soft and pleasing to the ear.

'I think there must be, your—your Illustrious Highness,' Allison mumbled. She looked up, past the skirts of his coat, which was fastened with a row of polished silver buttons across an impressive span of chest. The coat was braided with scarlet. A pair of epaulettes adorned a pair of very broad shoulders. Not court dress, but a uniform. A military man.

'Madam?' The hand extended was tanned, and though the nails were clean and neatly trimmed, the skin was much scarred and calloused. 'There really is no need to abase yourself as if I were royalty.'

His tone carried just a trace of amusement. He was not exactly an Adonis, there was nothing of the cupid in that mouth, which was too wide, the top lip too thin, the bottom too full. This man looked like a sculpture, with high Slavic cheekbones, a very determined chin, and an even more determined nose. Close-cropped dark-blond hair, darker brows. And his eyes. A deep Arctic blue, the blue of the Baltic Sea. Despite his extremely attractive exterior, there was something in those eyes that made Allison very certain she would not want to get on the wrong side of him. Whoever he was.

Belatedly, she realised she was still poised in her curtsy, and her knees were protesting. Rising shakily, refusing the extended hand, she tried to collect herself. 'My name is Miss Allison Galbraith and I have travelled here from England at the request of Count Aleksei Derevenko to take up the appointment of governess.'

His brows shot up and he muttered something under his breath. Clearly flustered, he ran his hand through his hair, before shaking his head. 'You are not what I was expecting. You do not look at all like a governess, and you most certainly don't look like a herbalist.'

Allison, dressed in the most sombre of her consulting attire beneath her travelling cloak, bristled. 'Ah, you were expecting a crone!'

'A wizened one with a hairy chin,' he said, with a smile that managed to be both apologetic and unrepentant.

'I'm sorry to disappoint you on both counts,' Allison replied, finding it surprisingly hard not to be charmed.

His smile broadened. 'I find your appearance surprising, but far from disappointing. In my defence, I should tell you that I have very little experience on which to base my assumptions. I've never hired a governess until now and I've never before required a herbalist's services. Forgive me, I am being remiss. I am Count Aleksei Derevenko,' he said, making a brief bow. 'How do you do, Miss Galbraith?'

Hers was not the only appearance to evoke surprise. This man did not look remotely like the father of three children in poor health and in need of English lessons. Portly, middle-aged, whiskered, red of face, bulbous of nose, is how she would have pictured such a man if she was in the habit of making sweeping assumptions. He would not have long, muscled legs that so perfectly filled those ridiculously tight breeches as to leave almost nothing to the imagination. He most certainly would not have the kind of mouth that made a woman's thoughts turn to kissing. Or those eyes. Such a perfect, startling blue. Why couldn't they have been watery or better still, bloodshot? And why, for heaven's sake, was she thinking about him in such a manner in the first place?

'I am not at all sure how I do, to be perfectly honest,' Allison replied, inordinately flustered.

To her surprise, he laughed. 'No more do I. It

seems we have both confounded expectations. It is to be hoped that the person who brokered our temporary alliance knows her business. Let us sit and take some tea. We have a great deal to discuss.'

Aleksei ushered the Englishwoman to the far end of the reception room where the tea things had been set out on a low table, the samovar hissing steam from its perch on the woodchips. Solid silver, enamelled with white, blue and gold flowers, the delicate cups a matching pattern, the service was, like everything in this huge palace, designed to demonstrate the Derevenko dynasty's wealth and lofty status. He had forgotten just how important appearances were, here in St Petersburg. No other European court—and on his travels, he'd been obliged to attend many—was as status conscious or such a hotbed of intrigue and ever-shifting alliances. No wonder that the woman now sitting opposite him on one of those ridiculously flimsy and uncomfortable little chairs had mistaken him for a prince, hearing that preposterous epithet. *His Illustrious Highness*, indeed.

She was clearly nervous, though she was trying not to show it, compulsively smoothing her gloves out on her lap. He still couldn't quite believe that *this* was the woman The Procurer had promised him would be the answer to his urgent plea, that *this* was the woman whose arrival would signal the end of his agonising enforced spell of inactivity and allow him, finally, to begin his search to uncover the truth.

It struck him uncomfortably, as he looked at her, that the problem with this particular woman was not that she didn't look like his preconceived notions of either a herbalist or a governess, but that she looked like his starved body's idea of the perfect woman to take to his bed. Her hair was the colour of fire. No, that was too obvious. It was the cover of leaves on the turn, of glossy chestnuts, of the sky as the sun sank. She was not conventionally beautiful, there was nothing of the demure English rose, so universally admired, about her. She was something wilder, untamed. Her skin seemed to glow with vitality, her figure was not willowy but voluptuous. She had a mouth that made a man think of all the places he would like those lips to touch. And then there were her eyes— what colour were they? Brown? Gold? Both? Was it her heavy lids that made him think of tumbled sheets and morning sunshine dappling her delightfully naked rump?

Aleksei cursed under his breath. Since Napoleon's escape from Elba, followed by Waterloo, and the formal mourning period he had just completed here in St Petersburg, he had been deprived of all female company, but this was most definitely *not* the time and place to be having such thoughts. Allison Galbraith was not here to satisfy his inconveniently awakening desires. He should be contemplating her suitability for the task, not her body. Though he could not deny that her body was one that he'd very much like to contemplate.

Would anyone believe her a credible replacement for Anna Orlova the previous, long-serving governess? A paragon, if the servants were to be believed, utterly reliable, and much loved by the children. Whether or not she returned that affection, Aleksei had no idea, since Anna Orlova had abandoned her charges and fled the Derevenko Palace long before he had had a chance to set eyes upon her.

He picked up the teapot which sat on top of the samovar, only to drop it with a muted curse as the heated silver handle scalded his palm. Covering the handle with the embroidered linen cloth designed for that very purpose, he saw that Miss Galbraith was staring at the urn with a puzzled look. 'You are not familiar with the ceremonial Russian tea ritual?' Happy to buy himself time to regather his thoughts, when she shook her head Aleksei concentrated on the performance. 'This is the *zavarka*, the black tea, which we brew for at least fifteen minutes, unlike you English, who barely allow the leaves to kiss the hot water before you pour.' Kiss? An unfortunate choice of verb. Touch, then? No, that was even worse!

He concentrated on pouring a small amount of *zavarka* into her cup, a larger, stronger amount into his own. The samovar hissed, reminding him that he had not completed the teamaking ceremony. 'This is *kipyatok*,' he said, 'which is simply another word for boiling water. Would you like a slice of lemon, some sugar?'

'Is that permitted?'

'It is not traditional, but I have both available if you wish. Our tea is something of an acquired taste.'

'I will take it as it is meant to be served. When in Russia, as they say.' Miss Galbraith picked up her cup and took a tentative sip.

She did not quite spit it out, but her screwed-up little nose and her watering eyes told their own tale. Biting back a smile, Aleksei held out the sugar bowl.

Using the tongs, she dropped three cubes of sugar into the tiny cup. 'I hope you don't think I'm being impertinent, but may I enquire why your wife is not here to greet me? I assume it is from her that I will take my instructions?'

'Her absence is easily explained. I'm not, and never have been married.'

'Oh.' Miss Galbraith coloured. 'I see,' she said, looking like someone who did not see at all.

'The children are not mine,' Aleksei explained, 'they are my brother's.'

She frowned. 'Then may I ask why you are— why I am not having this discussion with your brother and his wife?'

'Because they are both dead.' Drinking his own, thick black tea, a soldier's brew, from the ducal cup in one gulp, Aleksei registered the widening of her eyes, and realised belatedly how stark this statement sounded. 'Michael and Elizaveta died in May this year, within a few days of each other.'

Which attempt at tempering the shock made things worse. Miss Galbraith blanched. 'How awful. I am so terribly sorry.'

'Yes.' Aleksei curbed his impatience. It *was* awful, but he'd had almost four months to accustom himself to it. 'However, the formal mourning period is now over.' *Did that sound callous?* 'My brother and I were not particularly close.' *Even worse?* Best to just get on with the matter in hand. 'It is the consequences of his death which concern me, Miss Galbraith, and that is the reason you are here.'

'Consequences?'

Though he was relieved to be back on track, Aleksei found himself in a quandary. It was already clear that the distractingly luscious Miss Galbraith had been only partially briefed by The Procurer woman. Her reputation for complete discretion was well founded, thank the stars, which meant he had the luxury of not having to launch into a full exposition of what he euphemistically referred to as consequences to a complete stranger just off the boat. But precisely how much to tell her?

Aleksei decided to proceed with caution. 'Michael bequeathed me the guardianship of his offspring in his will—I have no idea why, for he did not consult me on the matter. I am, as my brother knew perfectly well, as unsuitable a guardian for his children as it's possible to imagine, and have no intentions of continuing in the post once I can secure a more suitable candidate. At which point, Miss Galbraith, your duties will come to an end.'

'Oh. Then my appointment as governess—you envisage it being of very short duration?'

'I sincerely hope so. What I mean,' Aleksei continued, noting her slightly startled expression, 'is that I hope *my* appointment will be of short duration. Four months ago, when I received word of Michael's death, I was preparing to do battle with Napoleon's army. Having done my duty by my country and my men at Waterloo, I was obliged to return immediately to St Petersburg to take up my new, unasked-for duties. As you have no doubt surmised, I did not take kindly to having been bounced from battle to babysitting without a moment to catch my breath.'

'Though Napoleon's defeat has made it unlikely that you'll have to fight any battles any time soon, has it not? Now that Europe is at peace you can surely be more easily spared to devote yourself to your new duties.'

Aleksei blinked at this unexpected riposte. Miss Galbraith, it seemed, had recovered her composure, and inadvertently unsettled his by pointing out a truth which had not occurred to him and which he had absolutely no desire to contemplate. 'I am a soldier, have always been a soldier, and have no wish to be anything other than a soldier. Peace has certainly granted me the freedom to fulfil the obligations my brother forced upon me, but that does not mean I wish to spend the rest of the foreseeable future acting *in loco parentis*.'

'I see.'

She did not. She thought him callous. Aleksei bristled. He did not need to justify himself to her. 'The children will be far better off in the care of a guardian who understands the workings of the court, and how best to raise them to take their place in it.'

'To be perfectly frank, I know nothing of royal courts and their etiquettes. I hope you were not expecting…'

'You need not concern yourself about that. Apart from anything else, the children are too young, though Catiche…'

'Catiche? I'm sorry, but I know only that there are two girls and a boy, I have no idea of their names and ages.'

'That, I am pleased to tell you, I can easily remedy,' Aleksei said. 'Catiche—that is Catherine—is thirteen. Elena is ten. Nikki, my brother's heir, is four. You will make their acquaintance the day after tomorrow. When I had word that your ship had docked this morning, I packed them off to stay with friends for a couple of nights, to allow you time to settle into your new surroundings.'

'Thank you, that was thoughtful. May I ask how the little ones have coped with the loss of their parents? They must have been devastated.'

'They seem perfectly well to me,' Aleksei replied, frowning, 'though my time is so taken up with my brother's man of business that I see very little of them which, assuming they are being raised as my brother and I were, is no change to the status quo. They have a nanny, a peasant woman as is the tradition, who has cared for them since they were in the nursery. If they were devastated by anything, it's more likely to have been the loss of Madame Orlova, their governess of some years' standing.'

'Loss? Good gracious, don't tell me that she too perished? Was there some sort outbreak in the palace, a plague of some sort?'

'No, no—you misunderstand. Madame Orlova left her post somewhat abruptly the day before my brother died.'

Miss Galbraith said something under her breath in a language he did not recognise. 'Those poor little mites. What appalling timing. What prompted her to leave?'

'I have absolutely no idea and nor have I been able to discover a single person in the army of servants here who does. I've tried to locate her, but if she's in St Petersburg then she's very well hidden, and I've been unable to widen my search since I am loath to leave the children for any sustained period without proper supervision. Now you are here, I intend to make tracking her down a priority.'

'You intend to reunite her with her charges?'

Aleksei hesitated, reluctant to blatantly lie. 'I must establish why she left in such haste before deciding anything.' That much was true enough.

'I don't know why it didn't occur to me before, but while I was assured that both English and French are widely spoken in polite society here, I didn't ask specifically about the children. Obviously I speak no Russian.'

'There will be no need for you to do so. The children will have picked up Russian from their nanny as we all did, but they have been taking French and English lessons from Madame Orlova from a very young age, so you need not fear you will be unable to make yourself understood.' Indeed, Aleksei thought, Catiche's fluency was such as to render any English tutoring virtually redundant. No matter, by the time Miss Galbraith discovered this for herself, he'd have explained the true reason for her presence here.

Which he most decidedly did not wish to do just yet. It was time to conclude this most extraordinary conversation. Miss Galbraith had already demonstrated that she had a sharp mind. It would not be long before she asked him why the devil he had not found someone closer to home to perform what must seem to be a fairly straightforward task, and he wasn't ready to answer that question just yet. Not until he'd made sure that St Petersburg society, that hotbed of scandal and intrigue, took Miss Galbraith, English governess, at face value and did not question her presence in the palace.

Aleksei had intended to introduce her at a soirée or a small party. There was, in the euphoric aftermath of victory at Waterloo, no shortage of social events to choose from. As it so happened, this very night a much grander affair was taking place. It would be a baptism of fire, but he was confident that she would emerge unscathed. It wasn't only the guarantees he'd received from The Procurer—though they certainly helped. No, it was Miss Allison Galbraith herself. She was confident—once she had got the better of her quite understandable early nervousness. She was without question clever. And feisty, a woman whose fiery temperament matched her red hair. He reckoned she would fight her corner, so he'd better make sure they were in the same corner. And as for her other qualities? Irrelevant. Absolutely, completely, ravishingly irrelevant.

But also, without question, an absolutely completely, delightful bonus. A most unwelcome distraction from the task in hand undoubtedly, but from a personal point of view a very welcome one. For the first time since he had read that life-changing letter from Michael's man of business, he felt his spirits lift. 'If you have finished your tea, I will have a servant show you to your quarters. You have...' Aleksei consulted his watch. '...three hours to prepare.'

She stared at him blankly. 'To prepare for what?'

'Your introduction to society,' he informed her blithely. 'I did not expect The Procurer to send me a sultry redhead, but your appearance could actually work in our favour. By tomorrow morning, all of St Petersburg will know that there is a new English governess at the Derevenko Palace.'

Chapter Two

Four hours later, Allison found herself standing in the foyer of the Winter Palace, the official home of the Russian royal family. Her hand was resting lightly on the arm of a disturbingly attractive man she had met for the first time today. And she was wearing a dead woman's ball gown. Not, the maid Natalya had hastened to assure her, that the Duchess Elizaveta had ever worn the garment, it was one of many gowns the Duchess had owned but never worn. All the same, were it not for the fact that she possessed only one evening gown, and that not at all suitable for a ball at a royal palace, Allison would have refused to have worn it. It felt both inappropriate and slightly macabre.

She had had no option, however, and though she selected the very plainest of those offered to her, the luxurious garment was outrageously glamorous and utterly unlike anything she would ever have chosen to purchase. White silk with an overdress of creamy net, the evening dress was embellished with tiny gold-thread flowers, a seed pearl at the centre of each. There was a demi-train, the puff sleeves and the surprisingly modest décolleté were trimmed with scalloped lace, and a narrow sash of gold ribbon was tied just under her bust, in the style made popular by the Empress Josephine. The layers of satin-and-lace petticoats made a faint rustling noise when she moved, like fronds swaying in the breeze. For long moments, staring at her reflection in the mirror earlier, Allison had been quite transported by the idea of gliding round a ballroom in such a very beautiful garment. Beautiful but absurdly complicated, mind you. She'd had to fight the urge to ask Natalya for donning instructions.

Hooking the last of what seemed to be about a hundred tiny buttons, the maid had brought Allison firmly down to earth. 'This is a very simple gown in which to attend the Winter Palace, but since the Emperor will not be in attendance, then it will suffice. Do you have no other jewels, madam, other than one locket?'

A disapproving purse of the lips was the response to Allison's shaking her head. She had looked similarly disapproving at the dullness of Allison's wardrobe when she had unpacked her luggage. 'Perhaps madam intends to shop in St Petersburg,' she had said. And when Allison had answered that she doubted she'd have need to, Natalya had looked positively shocked. 'With mourning over, the children will be expected to attend any number of functions,' she had said. 'Catiche is old enough to make her debut appearance at the children's balls, and you will be expected to accompany her.'

Children's dances, for heaven's sake! What other duties would she be expected to carry out? But with this very adult ball looming, Allison had decided it was better not to know, and to concentrate on surmounting each social hurdle as it arose.

There was no doubt that this was a social hurdle where the bar had been set very high, she had thought as their carriage arrived at the vast edifice that was the Winter Palace. Light blazed from all four sides of the courtyard as their carriage passed through the imposing arched entranceway, light which became positively blinding as they entered the palace itself, where someone removed their cloaks, and they joined the throng waiting to ascend the most magnificent double staircase of marble and gold that Allison had ever seen.

Which was where she was now standing, her eyes drawn upwards, past the double row of arched windows, the pilasters and statues, the profusion of gold-leaf laurel and acanthus leaves, to the ceiling, where cherubim and seraphim peeped down at her from puffy white clouds in a celestial blue sky.

The crowd was moving very slowly. Allison clutched at Count Derevenko's arm, willing herself not to succumb to nerves. She had travelled over a thousand miles to reach this cosmopolitan city armed with questions, questions which she had been unable to ask the woman who appointed her, in the rush to make her arrangements. Questions which should have been answered by the man standing beside her this afternoon. And they had, most of them. Save one question so fundamental she couldn't believe it hadn't occurred to her until today. But which she could no longer ignore. 'Why did you send all the way to England for me?'

The Count frowned down at her, raising his

eyebrows at her peremptory tone. 'I don't understand what you mean.'

She would have missed it, were she not studying him so carefully, that tiny flicker in his eyes which told her he understood perfectly. 'There must be any number of females right here in St Petersburg qualified to fulfil my role.'

'You underestimate yourself, Miss Galbraith. I require a governess who is also a skilled herbalist. That is an elusive combination.'

'But surely not unique in a city the size of St Petersburg. Was the previous governess also a herbalist? I presume the children are sickly, or perhaps suffering from some inherited malaise?'

'You presume because The Procurer wasn't specific?'

Allison nodded, her brow furrowed. 'Was I mistaken?'

'Miss Galbraith, this is hardly the time or place for such a discussion.'

'Which confirms that there is a discussion to be had.'

He acknowledged this hit with a small smile. 'You have a sharp mind.'

'Yes, I do, so don't attempt to pull the wool over my eyes.' She treated him to her best *Take your medicine or else, young man* face. It didn't work on this particular patient. He laughed. His eyes crinkled when he laughed. She bit her lip, determined not to soften her stance. 'Well?'

'Not here. No, please spare me another of your schoolmistress glares.'

'The glare of a herbalist who wishes her patient to take his pill, actually.'

'Does it work?'

'Almost every time. And I should warn you, Count Derevenko, I'm an expert at detecting procrastination.'

'I'm not procrastinating.' They shuffled up two more steps. The Count pulled her closer, placing his lips disconcertingly close to her ear. 'The truth is,' he whispered, 'that I cannot trust anyone in St Petersburg. I need an outsider... someone I can be sure has no connections to the court.'

They mounted another step. 'Well, I certainly fit the bill on that score, but...'

Two more steps. 'This really is *not* the time. Look, I promise that I'll explain everything in due course. Trust me.'

'Trust has to operate in both directions.'

He smiled enigmatically. 'You can have no idea of the amount of trust I am about to invest in you, but for now, let us concentrate on making a success of your introduction into polite society.' Count Derevenko ushered her up the final two shallow steps. 'Your audience awaits, Miss Galbraith.'

She had enjoyed their verbal sparring, even if the Count had once again avoided answering her questions, but as they approached the wide-open double doors at the entrance to the ballroom, Allison's confidence faltered, her stomach became queasy with nerves. She had never had cause to attend any ball, let alone a royal ball, but she was *damned* if she would fail at this, the very first challenge. A deep breath, a straightening of her shoulders and her nausea subsided.

As they stepped across the threshold, she realised how large a gathering she was about to face, and just how awe-inspiring the setting. The formal staircase was but an amuse-bouche, a mere taster for the magnificence of this ballroom, so elongated that Allison struggled to see where it ended. Two tiers of windows, one tall and arched, one square, faced each other across the expanse of dance floor, with massive marble Corinthian pillars spaced between each set. The walls themselves were plain, but the ornate, gilded and corniced ceiling was reflected in the intricate pattern of the parquet flooring. Light flooded the chamber from innumerable glittering chandeliers, and from the branches of candles which stood at each window. Aside from a few flimsy-looking gilded chairs upon which no one sat, the room was empty of furnishings and filled to the rafters with milling people.

People who glittered with diamonds and jewels in many forms and incarnations—ornate tiaras, necklaces, opulent rings, bracelets and bangles, military and ceremonial orders and medals. It was no wonder, she thought, resisting the urge to touch her grandmother's simple gold locket, that Natalya had been horrified at her lack of baubles. She need not have worried about being overdressed. The gown, which she had thought so fussy, was almost puritan compared to most here, encrusted as they were with pearls and embellished with gold thread. And the men! Most were garbed in magnificent dress uniforms, tassels and sashes, boots so polished they reflected the light. 'Is the entire Russian army present?'

She spoke flippantly, but Count Derevenko's

smile tightened. 'The real soldiers, the ones who did the fighting, would be lucky to be given bread at the kitchen door, if General Arakcheev has his way. That's him over there.' He nodded at a tall, gaunt man with heavy brows and even heavier gold epaulettes. 'The Emperor's second in command. They refer to him as the Vampire for his bloodlust, though in the field, we nicknamed him the Ape in Uniform. A man who punishes every slight, real or intended, with ever more inventive barbarity. Come, we may as well get the ordeal over with.'

'Aleksei. Out of mourning at last, I see. And cementing our entente with the English with an alliance of your own, too. Or should that be dalliance?'

Allison repressed a shudder as a claw-like hand brushed hers, and a pair of soulless brown eyes under hooded lids glanced indifferently over her. The Vampire was aptly named. A man who would take pleasure in sucking the lifeblood from his enemies.

'Miss Galbraith is the new governess,' the Count answered haughtily, 'here to help my wards perfect their English.'

'And to give you French lessons, no doubt,'

General Arakcheev responded, making his double entendre clear with a lascivious look in Allison's direction, noting her shocked countenance with a small, satisfied smile before returning his attention to the Count. 'You will find many of your comrades are present tonight, anxious to celebrate the end of your emergence from mourning. It seems you were quite the hero at Waterloo. I grow weary of hearing your exploits recounted.'

'Perhaps if you had deigned to make an appearance on the front line you would have spared yourself that tedium.'

'Very droll. As you well know I had the honour of being asked to deputise for the Tsar here in St Petersburg. A more important task than killing a few Frenchmen, I'm sure you'll agree. Our Emperor is anxious to bestow several medals on you in recognition of your contribution to our victory.'

'It was an honour to serve my country,' Aleksei replied. 'That is reward enough.'

'Any other man, I would disbelieve, but I think you actually mean it. I will inform him of your wishes. Besides, you will have no need of any token of his gratitude, will you, Aleksei? Not now that you have the choice of two such pretty little nieces to marry. There's nothing like keeping it in the family, is there? Oh,' Arakcheev said, feigning surprise when the Count took an impetuous step forward, 'come now, if it's good enough for the Romanovs it's surely good enough for you? Now, if you will excuse me?'

With a smug smile, the general turned away, leaving Count Derevenko rooted to the spot. 'People are staring,' Allison said, tugging at his sleeve.

He cursed viciously in what she assumed must be Russian under his breath. One hand was clenched into a fist. The other dug painfully into her arm. 'He deliberately set out to rile me.'

'He succeeded,' she told him tartly, drawing him aside to the shelter of a small alcove, 'and you are ensuring that he and everyone else knows it.'

The Count cursed again. 'If Arakcheev were not in our Emperor's pocket, that man would long ago have been at the bottom of the Neva River.'

'He took me for your mistress!' Now that the encounter was over, Allison was furious. The slander was a horrible reminder of the scurrilous slurs that had been published in the London gutter press. 'He assumed that I—that you and I—you must put him straight.'

'And give him the satisfaction of knowing his barbs had hit home? The Count eyed her flushed countenance. 'You must not take what he says to heart. Arakcheev is a man who thrives on insults, and as taunts go, that was pretty mild. This is St Petersburg. The fact that we are not having an affair would raise more eyebrows.'

Allison mustered a smile. She had overreacted. It wasn't as if it mattered what people thought of her here, far from home. 'You make the city sound like a den of iniquity.'

'You think I'm exaggerating? You see that woman over there?' the Count said, with a sneer. 'The famous—or should I say, infamous—Princess Katya Bagration. I thought she was settled in Paris. I am surprised to see her here.'

Princess Katya, surrounded by a swarm of officers, was very beautiful, with dusky curls, cupid lips and skin like milk. 'Her gown is quite translucent,' Allison whispered, for the Princess's shapely legs could clearly be seen under the filmy gauze of her attire. 'Under the light of these chandeliers—I wonder if she is aware...'

The Count snorted. 'She is perfectly aware.

In Vienna she is known as the Naked Angel or sometimes the White Pussycat.'

'The White Pussycat?'

To Allison's surprise, he looked abashed. 'Something to do with her particular talents. Forgive me, I have been too long in the company of soldiers.'

'Particular talents?' As realisation dawned, Allison gazed over at the beauty in astonishment. 'Do you mean she is a courtesan?'

'Not of the type you mean. She demands secrets rather than gold in return for her favours, I am told. Pillow talk of the most dangerous sort,' the Count clarified, his tone making his feelings very clear. 'During the Congress, she had both our Emperor and Metternich in tow, amongst others.'

'She was Tsar Alexander's mistress? Yet she is received here in the Winter Palace?'

'That is nothing.' Taking a glass of champagne for each of them from a passing waiter, Count Derevenko proceeded to give her a sardonic résumé of who, in the ballroom, was involved in clandestine liaisons with whom. 'As to our Emperor, I would need more than two hands to count the number of women here who have warmed his bed. His Highness is notorious for behaving as if *he* has more than two hands. If his mistresses were excluded from court on grounds of propriety, this ballroom would be empty. But it is the same in England, is it not? Save that the court there pretends to ignore your Prince George's indiscretions, including, I am told, his flirtation with our Emperor's favourite sister, Catherine. In the Court of St Petersburg, indiscretions are part of the fabric of life.'

'I don't move in such exalted circles,' Allison said, feeling like a prude, 'though my work has taken me to the heart of many high-born families. Is fidelity truly so outmoded?'

'Once again, the Emperor leads by example. He and Madame Maria Naryshkhina over there have had several children, much to the chagrin of the Empress who remains childless.'

'There are many women among the poor who would envy her barren state. Mother Nature is often over-generous to those who can least afford it.'

'But that state of affairs is something which a herbalist could easily remedy, is it not?'

Allison stiffened. 'What you are implying is not, and has never been a service I provide. Though there are some who do, and some very desperate women who turn to them. *I* do not judge.'

'Despite what you think, no more do I. I may be a mere man, but I am aware, Miss Galbraith, that it is women who are forced to bear, most unfairly, the consequences of our masculine desires—whether they want to or not.'

'Then you are a very singular man to have considered the problem at all,' Allison replied, mollified. 'I confess, there have been occasions when I have advised—not after the fact, but before—there are ways to prevent—but really! I do not know how we came to be discussing such an intimate topic.'

'It is my fault for drawing your attention to Madame Maria Naryshkhina. My apologies.'

She was forced to smile. 'You seem to be very well informed considering that you have not lived in St Petersburg for some years.'

'The Romanovs are related to every other royal family in Europe. One does not have to reside in St Petersburg to remain *au fait* with their machinations,' the Count replied, not bothering to hide his contempt for the Imperial family. 'And my brother kept me informed with the latest court gossip in his occasional letters. Actually, if one were looking for a rare example of a faithful and devoted husband and father, Michael was your man.'

'You were not—not overly fond of your older brother?'

The Count shrugged, a habit he exhibited, when he did not care to answer, but after a few moments staring down at his champagne flute, he surprised her. 'Of course I cared for him, as one naturally cares for one's family— he was my only sibling, after all. But we were never close, had little in common and as adults spent very little time in one another's company. Which is why I find it so utterly confounding that he nominated me—' He broke off, draining his champagne in one draught. 'But it is done now, no point in lamenting over what cannot be changed. Come, it is time for the great and the good of St Petersburg to meet the new Der-evenko governess.'

The Count set his empty champagne glass down on a window ledge. Allison, surprised to find her own flute also empty, followed suit. 'I will never remember all these names and faces.'

'It doesn't matter, the objective is to ensure that they know yours.' He covered her hand with his, angling his back to the room to obscure her from view. 'You need not be so nervous, you are performing admirably.'

His smile was meant to be reassuring, she told herself, as was the clasp of his fingers. They were both wearing gloves, but her skin was tingling in response to his touch all the same. And his smile—no, it wasn't at all reassuring, it was—she wished he wouldn't smile like that, because she couldn't resist smiling back, and if her smile was anything like his, he'd get the wrong idea entirely. 'Thank you.'

She smiled. He inhaled sharply. Their eyes locked. 'Under different circumstances,' the Count said, 'I would have been delighted if Arakcheev's assumptions had foundation.'

There was no mistaking his meaning. No mistaking the unexpected, delightful *frisson* of her response. An inappropriate response which needed to be quelled. 'You cannot mean you would like to marry one of your nieces!'

'You know perfectly well that's not what I meant.' His fingers tightened on hers as he leaned towards her. For a dizzying moment, she thought he was going to kiss her in full public view. And she wanted him to, for that dizzying moment.

Then he snapped his head back, dropping her

hand. 'Unfortunately the circumstances are not different. We must make a circuit of the room. I would recommend another glass of champagne to fortify you for the circus you are about to experience.'

It had indeed been a circus, and under the scrutiny of St Petersburg society, Allison would have felt as stripped bare and vulnerable as an acrobat on a tightrope were it not for the Count's reassuring presence by her side. By the time they left the ball it was late—or early, she could no longer tell which—and her head was pounding. But though she had fallen into a brief, shallow sleep as soon as her head hit the pillow, her churning mind did not permit her to rest for long.

Wide awake by dawn, her head whirled as she recalled the sea of faces, the inquisitive looks and the myriad of seemingly innocuous yet patently barbed questions aimed at herself and Count Derevenko as they made the circuit of the Winter Palace's ballroom. General Arakcheev—Allison shuddered, recalling the Vampire's empty eyes—had been only the first of many to assume the intimate nature of their relationship. In England, as she knew only too

well, society would have been scandalised—
or at least they would have claimed to be. In St
Petersburg, no one had batted an eyelid at the
notion of Count Derevenko's mistress playing
governess to his wards.

And if society did not care, why should she?
She was tired of railing against assumptions
and prejudice. She realised she had gradually
become—not ashamed, precisely, but she had
come to wish her appearance otherwise, for it
did not match what her patients expected of her.
But she was sick and tired of that too!

Pushing back the sheets, Allison struggled
down from the high bed and threw back the curtains. Outside, the sun was rising with her spirits. Inspired by The Procurer's example, funded
by the fee she would earn here, she would find
a way to take charge of her own destiny, and
she would not have to give any sort of damn
about what St Petersburg, or London, or any
other social elite thought of her. That was why
she was here. That was why she would do everything in her power to succeed, whatever it
was the Count required of her.

Curling up on the window seat, Allison
rested her cheek against the thick glass. Her
bedroom, on the third floor next to the chil-

dren's suite, looked due east. Through the gaps in the rooftops, she could see the glitter of the Neva River, where it flowed in an elegant curve before sweeping south through St Petersburg. The bedchamber was likely plain by the standards of the Derevenko Palace, yet it was opulent beyond her ken. The walls were covered in a dark-red paper embellished with gold. Her bed, a huge affair that required a step to climb into it, was dressed in velvet and brocade, the four posts gilded, the myriad mattresses and pillows designed to cocoon one in the cosiest, warmest embrace. Carpets of woven silk were soft underfoot. Her small collection of clothes was lost in the giant lacquered chest of drawers, her plain brushes looked like interlopers atop the matching dressing table.

Which was exactly what she was. An interloper. A stranger. A foreigner. Apparently the only person in this city that Count Derevenko could trust. Which begged the question, why couldn't he trust anyone else? And why did he require his governess to be a herbalist? She'd assumed the children were poorly. Neither he nor The Procurer had either confirmed or denied this, yet what other reason could there be? Even before she met her charges, Allison was beginning to feel very sorry indeed for them. Poor little orphans, they must be feeling wholly abandoned. Something she could certainly empathise with.

Pulling on her robe, she quit her chamber and walked the distance along the corridor to the series of connected rooms allocated to the children. It was the custom, in some English aristocratic households, to confine the children to the basement or the attic, to furnish their rooms as spartanly as those belonging to the lowliest of servants. She'd tended to sick children shivering in bedchambers where the wind whistled through the bare floorboards, children living like moles in windowless rooms below stairs. Ideal preparation, she'd been informed time and again, for the character-building privations of the boarding school which almost every little boy attended, and an increasing number of girls too. The process of estrangement happened, in many cases, from birth, when babies were handed immediately to a wet nurse, and thence on to a nanny, a governess, a tutor.

Or in her case a grandmother, an arrangement which had turned out to be permanent. Her mother had not even deigned to turn up for Seanmhair's funeral seven years ago. Or perhaps she had simply not dared. Seven years, during which Allison had worked tirelessly to establish herself. And now that life too was gone.

But now, she had been given the chance to make a new future for herself. Her charges might well have lacked parental affection but their material needs were abundantly satisfied. The children's quarters were sumptuous, as richly decorated as the one she occupied. The playroom was an Aladdin's Cave of toys. Wondering why the doll's house looked familiar, Allison realised it was a miniature replica of the Derevenko Palace. The rocking horse which stood in the window had the look of an Arabian thoroughbred. A positive army of lead soldiers were lined up in one corner commanded, she noted with a wry smile, by an officer wearing Count Derevenko's regimental colours. Next door to the playroom was a schoolroom complete with three desks and a large slate board, a cupboard full of text books, all in French and English. And next door to that, what must have been the nursery, but which now seemed to be the nanny's room. There was no evidence of any sort of sick room.

Allison made her way back to her own chamber. She had thought herself accustomed to children, but really, she was only accustomed to children in distress, in the throes of illness. Fractious children, sobbing children, suffering children whose pain she relieved, whose maladies she remedied. Children who were grateful for her soothing presence, and whose parents too were grateful. But these three orphans were an entirely different proposition. Her presence would surely emphasise the absence of their mother and father. No matter how distant those parents had been, the children must be grieving. And then there was the governess who had also, mysteriously, deserted them.

There was no getting away from it, Allison must prepare herself to be perceived as an unwelcome intruder, and an inadequate one at that. Empathy did not make a teacher of her, and one thing she did know about children was that they were not easily fooled, seeing a great deal more than most adults realised. Her charges would likely sense she was a fraud.

Oh, for heaven's sake! She was overthinking the situation. Honestly, Allison chastised herself, how hard could it be, really? Her life had been dedicated to caring for sufferers. Sympathy and understanding were as much a part of her armoury as her precious herb chest. What's more, she had been selected, interviewed and judged capable. She had passed muster last night, she knew that, for if she had failed, she would have been ushered out of that hot, glittering ballroom *tout de suite*. The Count was not a man to tolerate failure. He hadn't exactly relaxed by the end of the evening, in fact he'd been watching her like a hawk, but several times, when she had found the confidence to riposte some of the sly remarks, he had pressed her hand in approval or given her the most fleeting of nods.

Everyone to whom he introduced her had been informed that she was the new English governess. Everyone assumed she was also her employer's mistress. 'You are the envy of every unmarried lady in St Petersburg, Miss Galbraith,' one of the courtiers had confided *sotto voce*. 'As next in line to the dukedom, Aleksei is now one of the most eligible bachelors in the city. How unfair of you to force us to wait until he is done with you. You will understand why I hope that your liaison is short-lived. Though I cannot blame you for wanting to keep him to yourself. There is something about an officer in uniform, is there not? It makes one almost indifferent to the possibility that a ducal coronet may follow. Almost.'

That the Count was sought after did not surprise Allison. That she herself was drawn to him however, surprised her very much. That the attraction was mutual—now *that* was the biggest surprise of all.

Time and again, she had been propositioned, by husbands and fathers and brothers of her patients, by apothecaries and physicians. Not once had she been tempted, knowing full well that her reputation must be above reproach. All very well for a man in her profession to take a lover, but as a woman, she must be either an angel or a whore, to paraphrase The Procurer. Save for that one secret, salutary entanglement, Allison had never had any difficulty in opting to be the former. Which made it all the more infuriating that the gutter press had branded her a Jezebel with no more evidence than her hair and her figure and the vengeful mud-slinging of a few medical men intent upon protecting their own interests. It was so unfair it made her blood boil. At least, she thought sardonically, if it had been true she would have had some pleasurable memories to bolster her. Instead, ironically, she was a fallen woman with a past that was only one step removed from the virginal. Though as far as London society was concerned, she was irrecoverably ruined.

Which was, if one turned the idea on its head, rather a liberating thought, for the worst that could be said of her had already been said. Allison smiled slowly. What's more, what was damned in London was positively encouraged in St Petersburg. Why should she make a virtue of resistance?

She enjoyed sparring with the Count. He brought out a teasing, playful side of her that she didn't recognise. Another sign that she was emerging from the fog of the last six months? Smiling to herself, Allison sat down at the dressing table and took a brush to her hair. Perhaps so, but it wasn't only that. It was him. Count Aleksei Derevenko. If she was being skittish—and she did feel rather skittish—then she'd have said that he had been fashioned to her precise design. She'd responded to his body on a basic, visceral level that was unknown to her, and she had flirted—yes, unbelievably, that is what she had done, she'd flirted with him. What's more, she'd enjoyed it.

And so had he. He'd wanted to kiss her last night. Had they not been in the ballroom of the Winter Palace—Allison paused mid-brush-stroke. She couldn't believe they had nearly kissed in the middle of a ball in the Winter Palace.

She resumed her brushing and rolled her eyes at her reflection. She had far too much to lose to make a fool of herself over a man who was her employer, but provided she kept that salient fact in her head, where was the harm in indulging in a light flirtation, if he too was so inclined? She had nothing to lose. She was in St Petersburg, after all. It was pretty much expected of her. What the hell, why not!

Chapter Three

The Square Room, where Aleksei had first encountered Allison Galbraith, was a suitably private and soberly oppressive venue for their next, crucial meeting. A room which epitomised the suffocating world of the Imperial court. A world which he had rejected and in which his brother had flourished, strangely enough, for though Michael had been a pompous prig, he'd had integrity and he had been scrupulously honest, both qualities in short supply in the court of the Tsars.

The aristocrats he had mingled with last night at the Winter Palace ball seemed like strangers to Aleksei. It was not on their behalf that he had fought for his homeland. Last night had confirmed what his gut had told him from the moment he arrived: he did not belong here in this chaotic city so singularly lacking the rules, discipline, the sense of order to which he was accustomed. The sooner he could escape it the better. Which meant getting to the bottom of the conundrum he faced.

He checked his watch. Five minutes before Miss Galbraith was due. He got to his feet. One thing to be said for the sprawling Derevenko Palace, it provided abundant opportunities for anxious pacing. He hadn't expected to enjoy the company of the woman who would assist him in his search for the truth, but he had, very much. She had resolve, she had a ready wit and a great deal of poise. Her early encounter with Arakcheev had unsettled her, the general's salacious remarks had made her furious, but she had quickly regained her composure, deftly handling the gossip and speculation which had followed them around the ballroom for the rest of the evening.

Gossip and speculation which, given her appearance, he ought to have anticipated. Allison Galbraith had a lush sensuality that was all the more enticing because she seemed blissfully unaware of it. No doubt she received more than her fair share of unwelcome propositions. And last night, he'd actually suggested that if circumstances were different…

Aleksei winced. He hadn't actually propositioned her, but the implication had been there. To be fair to himself, he was pretty certain that the attraction was astonishingly, delightfully—and extremely inconveniently, mutual. Though by all that was precious, wasn't the situation complicated enough without that!

It had been too long since he'd been able to enjoy the company of any woman. Frustration, that was all it was, he told himself. Though if that was true, why hadn't he been attracted to one of the many other beautiful women he had been introduced to last night?

Because he couldn't trust any of them, of course. And because none of them had that—that certain something which Allison Galbraith possessed. Something which made him sure, absolutely certain, that together they would be…

Dammit! She was here for a very specific purpose, and if he wanted to take advantage of her skills, he could not risk being distracted by her body. He was a rational man, he was a man who had forged a very successful military career by putting discipline above all else.

Now was not the moment to change the habit of a lifetime.

But on the other hand, must a desire to conclude his business here as quickly as possible preclude enjoying the company of the woman who would help him do just that? How long had it been since he'd been able to indulge in even the lightest of dalliances? Months? It felt more like years. He would not go so far as to say he deserved the tempting Miss Galbraith, but didn't he deserve some sort of mild flirtation?

But what if he was mistaken? What if he was imagining the attraction to be mutual simply because he wanted it to be? And really, wasn't he getting his priorities all wrong?

As if in agreement with this very point, the double doors were flung open, the servant announced her, and Allison made a curtsy. 'Good morning, your Illustrious Highness.'

He looked just as striking as he had at the ball, Allison thought to herself. Last night had not been a dream, then.

'Good morning,' the Count said, 'and it is Aleksei while we are alone, if you please. In company, Count Derevenko will suffice. Hearing *Your Illustrious Highness* makes me want to glance over my shoulder to see my brother enter the room. Though actually he preferred *Your Serene Highness*. Michael was a stickler for etiquette, with a predilection for pomp and ceremony. As you'll have gathered from our surroundings,' he added, waving vaguely at the huge reception room in which they were ensconced.

'What I gather, is that it is decidedly not to your taste,' Allison said, crossing the room to join him.

'I've been away on active service for so long, I have no idea what my taste in interiors is,' the Count—Aleksei—replied with a faint smile. 'It mostly revolves around canvas tents and wooden trunks. Last night at the Winter Palace, I felt even more of a foreigner than you.'

She took the seat opposite him, the same one she had occupied yesterday. He handed her a cup of black tea into which, to her relief, he had already added three sugars. Allison took a tentative sip from her cup. The taste of the tea was odd, the contrast of the sweet and bitter one that she could, despite her reservations, grow to like. Opposite her, the Count—no, Aleksei! She tried his name out for herself, mouthing it silently as she studied him. It suited him. Strong. Forthright. He was not wearing his uniform today, for which she was—shamefully—grateful, for it was true, what the courtier had whispered salaciously last night, there was something about a man in uniform. Or at least, something about this man in uniform. Though if she was being scrupulous about it, his attraction was in no way diminished by the austerity of his breeches and short boots, the long black coat and pristine white shirt with its starched collar. There was a rebellious and endearing kink in his hair, almost silver compared to the dark blond, which stood up on his brow like a comma. The slight frown which seemed to be permanently etched into his face was bisected by a faint scar which she hadn't noticed yesterday. He sat awkwardly in the little chair, his long legs crossed at the ankles, his shoulders hunched, grasping the delicate teacup with both hands.

'What is it that you find amusing?'

She hadn't realised she was smiling. 'You look like a giant squatting on a child's seat.'

He grinned. 'The furniture in this room is designed to discourage use.'

'Similar to the chairs in the ballroom last night.'

'No one would dare sit in the presence of the Emperor—or his deputy.'

'Arakcheev.' Allison couldn't repress a shudder. 'I most sincerely hope that was my first and only encounter with that odious man, if you don't mind me being so blunt.'

'I don't, it's what I much prefer, and you're the only person in this city who's likely to indulge me.' Aleksei drained his tea in one gulp, a soldier's habit, Allison assumed, and set the cup on the tray before leaning forward, his elbows resting on his knees. 'So! I promised you last night that I'd come clean with you, and I'm a man of my word. But before I do, I must stress that everything I'm about to tell you is in the strictest confidence.'

'As I said last night, you can trust me, Count—Aleksei.'

'And as *I* said last night, you can have no idea how much trust I'm about to place in you. The Derevenko name is a venerable one. My brother was one of the wealthiest men in Russia. He was also the figurehead of one of the most powerful dynasties in the country, with the ear and the protection of the Tsar himself. If anyone in this city got wind of my suspicions, all hell would break loose, whether I'm right or wrong.'

Allison stared at him, quite confounded. 'I am not sure—what is it you suspect?'

'Assassination.'

Her jaw dropped. 'I think perhaps I misheard you. Or perhaps your English—though it is most excellent. But you can't have meant...'

'I suspect my brother Michael was murdered,' Aleksei informed her matter of factly, 'and I need you to help me to discover whether or not I am correct.'

Utterly thrown, Allison ran her fingers through her hair, forgetting that it was not tied simply back but in a tight chignon, disrupting several pins in the process. 'How on earth can I help? I am no Bow Street Runner, I'm a herbalist.'

'Precisely! As far as the world is concerned, my brother died of natural causes, and that is what the world must continue to think until we can prove otherwise. I suspect he was poisoned, which is where you come in.'

'Couldn't you have consulted a local expert? Why send halfway around the world for me.'

'I thought I'd made that clear,' Aleksei replied with a hint of impatience. 'You had a glimpse of what St Petersburg is like last night. Gossip is a way of life here, everyone's life is an open book. I need an outsider with no ties here. No one knows you. Though the reality is that my wards require neither English lessons nor nursing, no one will question your notional title of governess.'

And all would assume that her duties extended from the schoolroom to Aleksei's bed. Allison rubbed at her temples, distractedly pulling out several more hairpins. 'Did The Procurer know your real requirements?'

'She did. I heard of her from a fellow officer. He did not tell me the particulars of his own case, only that he had been obliged to be scrupulously honest in his dealings with her. He'd tried to pull the wool over her eyes, and she almost refused the commission. I decided I couldn't take that risk, and so I was brutally honest.'

'She was not quite so truthful with me.'

'Clearly.' Aleksei eyed her quizzically. 'Would you be here, if she had been?'

Her hand instinctively clutched her locket, concealed beneath the neckline of her day gown. The Procurer had given her the opportunity, but it had been her grandmother's belief in her which had given her the strength to take it. Now it was up to Allison to make the most of it. 'I can't tell you how glad I am that I did.'

Aleksei smiled at her, and she could have sworn that his smile tugged at something, an almost tangible connection between them. 'I've no idea if I can help you,' Allison said, 'but I can promise, hand on heart, that I will do my utmost to do so. Tell me, in plain and simple terms exactly what it is that you suspect and why.'

'Plain talking.' Aleksei automatically made for the samovar, in need of another cup of tea, that panacea for all ills and aid to clear thinking. 'What I have always preferred, though it is anathema here in Machiavellian St Petersburg. The starting point,' he said, resuming his seat, 'was when I received a letter from Michael's man of business informing me that my brother and his wife had died within a few days of each other. I was shocked of course, and deeply saddened, but our imminent encounter with Napoleon at Waterloo was my priority, and so I gave little thought to the circumstances beyond assuming there must have been some sort of carriage accident. The matter of my guardianship was, as I've already told you, a most unwelcome surprise, but not one that I had much time to consider in the bloody aftermath of Waterloo, and the urgent need to look after the welfare my troops. It was only when I finally arrived here in St Petersburg that I began to worry that all was not what it seemed.'

Allison was listening intently, her teacup clutched, still full, in her lap. Aleksei set his own aside. 'The first thing I discovered was that there had been no accident. Michael appeared to have died of an apoplexy, a violent heart seizure which killed him before the doctor could be summoned. Elizaveta then fell ill shortly thereafter, but her symptoms were quite different. A flux, breathlessness followed by palpitations, caused by a severe intolerance, the doctor confirmed. Here is a copy of his report.'

He handed over several pages of notes, which Allison quickly scanned. 'The cause of the Duchess's death is very clear. What is a coulibiac?'

'A sort of fish pie, peasant food which my sister-in-law consumed on impulse at the market. She had been advised to avoid eating fish following previous adverse reactions as a child, as it says in the notes. It's clear her death was nothing more than a tragic coincidence. Her reaction, as the doctor states, was severe, but not in the least bit suspicious.'

Allison frowned over the report. 'But there is no suggestion that your brother's death was attributable to any sort of poison. The doctor is quite clear, as you said, that he thinks it was due to an apoplexy.'

'*Thinks*. But he is not certain,' Aleksei said. 'In fact, he told me that he was most surprised, because not only was my brother in rude health, Michael had just turned forty, a notoriously abstemious man and most unfashionably fond of taking exercise. What do you make of it?'

She spread her hands helplessly. 'In my experience, apoplexies are more common in older men, or those who indulge in excessive consumption of food or wine, but it could simply be that your brother had a weak heart. Isn't the more obvious conclusion what the doctor has described in his notes—a seizure of the heart?'

'An obvious conclusion in London perhaps, but not in St Petersburg where poison and power are often bedfellows. And if it was not an apoplexy, it must have been poison, don't you think?'

Allison scanned the report again. 'No lesions or rashes. No signs of blunt force or trauma. Clear signs of stress of the heart but none to any other vital organs. I would have to study it more carefully, but—'

'I know, it is not much to go on,' Aleksei interrupted her, 'but the manner of Michael's death is not the only factor which aroused my suspicions. There is also the sudden disappearance of Anna Orlova, the children's governess, which I mentioned yesterday.'

'You can't mean that you suspect the governess capable of murder?'

'I know, it sounds far-fetched, but it is even more far-fetched, when you take account of the circumstances, to conclude she was not complicit in some way. Why else would she abandon her charges, whom she is purported to be devoted to, so suddenly and the day before Michael died? And if she has nothing to hide, why is she, paradoxically, in hiding?'

'I assumed that you wanted to find her for the children's sake,' Allison said, sounding quite dazed. 'I agree, in the context you have described that it looks suspicious, but she was not even present when he died. Not that that means—for there are poisons which are slow acting or have a delayed effect, but—what had she to gain from killing her employer? And such an illustrious one—a duke, for heaven's sake.'

'The Orlova woman was due a small bequest, but it has not been paid, since her whereabouts are unknown, and as a motive for murder, where the punishment would not only be death but torture—no, it beggars belief.'

'What of the other beneficiaries of your brother's will?'

'Aside from the legacy to myself, there are no other significant beneficiaries. Michael left everything to his children, as indeed, did Elizaveta, which leaves my nieces and nephew extremely wealthy indeed, but I think we can rule them out.'

'Aleksei!'

'A poor joke,' he said with an apologetic smile. 'The children's guardian has the most to gain, for he has their vast assets and their malleable minds entirely at his disposal.'

'But *you* are their guardian.'

'Which brings me to the root cause of my suspicions. Michael changed his will about a week before he died. According to his man of business, the change was to be kept under wraps until such time as Michael chose to inform the relevant parties. I've no idea if he informed Elizaveta, but as you know, I was in the dark, as was my first cousin, Felix Golitsyn, who until the change was the nominee of long standing.'

Aleksei drummed his fingers on his thigh, frowning off into the distance. 'Felix was the first person to call on me to pay his condolences, though he was so grief-stricken himself, it was I who consoled him in the end. Michael's man of business had fetched him from Peter-hof Palace, some distance down river of here, where he had been staying when my brother died. It fell to my cousin, as Michael's nearest male relative, to take charge of the funeral arrangements in my absence. Felix fully expected to take custody of the children too, and when he was informed of the change of guardianship it came as quite a shock.'

'But if your logic is correct,' Allison said, clearly struggling to keep track, 'if this cousin did not know your brother had changed his will, then surely that makes him the prime suspect?'

'Aside from the Orlova woman, you mean? Yes, I'm afraid that it does,' he agreed heavily. 'I find it very hard to believe, but as you point out, the logic is inescapable. I would give almost anything to prove his innocence, however.'

'You must care a great deal for your cousin.'

'The truth is I care more for what my cousin

can do for me,' Aleksei replied, 'which is take my wards off my hands. Felix understands the workings of the palace and the court, and he's much more familiar with the family estates than I am.'

'Yet your brother clearly thought he was no longer suitable.'

'I know, dammit. But until I find out why he changed his mind I cannot discount the possibility that it is somehow connected with his death.'

Allison was toying with one of her hairpins, absentmindedly bending it to form a circle. 'Do you suspect anyone else?'

'No one.' Aleksei grimaced. 'And everyone. I have gone through Michael's accounts with a fine toothcomb and found no evidence of extortion, of shady dealings, property transactions or unusual payments or deposits. The political posts he held were much coveted but they now lie within Nikki's gift—or mine, at the moment. No, if it was murder, and if it was not committed by either the Orlova woman or Felix, then the field is wide open. Assuming that we rule out a crime of passion which, believe me, knowing my brother, we can, the motive could be anything—revenge, a personal vendetta. Michael would have been privy to any number of potentially explosive secrets. Was he killed to silence him? Who knows?'

'My head hurts,' Allison said, screwing up her eyes.

Aleksei threw himself back heavily in the flimsy chair. 'A disappearing governess, an ambiguous doctor's report, a late change to my brother's will. I know, it is not much to go on. I've had weeks of enforced incarceration in this great barrack of a place to reason it out, to tell myself that I'm being illogical, that everything is exactly as it seems, but I simply can't bring myself to believe it. What it comes down to is that my gut is telling me something is not right, and I owe it to Michael to establish the true facts surrounding his death, no matter what that turns out to be. Can you help me get to the truth?'

She wanted to, very much. Aleksei might not have been close to his brother, but he was an honourable man who wanted to honour his brother's memory, and a desperate man. She was entirely unprepared for the impossible task he had thrown at her, but what was it The Procurer had said, something about making the impossible possible? That mysterious woman had believed in her when all of London scorned her. And Aleksei believed in her too. So Allison had better start believing in herself.

She stared down at the hairpin which she didn't remember mutilating. 'Let me get this straight. You want me to establish whether or not your brother could have been poisoned?'

Aleksei nodded encouragingly. 'And if he was, what was used, and how was it administered.'

Away and boil your heid, ya tumchie, was how her grandmother would have responded, but Allison did not have that luxury. Start from the basics, she told herself. 'Is there a physic garden here at the palace?'

'I know there is a herb garden, if that is what you mean?'

'It could serve. I need to understand what plants grow locally, and whether they are different from what is available at home. But I'll also need to know what can be purchased from an apothecary. I can easily visit a few, under the guise of stocking up my own herb chest.'

'But surely apothecaries sell medicines not poisons?'

'Some can act as both. Arsenic, for example, is used in many treatments including a whitening powder for the skin, though that is one of the most common poisons we can dismiss, because the symptoms don't match. I shall compile a list, once I have studied the doctor's report in more detail.' She frowned. 'How any poison could have been administered is a much more complicated question. I take it no one else in the palace displayed any symptoms similar to your brother?'

'No. So if it was something he ate, only he alone ate it.'

'There are other methods—but that is for me to investigate.'

'Excellent!' Aleksei clapped his hands together. 'Which brings us to the second part of your duties, which is to take charge of my wards while I try to locate the missing governess. I plan to start with a visit to her family home, which is about three days' travel from here. I have no idea how long I will be gone, a few weeks at most. I will have it put about that I'm touring the Derevenko estates, which are numerous and far flung. Don't worry, I've made arrangements—'

He broke off, scowling as the grandfather clock in the corner chimed the hour. 'Talking of which, I have another appointment with Michael's—Nikki's—man of business which is bound to take up the rest of the day. Join me for dinner tonight,' he said. 'We can talk. Not about murders and poison. I've been starved of company for an age. And you, Allison Galbraith, are unexpectedly delightful company. I'd like to get to know you better.'

It didn't cross her mind to turn down his offer. Hadn't she too been starved of company? And wasn't Aleksei also unexpectedly delightful company? 'I'd like that.'

He smiled then, that smile that made her think of kissing, and she couldn't help smile back at him, just as she had done last night. And just as he had done last night, he inhaled sharply. And then, unlike last night, he kissed her. Not a real kiss. Just the merest brush of his lips. Enough for her to smell the citrusy lemon tang of his soap, feel the almost-smooth skin of his freshly shaved cheek, the silk of his waistcoat, the warmth of his body, a flare of desire. And then it was over. For which she should be thankful. Though thankful was very far from the emotion she was feeling.

Chapter Four

Allison's only evening gown had been a gift from a very grateful mother whose child she had successfully treated, a woman who apparently laboured under the misapprehension that herbalists had any number of functions to attend which required a lavish silk robe. Tonight would be its first and likely its only outing.

The gown was olive-green and, compared to those on display at the Winter Palace last night, a simple affair, the decoration confined to one pleated ruffle around the hem and some intricate smocking in the short puffed sleeves. But the skirt, below the narrow sash was composed of acres of silk, and the quality of the fabric itself infinitely superior to anything else that Allison had ever owned.

She wore silk slippers on her feet. Her best

silk stockings were held up by garters tied with green ribbons. The many layers of petticoats under her gown rustled with every step she took. Though Natalya had protested that her corsets were too loosely laced, Allison was convinced they were too tight. The décolleté of her gown was modest, but she was conscious of the quivering of her exposed cleavage, the way her locket nestled in the valley between her breasts. Natalya had piled her hair high on top of her head, threading it through with ribbon and an extraordinary number of pins, allowing one long curl to fall artlessly over her bare shoulder, achieving an elegant, deceptively simple coiffure that Allison could never have attempted and which made her look considerably more sophisticated than she felt.

'Parfait, mademoiselle.' Natalya fastened the buttons at the wrist of Allison's long evening gloves. 'I hope you have a pleasant dinner.'

Madame Orlova had habitually dined alone in her private sitting room, Allison knew, because Natalya had outlined the domestic arrangements to her yesterday. Yes, Natalya had admitted, there were occasions when Madame Orlova had attended a dinner with their Serene Highnesses in order to make up the numbers,

Madame Orlova being sufficiently high born not to lower the tone of a duke and duchess's table.

Allison, whose blood was bright red and not remotely blue, would most certainly not have been invited. And in any case, she was not making up the numbers on this occasion, she was dining with the acting head of the Derevenko dynasty tête-à-tête. What Natalya made of this, she did not say, but Allison had no doubt it would be the main topic of conversation at another dinner, in the servants' hall.

Was it foolhardy and reckless? If so, it was too late to do anything about it. Besides, she didn't want to cancel.

'*Mademoiselle?* The footman is here to show you the way.'

Allison took a final glance in the mirror. The woman who gazed back at her was not only elegant, she was a sultry creature, a vibrant one, the colour of her hair, her eyes, even her lips, enhanced by the gown. She looked, ironically, like the sophisticated twin of the harlot Allison depicted in the London gutter press. Those caricatures had shamed her. But this version of her—Allison smiled at herself—she liked what she saw.

'You are ready, *mademoiselle*?'

'Thank you, Natalya. I am more than ready.'

The Green Dining Room, Allison thought, as she entered the empty chamber, I have certainly dressed to match.

The room was decorated in the classical style. Pale green walls were embellished with white moulding of various toga-clad figures and Etruscan vases, above which was an elaborate cornice of trailing vines, fruits, birds and cupids. A lion rampant propped up either side of the marble fireplace. Candles on the mantel and the table gave the room a soft glow, but the huge candelabra suspended from the ceiling was unlit.

Two places had been set at the table, one at either end. Though this was, she presumed, one of the Derevenko Palace's less formal dining rooms, the expanse of white linen, silver epergnes, and crested china plate between the settings would make conversation difficult. In fact they'd probably have to shout. Not exactly intimate then. Deliberately so?

The kid soles of her slippers skidded slightly on the highly polished parquet flooring as she crossed to the tall French windows which took up most of one wall. Pulling aside the voile, she peered out, hoping to get a glimpse of the gardens, but it was too dark to make out anything save shadowy shrub-shaped silhouettes.

'My apologies, I was detained, interminably as ever, on estate business.'

Aleksei had changed into a burgundy tailcoat with a black collar and cuffs. A burgundy waistcoat, black pantaloons and top boots, and a pristine white shirt with a neatly tied cravat completed this plain but extremely well-cut ensemble, the tailoring making the most of the breadth of his shoulders and chest, Allison thought, eyeing him appreciatively.

He made a bow over her hand, the look in his eyes making it very clear that the appreciation was reciprocated. 'You look quite ravishing.' Aleksei frowned at the table setting. 'I must presume that Michael and Elizaveta preferred not to talk when dining alone,' he said, ringing the bell. 'Miss Galbraith will sit by my right,' he instructed when the footman answered his summons. He had not been responsible for the slightly frosty seating arrangement, then.

It took ten minutes, three footmen and one butler to pour the wine, rearrange the table and lay out a vast array of silver-covered salvers. 'Thank you,' Aleksei said, when the butler made to lift the lid on the first of those, 'we will serve ourselves.' Adding firmly when the outraged butler would have protested, 'I will ring if I need you.'

'Poor man, he's probably gone to weep in his pantry,' Allison said, as Aleksei took his seat beside her. 'Not only have you broken with protocol by dining alone with a lowly governess, you have had the audacity to feed yourself.'

Aleksei chuckled. 'I'm already in the bad books for refusing to allow Michael's valet to shave me or dress me. Now,' he said, lifting the lids on the nearest salvers, 'would you like me to help you to some food, or do you prefer to serve yourself? The chef is French, and very good. Here we have consommé, and this looks like lobster in some sort of sauce. A *blanquette de veau*, *choux farcis*, a white fish—I think that must be carp—or an omelette *fines herbes*, artichokes, carrots…'

'Thank you, that is more than sufficient.' Allison surveyed the remaining covered dishes. 'Is this what you would call a small informal dinner?'

Aleksei laughed. 'By Derevenko Palace standards, certainly. I am accustomed to much more basic fayre, cooked in one pot over a campfire, usually.'

Allison, momentarily distracted by the delicious lobster, drew him a sceptical look. 'During campaigns perhaps, but you are an officer, and no doubt dined like this in mess every evening.'

'Not every evening, and not for some time. One aspect of army life I don't miss. I am very glad to avoid the endless dinners being held in Paris to celebrate peace.'

'May I ask, what rank you are?'

'*Polkovnik*. Your equivalent of a colonel, and as such I was a great disappointment to my brother.' Aleksei grimaced. 'As the son of a duke, it was always expected that my family name would be my passport to rapid promotion. If I'd wanted to, I could be a full general at least, perhaps even an adjutant general.'

'But you don't wish?'

'I prefer to earn the respect of my men on merit.'

Having finished her portion of stuffed cabbage, Allison opted for some veal. 'You have also earned the respect of your fellow officers. That much was obvious at the Winter Palace ball.'

'Oh, that. Between ourselves, the respect of

most of that fawning crowd means little to me. Their experience of war, with a few notable exceptions, is confined to watching battle from the side lines, for which I am very grateful, given their ineptitude.'

Allison smiled, raising her champagne glass. 'A toast! To succeeding on your own terms.' There was a trace of bitterness in her voice that she had not meant to express. She set her glass down. 'So, what does the future hold for you now that there are no more wars to fight, Polkovnik?'

'Unfortunately we live in a world where there will always be more wars to fight.' He was silent for a moment, concentrating on his food, and she hoped that he hadn't picked up on her tone. She was wrong. 'You have had to make compromises in your life?'

Allison attempted one of Aleksei's indifferent shrugs. 'I'm a woman in a man's world.'

He laid his fingers on her arm. 'I'm interested, if you're willing to talk about it.'

No one had ever asked her before. No one, not even Robert, had ever shown any interest. 'You touched on it yourself, when we met yesterday,' Allison said. 'My appearance works against me.'

His eyebrows shot up. 'In my opinion, your appearance is very much to your advantage.'

Though she smiled, it was dismissive. 'Not when one is trying…' She sighed, shaking her head. 'Imagine, if you can,' she began, frowning, 'that you are a woman, a skilled herbalist, and an experienced healer. You have worked tirelessly for seven years to establish yourself in society. You have proven results, sound methods, have become sought after by women in particular, to deal with feminine complaints, and with the illnesses which beset their children.'

'I remember the doctor who attended us when we were little. We called him the Raven, though his cures—to be honest, I'm astonished he didn't kill us with his harsh treatments.'

The shadow of the past fluttered over her, and Allison shuddered. Resolutely, she quashed the memory, slipping her hand free from Aleksei's clasp to take a sip of champagne. 'Bleeding, cupping, purges—I agree they can all be extremely unpleasant, but in the majority of cases they do no major harm.'

'But you do not advocate their use?'

'No, I do not, and that is part of the problem,' she said, with a bitter smile. 'My methods and my remedies are quite different from those prescribed by physicians and apothecaries. I do not claim they are always more successful, I do not claim to have the skills, for example of a surgeon, but I am an excellent healer. Yet despite that, my sex prevents me from being recognised by the exalted Society of Apothecaries, which means I have no legal right to practise. My clients turned a blind eye to that, but society viewed me differently.' She felt herself colour. 'My appearance and my vocation—men take me for a woman of—of loose virtue. No, let us be plain. Men assume I'm a harlot. It is but a short leap from herbalist to sorceress, you see, and there is something about me...'

'There is, most definitely, something about you,' Aleksei said with a rueful smile. 'Though I suspect that is something you have heard too many times and have no wish to hear repeated.'

'What I wish is to be judged on my skills as a herbalist and not my appearance. Such a simple ambition, you might think,' Allison continued, almost to herself, 'and so it would be, were I a man. But as a woman, I must not only prove my skills, I must prove myself a paragon of virtue.'

She blinked. Her hand was curled tightly around her champagne glass. 'I'm sorry. I did not intend the conversation to take such a sombre tone. It is ancient history and has no relevance now. You do realise that we will be the subject of lurid speculation in the servants' hall?'

'I don't give a damn what they are saying about us. Unless you do?'

'No.' She smiled. 'I really don't. Let them talk.'

But it was they who talked. Aleksei pulled a *chaise longue* in front of the fire, and they sat together before the flames, sipping wine and chatting.

'From Seanmhair—that is, my grandmother,' she told him with a tender smile, when he asked her how she acquired her knowledge of herbs. 'Seanmhair is what is known as a fey wife or wise woman in the Highlands of Scotland. It is from her that I inherited my love of herbs and healing, though she always said I derived my ambition from Lady Hunter.'

'Lady Hunter?'

'The laird's wife. She took a shine to me. My grandmother said it was her having no daughter of her own. It was from Lady Hunter I had my English lessons, and learnt to go about in polite society, learnt also to use my skills there with discretion. When Seanmhair died, it was Lady Hunter who encouraged me to seek my fortune in London.'

'And what of your mother?'

'She left me in my grandmother's care when she married. Her husband was not my father, you see. I would have been a great inconvenience to the pair of them.' Allison was curled up on the *chaise longue* beside him, her feet tucked under her. 'You must not be feeling too sorry for me, mind. If she'd taken me with her, I'd never have become a herbalist, and if I were not a herbalist, I would not be here in St Petersburg. What was your own mother like, Aleksei?'

'Very beautiful. I'll show you her portrait tomorrow.'

'And do you look much like her?'

'Now how am I to take that?'

'Are you fishing for a compliment now, Polkovnik? Then I will tell you that I've not seen a finer figure in uniform. An opinion shared by every other woman I talked to in the Winter Palace the other night, I might add. They would be as green as this dining room with envy if they knew I was sitting here alone with you, round the campfire, so to speak.'

'I can honestly say that I've never sat around a campfire with such a charming companion.'

'Now how am I to take that, given that my competition consists of gnarled, battle-hardened soldiers?'

'Soldiers whose penchant for singing folk songs is rarely matched by their musical ability.'

'Ah, then that is something I must confess to sharing with them. I too love singing Scottish folk songs, but I am, in my grandmother's words, tone deaf.'

He could not resist testing her. 'I don't believe you.'

Allison, to his delight, responded to the challenge by getting to her feet and clearing her throat. There was a gleam in her eye that made him want to laugh, and he bit his lip. 'This is a wee song in the Gaelic,' she said, 'which is my native language. It is about a woman whose sailor husband has been lost at sea. She goes down to the beach every day and sings to the seals in the hope that her husband is a selkie— a drowned man returned in seal form.'

'And is he?'

'Well, now, he might be, for there is one particular seal with big brown eyes who gazes at her longingly, and she is fairly certain it is her dear one.'

'But don't all seals have big brown eyes?'

'Indeed they do,' Allison said, nodding sagely. 'And all Gaelic folk songs have a tragic end. I'm sorry to have to warn you that in this one, our poor widow throws herself into the sea and is drowned.'

'Not saved by her seal husband?'

'That is for you to decide. Are you sure you want to hear this tragic tale? I warn you, it is a great deal more tragic when I sing it!'

'I'll be the judge of that,' Aleksei said. 'Miss Galbraith, the stage is yours.'

She swept him a curtsy that inadvertently gave him a delightful view of her cleavage. She took a deep breath that made her very distracting cleavage quiver, exhaling in a fit of the giggles. Then she clasped her hands, and assumed the mournful, yearning look that all singers of folk songs seem to think de rigueur, and began the lament.

And it was truly lamentable. Though the Gaelic language was likely suited to a breathless wavering voice, Allison's sounded more like the wind whistling through the sails of a ship in a tempest, or the howl of a wolf across the steppes. Every time he met her eyes, he was almost overset, struggling between appalled disbelief and laughter, but she made it through to the widow's final shrill wail to her seal husband, before collapsing in a heap beside him on the *chaise longue*. 'Oh, dear heavens, I can't remember the last time I laughed so much.'

'And I can't remember the last time I heard such a bloody awful racket,' Aleksei said with feeling.

'I did warn you.'

'You did indeed.' He handed her a glass of lemonade. 'I think you have earned that.'

She took a deep draught. 'What I've earned is a traditional Russian folk song in response. Don't be shy now, you can't possibly be as useless as me.'

'Give me a moment to think of something suitable.' He cleared his throat. Emulating her performance, he got to his feet and made a bow. 'Madame Galbraith, I give you that tragic Cossack ditty: "I lost my leg, my own true love".'

I lost my leg, my own true love, in a battle far away.

*I lost my leg, my own true love, a price I
was glad to pay.
When I return, my own true love, you'll
kiss the pain away.*

*And now you're back, my own true love,
and what am I to say?
I cannot bear to see your pain, to see you
maimed this way.
So I'm afraid, my own true love, that you
must hop away!*

'You made that up!' Allison shrieked, in fits
of laughter.

'Believe me, some of the real ones are worse.'

Aleksei sat down beside her, taking her
hands in his. She had long abandoned her evening gloves. The fire and the wine had put a soft
glow in her cheeks. The songs and their shared
laughter, and the flickering candles wrapped
them in an intimacy that made a mockery of the
very short time they had known each other. Tomorrow he would leave her to begin his search
for the missing governess, and who knew how
long before he would see her again? Who knew
how long after that it would be, before she returned to England? So little time. And he could
not recall wanting anything so much as this.

This woman in his arms by the firelight. And her kiss.

'Allison,' he said, a question and a caress.

'Aleksei,' she said, in a manner that left him in no doubt.

He slid his arm around her waist, but she needed no urging, leaning into him, her own arm around his neck. It started as the most fragile of kisses. Their lips met. Touched. Hesitated. Then their eyes drifted closed, their mouths softened into each other, opening to each other, and the kiss transformed into a very adult kiss. There was no awkwardness, no clashing or jarring, only a sweet melting sensation, the lightest of friction.

His tongue traced the length of her bottom lip. She sighed, parting her lips in wordless encouragement. He took it, his mouth covering hers, the kiss deepening, kindling a fire low in his belly. His tongue touched hers and he groaned, sliding his hand from her waist to cup her bottom through her skirts, and the smoking coil of desire inside him began to burn more brightly and he closed his eyes and surrendered to the dangerous, delightful taste of her.

Kisses. He had forgotten what it was like, to lose himself in kisses. Or perhaps he had not been so lost before. He trailed kisses down her neck, over the soft swell of her breasts, into the tantalising valley between them. And then he kissed her mouth again, and their tongues tangled, and he felt such a jolt of desire as the blood rushed to his groin, that it shocked him. Forcing himself to slow down, to ease himself free, he saw his shock and his desire reflected in her face, in the lambent light in her eyes, the flush of her cheeks.

'I have wanted to do that from the moment you walked into the palace,' Aleksei said, his voice rough with passion.

'I have wondered what it would be like,' Allison replied, her voice as husky as his. 'And now I know.'

'I can say it won't happen again, but I don't want to.'

'Then don't say it. And please,' she said, catching his hand, 'don't warn me that it can mean nothing, for I am perfectly well aware—our paths have crossed only very temporarily.' Her face fell. 'And for a very specific reason. I did not expect to be—Aleksei, you know that I would never be so foolish as to compromise what it is you brought me here to do. This…'

'Is an unexpected bonus, as far as I am con-

cerned.' He kissed her hand. 'I have been counting the days till your arrival. Nothing is more
important to me than uncovering the truth,
whatever the hell it is.'

'Then we should get some rest. It is very late,
and we both have a long day ahead of us.'

'You are right.' He got to his feet, helping
her up. 'I wish it were otherwise, but you are
correct. Tomorrow, Miss Galbraith, Count Derevenko will meet you after breakfast for a formal tour of the house and gardens, after which
I will introduce you to your charges. But tonight…'

He pulled her into his arms, kissing her
deeply. 'For now, Aleksei bids the delectable
Allison goodnight.'

The next day, Allison was not feeling in the
least delectable, but rather a completely confused Miss Galbraith by the time they had
finished the tour of the palace. Her head was
reeling with the magnitude of the task she
faced, and she had no difficulty whatsoever in
forgetting all about the previous night.

'Have you seen enough?' Aleksei asked as
they re-entered the huge central rotunda on the

second floor which she thought, but could not be certain, had been their starting point.

'Enough to conclude that it's highly unlikely any poison—if there was poison—was contained in food from the kitchens,' she said, relieved to be able to make even this basic deduction. 'All the food that is sent to the dining room is delivered in communal platters, and the leftovers are returned to the kitchens, where they are given to the servants. Since they are all still hale and hearty then it seems reasonable to conclude—well, a different method must have been used. The poison may have been mixed with a drink. Or it may have been administered directly on to the skin.'

She bit her lip, desperate to reassure Aleksei before he departed, but unwilling to create a false sense of hope. 'That implies a level of physical proximity. Poisoning is often an intimate crime. If it was a servant, then it must have been a trusted one—butler, valet, that kind of person.'

Alexei frowned. 'But we come back to the fact that my brother was a duke. If he was murdered, then it must have been for a very good reason. And if you did commit such a murder, whatever the reason, you'd flee the scene of the crime, wouldn't you? And since all of Michael's personal servants are still here…'

'Save for Anna Orlova. You don't think she could be hiding in the palace?' Allison said, only half-teasing. The rotunda was an immense domed space with two rows of Doric columns marking its circumference, and a highly polished and treacherously slippery wooden marquetry floor. A second row of columns stood sentry around the shallow gallery which ran around the rotunda at the next level, and above that, light coursed down through the central glass skylight. 'This place is so huge, I'm sure I would get hopelessly lost if left to find my way about alone.'

'Just don't wander down any of the back stairs,' Aleksei joked. 'It could be months before your skeleton is discovered.'

'How very reassuring! In England we tend to keep our skeletons safely hidden away in closets.'

'Is that where yours reside?'

For a split second, Allison wondered if The Procurer had betrayed her, but that was foolish. Aleksei was simply teasing, and a welcome relief it was too. 'If what you say about St Petersburg is true,' she retorted, 'there must be a spacious skeleton closet in every home.'

'It is de rigueur.'

'Are yours behind this set of doors? I don't think that we've been inside, though I could not swear to it.'

'You're right. Not a skeleton closet alas, but in fact the largest room in the palace.'

'Then it must be vast. No one could ever accuse this place of having a homely feel.'

'Certainly not. This is the Derevenko Palace, the residence of one of the richest families in Russia, and this room is designed to ensure that anyone who enters it is left in no doubt of that.' Aleksei threw open the double doors with a flourish, bowing low before her. '*Pazvol'tye mnye predstavit*, Miss Galbraith,' he said, with a theatrical bow. 'Which means, may I present to you, Miss Galbraith, the Gala Reception Room.'

The chamber was quite empty, which made it seem even more immense. The marquetry floor was worked in a complex pattern which seemed to lead the eye to the line of tall windows at the far end of the chamber, looking out on to a huge formal garden which, Allison deduced, must be at the rear of the palace. Arched windows alternated with matching arched doorways, adding to the sense of symmetry and grandeur, with Corinthian pillars of dark-red marble set in between. The doors were worked in gilt—or what might well be gold leaf. And above, the frieze depicted a series of scenes from…

'Homer's *Iliad*,' Aleksei told her, his gaze following hers. 'What do you think?'

Overblown and slightly preposterous, if truth be told. 'I think if the objective is to overwhelm the visitor then it succeeds admirably.'

Something of her distaste came through in her tone, but rather than take umbrage, Aleksei burst out laughing. 'You don't feel inclined to fall to your knees in obeisance, I take it.'

'Is this what it's used for? Is there a throne?'

'Actually, there is, though it's not always here, because mostly this room is used for receptions and balls. My mother had all those mirrors hung. She liked to see her reflection, she was as vain as she was beautiful.'

'And you do resemble her,' Allison said, recalling the portrait, 'though I don't think anyone would ever call you beautiful.'

'*Spaseba,*' Aleksei said. 'I think. Shall we go?'

'I'm sorry. It hadn't occurred to me that this might be painful for you.'

'Every room redolent with memories?' Aleksei's smile was twisted. 'My mother died ten years ago, and my father five years before that. As an adult, I've spent very little time in St Petersburg and of late, thanks to Napoleon, none.'

'But this was your childhood home. You must have some happy memories of the palace.'

'I remember Michael and I used to ride our wooden horses here in the winter. You have to understand, Allison, over the years, we spent very little time in one another's company. By the time I was sent off to military school at the age of six, Michael, at ten, was already spending most of his day taking lessons in our family history, in etiquette and the traditions and rules of the court, in the running of the estates and many palaces he would one day inherit.'

'An unfair burden on one so young.'

'My thoughts exactly. You can have no idea,' Aleksei said wryly, 'how relieved I was when Elizaveta finally gave birth to a son.'

'And will your nephew receive the same upbringing as his father?'

'He is the Duke, it is how things are done here.'

'Poor little Nikki.' Allison grimaced. 'I confess, I never thought I'd feel sorry for a duke.'

'The boy knows no different. Most people would think him very fortunate indeed, though not I.' He gazed around the vast space of the Gala Reception Room. When he spoke he made no attempt to disguise the sneer in his voice. 'St Petersburg was built on vanity, and it thrives on it to this day. They say that tens of thousands of serfs and Swedish prisoners of war died building the city. Or rather whisper it behind their hands and their fans, as they do when they gossip and speculate endlessly.'

'You really don't approve of polite society, do you?'

'No more than you, from what you told me last night.'

Last night. The atmosphere between them changed in an instant. Or was it her imagination? The air between them wasn't really crackling. There was no actual cord pulling her towards him. She could easily brush away his hand as his fingers trailed lightly over her cheek. His touch was cool, that was why she shivered in response. When she reached up to mirror his action, to touch his cheek, it was a reflex, that was all.

'We should not. Not here. We are working,

we agreed we need strict demarcation lines,'
Allison said.

'We did.'

His hand smoothed down the back of her
gown to rest lightly on her waist. He did not
urge her to step closer, but she did anyway.
'Yes,' she said, tilting her head and closing her
eyes.

'Yes,' Aleksei whispered, before his mouth
covered hers.

The most fleeting of kisses, too little and far
too much. They sprang apart.

'Time is marching on,' Aleksei said, 'we
need to concentrate on the matter in hand.'

'Yes,' Allison agreed, refusing to meet his
gaze. 'We should inspect the herb garden before the children return.'

'These are fabulous,' Allison exclaimed,
standing on the terrace which overlooked the
formal gardens at the rear of the Derevenko
Palace. 'How fortunate you are.'

Aleksei had only ever considered the gardens
of Derevenko Palace a vast playground, when
he was a boy. Now, he had no interest in them
whatsoever, and while he could see that the
expanse of green manicured lawn, the formal

flower beds, symmetrical paths interspersed with small fountains and statues were pleasing to the eye, he could see little in the vista to elicit the rapturous look in Allison's eyes. 'Not so very different from many gardens I've seen in England. Or France. Or even Italy, for that matter. In Spain, the climate is arid. There is less greenery,' he said vaguely.

'Gardens are not really your cup of tea, I take it,' Allison said, eyeing him with amusement.

'Not really.'

'Then I will explore them at my leisure, or with the children. Let us concentrate on the herb garden.'

Aleksei led the way down the steps and on to the path leading to the walled area. Opening the wooden door set into the high wall surrounding the herb garden, he stood back to permit her to enter first.

'Oh!' Allison gazed about her with delight. A wide paved path split the garden into two halves. Low, neatly trimmed box hedges set in groups of four formed planting areas, and smaller gravel paths ran between each. Against each of the four walls, other borders were planted, and the walls themselves had been used to support a huge variety of small trees and shrubs. Aleksei could not put a name to a single plant, but even he could see that the riot of late summer colour was pretty enough, the perfumed scent heady.

'Oh, how wonderful,' Allison breathed ecstatically, before setting off down the path to the first box enclosure, grabbing his hand and forcing him to accompany her. 'Here are some of the most common herbs,' she said. 'Mint, peppermint, and skullcap. Various forms of thyme. Lemon verbena. Comfrey. Parsley. Chervil. Lovage. All fairly hardy, and so in the most exposed location, do you see?'

He saw only lots of plants, but fortunately Allison either expected no response, or else took his silence for acquiesce. 'Here we have fennel, dill, comfrey. Angelica. Oh, and St John's wort, valerian, and you don't need me to tell you that is lavender,' she added, gesturing at the silvery line of plants which marched along one long border. 'Rosehip here, and rosemary too, in the sunniest part of the garden.' On she dragged him. 'Those flowers that look like daisies are echinacea, and over here we have the various berries, and there—'

She broke off, making a wry face. 'But you're not interested in a lesson in horticulture, are you? You want to know whether any of these plants could have poisoned your brother. And the answer is—oh, Aleksei, I wish the answer was straightforward, but it's not. Many of these plants, in the correct combination, could be lethal. Yet in a different combination they can act as curatives. The problem is though, that constructing the correct combination, of dried leaves or fresh, seeds or flower parts, roots—it requires a great deal of knowledge and skill.'

'Which neither of our suspects possess, you mean?'

'Which very few people possess, I mean. I think we must look for something simple and easily obtained. If your brother was poisoned, given what you have said of the risk and the consequences, then the murderer would have to ensure that he committed as near the perfect crime as possible—no one else involved in making a poison, no one suspicious of any poison purchased, and a poison which produced something which looked enough like an apoplexy to fool a very well-respected doctor.'

'A perfect crime, or a perfectly natural death. You think I am—what is the phrase, jumping up the wrong tree?'

'Barking,' Allison corrected, smiling, 'and

no, I don't. I think you need to be sure, one way or another. I will do my best to help you, and hopefully by the time you have found Madame Orlova, I will have something definitive to tell you.'

'I plan to head first for the Orlova family home and pick up the trail from there. You must not worry, Michael—dammit, Nikki's man of business will look after things.'

'It's the children I'm worried about. I am a complete stranger to them.'

'You know that I'm not really expecting you to teach them, only to ensure that they are taken care of? They have been perfectly content with their nanny and an escape from the schoolroom these last months. Time enough for them to return to their normal routine when this is over.'

'Yes, but I would like to help them in any way I can. My heart goes out to them.'

'I thought that you would be happy to be spared teaching duties, but you must do as you see fit. I trust you.'

'You do?'

He drew her closer. 'I do. I have every faith in you.'

She smiled up at him. 'Thank you.' Her fingers clutched his tightly. 'You have no idea how much that means to me.'

'Allison, before I leave I need to ask you if you regret last night.'

'No, I don't.' A blush stole up her throat, but she met his gaze fully. 'I am thirty-one years old. I will not pretend to innocence, though my experience is limited, for my vocation matters more to me than any man, and always will. But I am sick of the double standards which require a professional woman to be beyond reproach. I am tired of suppressing my feelings and I'm weary of having to disguise my looks. Last night was…'

She was blushing furiously now. 'I think it was perfectly obvious how I felt about last night, but for the sake of clarity, since we have no time to dance around the subject, then let me tell you that I would be more than happy to— to carry on from where we left off on your return, on the strict understanding that it doesn't interfere with our task.'

She looked so adorably flustered he wanted to kiss her. Which was the thing she'd asked him not to do. 'Then for the sake of clarity, let me reassure you that I am similarly more than happy to continue on those terms.'

'Then we have a deal.' She held out her hand, the gesture of an English gentleman, intending to shake his, but that was a step too far for Aleksei. He kissed her fingertips lightly. And she exhaled sharply. And despite their agreement, his resolution weakened. She stepped towards him. He moved towards her.

'Your Illustrious Highness. Forgive my interruption.' The servant's voice made them leap apart 'You asked to be informed immediately His Serene Highness Duke Nicholas returned.'

'Who?' Allison asked bemusedly.

Aleksei grinned. 'Nikki, and presumably his two sisters. Come, Madam Governess, it is time for you to meet your charges.'

Chapter Five

Aleksei had been gone almost three weeks, during which time Allison had made limited progress with her investigations and even less with the children. Which hurt. She knew she was being foolish, she had known they would view her as an interloper and what's more Aleksei had made it clear that he did not expect her to launch any sort of charm offensive, yet she opened the schoolroom door each morning with a sinking heart.

Nikki stood to attention at his desk, looking as if he was about to salute her. Catiche and Elena rose reluctantly, dropping the most grudging of curtsies and sank back on to their chairs before Allison had even reached hers. Nikki's nascent smile faded as Elena yanked him unceremoniously back into his seat, hissing something at him in Russian.

'Good morning.' Allison's smile was fixed. She knew it was too wide and too rigid. She also knew it would not be returned.

'Good morning, Miss Galbraith,' the three children chorused in perfect and perfectly expressionless English.

Allison made a show of shuffling the papers and books stacked on her desk, studying her charges from beneath her lashes. She had been prepared for reserve, expected tantrums, these were troubled orphans after all, but this sullen display of outward compliance, she was finding very difficult to penetrate.

Catiche, at thirteen, was coltish, at that awkward stage between girl and young woman. She seemed to be tangled in legs grown too long, both embarrassed and proud of her burgeoning curves. Her features were maturing from childhood cuteness, too raw to be beautiful as yet, though with all the signs of beauty to come. As the eldest, it was to be expected that she would be most affected by the loss of her parents and governess, but Catiche hid it inordinately well, doing her crying in private, and refusing point blank to acknowledge any redness in her eyes when Allison had gently raised the subject. For the most part her expression was taciturn. Her eyes were disconcertingly Baltic blue, exactly like Aleksei's and every bit as icy. The only emotion she made no attempt to disguise was a contempt for the English intruder.

Elena, on the other hand, was less troubled but more troublesome. The middle child, angelically fair and very much aware of her charm, it was she who pulled her siblings' strings. If Allison wasn't so set upon being charitable, she'd have labelled Elena a precocious brat in need of a good setting down. A true child of St Petersburg was Elena, a consummate machinator who would baulk at nothing to achieve her objectives. And her objective was clearly to have their new governess dispatched back to England, the sooner the better.

Allison was no teacher, but she had dedicated her life to caring, and had always considered herself empathetic, yet she had signally failed to engage with her charges. She was most horribly aware that her overtures were becoming increasingly desperate and therefore increasingly transparent. The harder she tried, the more the children responded with what seemed to be contempt. Only Nikki seemed inclined to succumb to her attempts at friendly engagement, but Elena always made sure this weakness in her brother was short-lived, her sotto voce threats in Russian clearly intended to remind him of where his loyalties lay.

And then there was the dog. Allison shuddered with distaste. As if on cue, a noxious smell which was becoming revoltingly familiar wafted across the schoolroom, and Ortipo the bulldog gave a self-congratulatory bark. She knew it was ridiculous to think that an animal could be in cahoots with three children, but she was nevertheless sure that this was, somehow, the case. She didn't like dogs, though she had learnt to keep her feelings on the subject to herself, for the English, she had discovered, were inordinately fond of the creatures. Wives neglected by their husbands, and children neglected by their parents found, in the family lapdog, a comfort and companionship that Allison found odd but comprehensible.

Ortipo, however, was by no stretch of the imagination a tame lapdog. He didn't like to be petted, and took to growling menacingly at the least provocation. With the face of a failed pugilist, the breath of a dedicated drunkard, and a digestive system which would put an incontinent sow to shame, as far as Allison was concerned, Ortipo was as endearing as a decaying rat. Needless to say, the Derevenko children were besotted with him.

Ortipo, his expression impassive, extruded another noxious emission. Nikki giggled, holding his nose, and Allison only just managed to suppress a retch. 'Do you not think,' she said, trying not to breathe through her nose, 'the animal would be happier in the fresh air, rather than cooped up in the schoolroom?'

Catiche responded with a haughty look. 'Ortipo is not an animal, he is a bulldog with a very impressive pedigree. What is more, Ortipo is a Derevenko, and therefore does no one's bidding. Especially not an Englishwoman's.'

'Miss Galbraith is not English, she is from Scotland.'

Allison whirled around. Aleksei stood in the doorway, clad in riding clothes. His boots were dusty, he had obviously just arrived back for he was still carrying his gloves and whip, and judging from his expression, his search had been fruitless. 'Children, bid your uncle good morning.'

The request was unnecessary. All three were already on their feet, the girls dropping into careful curtsies, Nikki making a stumbling bow. Even Ortipo rolled upright from his bed with a welcoming yap to sit alert at Aleksei's feet, his stumpy tail thumping on the floor.

'What,' Aleksei said, wrinkling his nose, 'is that disgusting smell.'

'It is Ortipo,' Nikki said shyly, gazing up at his uncle with reverence.

Aleksei ignored the child, turning to Catiche. 'Get him out of here.'

'No!'

Aleksei turned his attention to Elena. 'I beg your pardon?'

The child, ignoring her big sister's warning look, held her ground under his steely gaze, much to Allison's admiration. 'Uncle Aleksei,' she said, 'Ortipo is our friend. He will be sad if he can't be with us.'

'Dogs cannot be sad,' Aleksei said, frowning down at his niece. 'And dogs as noxious as this have no place in the schoolroom.'

'But…'

'That is quite enough, Elena,' Allison said crisply, seeing that the girl was going to remonstrate further. 'It is inexplicable to me,' she whispered, drawing Aleksei to one side, 'but the children are extremely attached to the creature.'

'It is clear that you are not. Why subject yourself…?'

'Because the children love him, Aleksei. Because Ortipo is all they have left. When Elena said Ortipo will be sad, she meant that *she* will be sad.'

'Fine! On your head be it—or should that be your nose?' Aleksei said shortly. 'I have more important things to discuss with you than a dog. Call the nanny, I am anxious to hear how you have been progressing. Better than I, I hope.'

Allison's heart sank at the thought of explaining how her time had been spent in his absence while he was in such a foul mood. 'No need to call Nyanya just yet,' she said brightly. 'It is a lovely day. Children,' she said, turning to her charges before he could question her, 'we will take Ortipo for a walk in the gardens.'

The children, relieved to be released from another English lesson they didn't require, needed no encouragement, and ran ahead of them along the paths. 'I take it you found no trace of Madame Orlova?' Allison asked, eyeing Aleksei warily.

'As goose chases go it was a particularly wild one.'

He had discarded his hat and gloves and his greatcoat. In the bright sunlight, she could see the dark shadows under his eyes, his sculpted mouth drawn into a firm line, a frown knitting his brows together as he stared into the distance at the retreating backs of his wards. She wanted to touch him, simply to reassure him, but like the children, she was intimidated. He was not precisely a stranger, but at this moment he felt like one—remote, self-contained and very much the soldier. 'Her family could shed no light on her whereabouts?'

'None. They deny all knowledge of her, and seem genuinely concerned for her well-being. I believe them too,' Aleksei said, knuckling his eyes, 'for they were happy to provide me with a list of her friends, previous employers. Every one of them led to a dead end. The trail is cold.'

'Aleksei, has it occurred to you that she might be…?'

'Dead? Of course I've considered it, but if she is, then where is her body? She can't have buried herself. Though perhaps that is exactly what she has done in order to escape justice,' he said, grimacing. 'Or perhaps she is perfectly innocent and simply doesn't want to be found. I don't know. I need a hot bath and a sleep.' He sighed heavily, rolling his shoulders. 'But first, I'd very much like to hear how your investigations have been progressing. Assuming you have made progress?'

Allison steered him towards a bench set under a trellis on which the last of the summer's roses bloomed. Aleksei sank down without complaint, stretching his long legs out in front of him.

'If we assume that a natural poison was used,' she began, 'then we can eliminate a great many of the commonly available herbs which grow in this climate. Once matched with Michael's symptoms, the list of candidates is smaller still. While I could concoct any number of poisons from the contents of this garden and the succession houses, all require considerable expertise. But I did not confine myself to this garden.'

'Please tell me you haven't been prowling around the gardens of my neighbours.'

She laughed. 'Yes, that is exactly what I would have done if I'd wanted to arouse suspicion, but fortunately I had no need. There is a very famous Apothecary's Garden in St Petersburg,' Allison said. 'It was founded by Peter the Great, and from what I could gather when I visited last week, it seems to contain every medicinal species known to man—and a great many utterly unknown to this woman!' She clasped her hands together, momentarily distracted. 'You are so fortunate to have such a place right here on your doorstep. What I would give to be able to work there.' Her face fell. 'Though here, as in England, my sex prevents me. I was, however, able to speak to one of the apothecary gardeners, a relative of your own head gardener. Sergei, you know?'

'No. I did not.'

'No. Well, of course not.' Flustered, Allison shied away from explaining why Sergei owed her a favour, and returned to the salient point. 'In a nutshell,' she said, 'there is a plethora of poisonous plants available from the Apothecary's Garden which anyone could access, if they knew what they were looking for. Obviously, apothecaries sell ready-made potions, but a prospective murder is unlikely to risk discovery by wandering into an apothecary's shop and asking for a jar of deadly poison!'

'So the poison could have been stolen from the Apothecary's Garden but is unlikely to have been purchased from an apothecary, is that what you are saying.'

'Yes.' Allison frowned. 'One thing I have not

resolved is the gap between your two prime suspects' last-known presence here, and Michael's death. There are some poisons which have a delayed effect, but slow-acting poisons tend to produce slow-acting symptoms.'

'Then our prime suspects are not our prime suspects because they were not here on the morning Michael died?'

'The poison could have been in—say, a wine decanter, or a piece of fruit, or even in a cologne or some lotion, but if that is so, the perpetrator would have to be confident that he wouldn't poison someone else by mistake.'

'So it's more likely that it was administered directly?'

'I'm sorry, I know it's not what you want to hear, but...' Allison sighed. 'If I wanted to commit the perfect crime, I would not leave anything to chance. We know from the visitors' book that Michael had no callers that morning, but Derevenko Palace is so large, Aleksei, don't you think that someone could have got in without the servants knowing?'

'Someone he knew and trusted? Yes, it's possible, of course it is.' He thumped his leg with his fist. 'Any sane person would give up. I wish to the devil that I could give up, but I can't.

I know that there is something which doesn't add up to all this, I know it. If we could even prove that it was *not* murder,' he exclaimed. 'I would much *rather* prove that it was not murder, that there was some perfectly rational explanation for Michael's change of will, and for the Orlova woman's disappearance. But so far we have more questions than answers.'

She caught his hand as he made to strike himself again. 'I'm so sorry I cannot be more definitive.'

'No.' He unfurled his fist to clasp her fingers. 'Don't apologise. You have made more progress than I have.'

'For what it is worth, I do think you are right. There is something that does not add up.'

His expression softened. 'That is good to hear. Don't worry, I've no intentions of giving up just yet. I have come too far to do that.'

'As indeed have I!' She had given up once. She had stopped believing in herself once. Never again. 'I have come all the way from England, and I've no intention of going back there until I have completed the task you brought me here to do.'

'I believe I've told you before, but it bears repeating. I am very glad that you are here.'

Aleksei's smile was warm. He kissed her fingertips. 'We will regroup and talk later, when I am clean and rested. How have you been coping with the children? I presume they are behaving themselves?'

It was a perfunctory question. She could answer in kind, but what would satisfy Aleksei's conscience would not appease her own. 'I am finding them difficult,' Allison said, choosing her words with care. 'They are very reserved, extremely reluctant to warm to me.'

'What does it matter whether they like you or not? It's not as if you are to be any sort of permanent fixture in their lives.'

Which was perfectly true, but his coolness irked her. 'The tragedy is that the only permanent fixture in their life at present is that blasted dog,' Allison retorted. 'They need something—someone—to replace their parents.'

'Their blasted governess, you mean.'

'No, I don't! I mean their mother and father, Aleksei, both of whom, from what the servants have told me, were loving and attentive parents, and whose presence in those children's lives must be very much missed.'

'You seem to have been gathering a great deal of information from the servants.'

The second time this morning she'd had the opportunity to confess, but she did not want to divert the conversation from her charges. 'And from the children too,' Allison said, neatly avoiding the issue. 'Elizaveta and Michael were not the kind of parents who saw their children once a day in the drawing room after dinner. They read stories to them, sat through some of their lessons, played games with them.'

'Really?' Aleksei looked sceptical. 'If that is the case, Michael took a very different approach to rearing his offspring from our parents.' He shaded his eyes with his hand to block the dazzle of late sunshine, and watched the three children playing a game of fetch which involved both Ortipo and Nikki chasing a large stick. 'They don't seem noticeably unhappy.'

'Children are very resilient creatures, but I know that deep down they are grieving. Perhaps it's for the best, after all, that they continue to resent me.'

'Why do you say that?'

'Because then they won't mind when I leave. They have already lost the three people they care most about, so it is better that they don't come to care for me.' Or you, for that matter, Allison thought sadly, but did not say.

Aleksei frowned over at his wards, now gathered around the edge of a large fountain, attempting to cast pebbles into the open mouth of a large stone fish from which water spouted. 'Michael and I used to play that game. I always won, much to his chagrin.'

'At least those three have each other.'

'You think I don't care for them, but you're wrong. I care enough to know that I'd be a terrible guardian. Even if I wanted to weigh myself down with the burden of those three, it would be wrong of me. As you quite rightly implied, what they need is stability, a mother to rear them and a father to look after their interests.'

'Is your cousin Felix married, then?'

'No. I've never thought about it before, I wonder—but it doesn't matter. I'm sure, when—if—I clear his name and hand him custody of Michael's children, he'll find a suitable wife.'

'You could do that.'

'Take a wife, simply in order to provide Michael's children with a mother?' he exclaimed, looking appalled. 'Even if I could persuade any female to wed me on such terms…'

'Don't be so modest, Aleksei, there would be a queue from here to Moscow willing to take you under any terms, as Nikki's guardian.'

'You are mocking me.'

'Only a little. Are you really so set against marriage?'

'I am married to the army, and even if I was not—I have no intentions of remaining in St Petersburg.'

'Must the children remain here?'

He shrugged irritably. 'Michael would not contemplate them being raised anywhere else.' In the distance, a bell rang and the children and dog began to stampede towards the house in eager search of their lunch.

Which meant that Allison had an appointment elsewhere too. 'I should go and…'

'I'll come with you. We'll go through the garden-room door, it's quicker.' He checked the path to ensure that the children were out of sight, before sliding his arms around her waist. 'My thoughts have not been wholly consumed by my search for the Orlova woman. Thinking about you has been a very pleasant distraction.'

Her heart began to thump in her ribcage. How could she have found him intimidating? The way he looked at her now, it made her blood fizz with anticipation. She couldn't doubt that he found her attractive. It was a heady feeling. 'Really?' Allison said, smiling teasingly, 'I on the other hand have been far too busy to spend much time thinking about you.'

He laughed. 'So you admit to thinking about me some of the time?' His hand slid up her arm, coming to rest on her shoulder. His thumb began to stroke circles on the sensitive skin at the back of her neck, under her hair. She shivered. She reached up to trace the white line of the scar on his brow, relishing the way he responded to her touch.

'Allison.' He spoke her name as a caress. 'I do believe we have unfinished business.'

'Aleksei, I do believe you are right.'

He did not have to urge her to close the miniscule gap between them, she did that of her own accord. Their lips met, a tentative touch at first, as if they were worried that the three weeks would have dulled the attraction between them, but they need not have. Soft lips, rough stubble, and the tantalising touch of his tongue, and she melted swiftly into the heat of him. It was over too quickly. It left them both staring, breathing heavily.

'Tonight, do you think?' he asked.

'Tonight,' she agreed, without a second thought, allowing him to lead her towards the door of the garden room, momentarily forgetting what he was likely to find there.

A few moments later, Aleksei stopped short in front of the snaking line of servants queuing in the corridor outside the garden room. There seemed to be a full wardrobe of Derevenko livery represented, including an underfootman, a gardener, a scullery maid, two chambermaids and a stable hand, along with two individuals whose colours he did not recognise and a small, ragged urchin. All of them, including the strangers, flapped into a fluster of bows and curtsies, while the urchin simply gazed at him with wide-eyed wonder that made Aleksei want to laugh. 'What the devil is going on here?'

With one accord, every face turned to Allison. Whose face had turned a bright, mortified red. 'It is my fault.'

An inkling of understanding made him survey the gathering anew. Two bandages. One sling. Whatever was wrong with the others remained, probably most thankfully, obscured from view.

'I can explain.'

'I look forward to being enlightened.'

'I'm sorry,' Allison said, turning to her expectant patients, 'but I am afraid I won't be able to…'

'No, wait here. Miss Galbraith will be with you shortly.' Aleksei ushered her back into the garden room, folding his arms across his chest and leaning against the door. 'I'm waiting.'

'Aleksei, I want to assure you that I would never…'

'Put anything before your obligations to me? I know that.'

'I did not intend to keep my little dispensary from you. I would have told you later, if you had not insisted upon escorting me here—' She broke off, grimacing. 'I'm sorry.'

'There truly is no need. I told you before I left that I trusted you, and I meant it. If you wish to utilise your skills for the benefit of Nikki's servants—though I confess, there were some in the crowd who did not look as if they belonged to the palace?'

'No.' She looked ridiculously guilty. 'They have no one else to turn to and if I did not treat them, they would simply go untreated. These people cannot afford to visit an apothecary, never mind consult a doctor, and in some cases they have been living with their ailments for so long, they have quite forgotten what it is like to be without pain. But I should have consulted you, at the very least.'

'I wasn't here to consult.'

'No, but...'

'Allison, I understand.'

'You do?'

'I suspect you can't help yourself.'

'You're right,' she said, eyeing him with surprise. 'I had forgotten how much I enjoy treating patients.'

Which implied that she no longer did. When she was embarrassed, her cheeks flushed. When she was hiding something, colour stole up her throat, as it did now. He waited, giving her time to explain, but she so clearly didn't want to. 'Well then,' Aleksei said, 'tell me how this free service came about.'

'It started with Natalya, Elizaveta's maid,' Allison said, looking relieved. 'I thought she had been crying, her nose and eyes were so swollen, but it turns out she suffers dreadfully from hay fever, which is very easily treated with elderflower and marigold.'

'I presume that Natalya sang your praises to the other servants?'

'Only to your valet, who suffers from swelling of the joints in the fingers and toes. He recommended me to the housekeeper who is perpetually bilious. Then the chef came to me when he developed lockjaw from a cut from a meat knife—fortunately, you have wild garlic in the garden, since I have none in my herbal chest, and the chef himself procured the necessary mustard oil. Then, let me see, yes, Sergei…'

'The head gardener who, I presume owed you a favour, hence your introduction to the Apothecary's Garden?'

'Yes,' Allison admitted, with a sheepish smile. 'He had fallen into a patch of stinging nettles, and his wife's niece who works in the kitchen of the Vasiliev Palace came to me with a stomach complaint, and—well, it just snowballed from there. I come here at lunchtime when the children are with their nanny. There are not usually so many waiting, though some—the groom you saw—come every day for treatment. He suffers from stones, poor man, and my cure is likely to cause him some considerable pain when they pass. But you are not interested in—Aleksei, you truly are not angry?'

'How could I possibly be? Aside from the good you are doing, the suffering you are alleviating, and the gap which I was not even aware needed filling, you obviously—simply listening to you talk, it's very clear to me that you relish what you are doing.'

Her eyes lit up. 'I love it.'

'I can see that you do.' He could not resist kissing her, but forced himself to do so swiftly. 'I will not keep you, you must be anxious to attend to them. I will see you later.' Recalling the stack of post which had accumulated in his absence, and the latest list of questions from the over-zealous man of business, Aleksei rolled his eyes. 'Much later. Meet me here, after dinner.'

Another kiss would be a temptation too far. He opened the door, startling the waiting patients. 'Now, who is first in line?'

Chapter Six

'**W**here are we going?'

'I am taking you sightseeing.'

Aleksei led her out into the garden. The night sky was clear, the air chilly as he led her along a path to the perimeter wall, producing a key which opened a wooden door set into it. To Allison's surprise, they emerged on to the banks of the Moyka River. A large boathouse jutted out into the water. Aleksei produced a second key and, as she stepped warily into the gloomy interior, she could hear the gentle lapping of the waters against the wooden supports. She had no sense of the scale of the building itself until he lit a lamp, at which point she found her jaw dropping at this latest demonstration of the Derevenko's vast wealth. 'Good grief!'

'My father's idea,' Aleksei said of the huge

barge which took up most of the mooring, dwarfing the smaller, everyday boat moored alongside it. 'He took to heart the idea that St Petersburg was the Venice of the north, and had this built, modelled on a craft in one of the Italian painter Canaletto's waterscapes. It's monstrous, isn't it?'

'Magnificently so,' Allison agreed, reaching out to touch the high gold-painted stern on which was perched a carved image of the same bird which was carved over the entrance to the palace.

The barge sat low in the water, surrounded on three sides by wooden decking. Though the hull was painted white, it seemed to her that everything else, including the rudder, was covered in gold. A huge throne-like chair was built into the shelter of the stern, covered in crimson velvet. A cabin—if such a thing could be called a cabin—was constructed in the centre of the barge, the roof supported by wooden pilasters painted to look like marble. She made her way along the decking, counting the places for the oarsmen, Aleksei holding the lantern aloft for her. 'Eighteen. It must be tremendously hard work.'

'Impossibly hard,' Aleksei said. 'I took one

of the places once. It's far too heavy, utterly impractical. Unless you run with the tide, you need horses to help tow it. It's only used on state occasions, and then, obviously, only in the summer months. In the winter, every river and canal in St Petersburg freezes over. You ought to see the sleigh my father had built for those occasions,' he added, with one of his mocking smiles. 'Imagine something similar to this, only with runners. Come on, let me show you inside.'

It was a short step from the decking on to the barge, where Aleksei was already holding open the door to the covered area. Allison stepped through into a surprisingly small space, made sumptuous with velvet and furs, and glinting with more gold leaf.

Aleksei set the lantern down on the highly polished table, then threw himself on to the sofa. 'My head aches with questions. I was so sure that I would find that woman. I don't know what to do next.'

Allison sat down beside him, taking his hand between hers. 'It will come to you. What you need to do is stop fretting about it for a while.'

'You're right.' He rolled his shoulders, visibly relaxing, pulling her closer to him. 'Tell me, have any of the servants come to you seeking a love potion? Does such a thing exist?'

'Oh, they exist, all right, but they do not work. No elixir can compel someone to fall in love, though there are any number of quacks who will sell you something they swear will do just that. I never would. To have to ask for such a thing in the first place must surely mean that it's a lost cause. It is cruel to offer hope when there is none.'

'You think so, under any circumstances?' Aleksei asked seriously. 'I have had men— boys—mortally wounded, dying on the battlefield and begging to be told that they will live to see their loved ones again, while their lifeblood ebbs from them. I always lied, without compunction. Is that truly so wrong?'

The shadow of that last death, the mother's desperate pleas came back to her. Had she lied? She could not recall. 'No, I don't think that is wrong at all. I reckon I would do the same,' Allison replied. 'I cannot imagine the horrors and the suffering you have had to witness.'

'And inflicted, in the name of my country. It is ironic, is it not, that here we sit, you who have a vocation for healing, and I who have made a career out of killing.'

'You are a soldier, not a murderer.'

He shook his head, looking grim. 'There are times when there is a very fine line between the two. I'm not sure I have the stomach for the kind of wars our Emperor will wage now. More territory seized. More people put into servitude. More unnecessary deaths.'

'So you plan to leave the army, then?'

Aleksei sat up, shaking his head. 'I have not thought that far ahead,' he said dismissively. 'We're in danger of running out of sightseeing time. I thought we'd take a trip out on the water.'

'You're teasing me. Wouldn't we need another eighteen oarsmen?'

'I don't mean in this lumbering behemoth.' He got to his feet, pulling her with him. 'Being out on the water is the best way to see the true beauty of the city—and it is beautiful. When it is asleep, at peace under the stars, there is nowhere more beautiful than St Petersburg. Come, let me show it to you.'

Intrigued, she followed him to the far end of the deck, where he set about turning a large wheel which caused the riverside doors of the boathouse to slowly open. A set of steps led down to a small rowing boat, bobbing in the shadow of the barge. He leapt lightly into it, holding out his hand for her, though Allison needed no assistance, gathering the heavy folds of her cloak around her before climbing nimbly aboard.

'You've done that before.'

'Countless times,' she said, flashing him a smile. 'Fishing is a way of life where I come from. I can row too, I'm very proficient.'

'I don't doubt it, but you'll get a better view if you sit there.' He pointed at the wooden bench in the stern, which was strewn with pillows, a large blanket, neatly folded, placed on top.

She did as she was bid and tucked the blanket snugly around her, thinking that she did indeed have the perfect view as she watched Aleksei place the oars in the rowlocks and untie the boat from its moorings. He was wearing top boots and breeches, a wide-skirted coat, but no greatcoat. His movements were fluid, easy and graceful. Seated facing her on the middle bench, he nudged the craft away from the decking with the blade of an oar, expertly easing the little boat out of the boathouse and on to the river, heading upstream.

The sky above her was indigo blue, peppered with stars dimmed by the brightness of the full moon. On the opposite bank, a party of late-night revellers were singing something that sounded like a sea shanty. And in front of her, his legs braced, oars set, Aleksei smiled.

Allison smiled back. 'What are you waiting for, oarsman?' she said, with an imperious wave of her arm. 'Show me your city.'

He gave a little bow, then began to row with the seemingly effortless strokes of an expert, past two stone supports which were being constructed on either bank. 'The newest bridge, to be made of iron, and it's reputed it will be the biggest in St Petersburg,' he explained. 'When Peter the Great built the city, there were hardly any bridges. He imagined us as Venetians in the summer, making our way about the city in boats.'

'And sleds in the winter. I wish I could see that, but it's not to be unfortunately.'

'We're passing under the Red Bridge now. And the next one we come to is officially the Police Bridge, but everyone knows it as the Green Bridge.'

It was a beautiful night. She had forgotten how soothing the sound of oars dipping into water was, the rhythmic tug of the small craft easing forward with each pull. Though it was late, there were lights twinkling in the windows of some of the majestic buildings lining the quays. They passed numerous boathouses, large and small, any number of little jetties, boats nodding at their moorings.

'It is magical,' Allison said softly. 'It feels as if we are the only people in the city, as if it is laid out like this just for us, like some sort of dream world.'

Aleksei pulled the oars in, and let the little boat drift idly, holding out his hand to invite her to sit beside him. 'When I was a boy, I used to come out here at night to escape. I'd row for hours up river, all the way into the countryside. When you see it from there, the city is like a mystical island rising up from nowhere. It looks—I don't know, impossible that it could exist. Like a dream world, exactly as you said.'

'I'd love to see that. It's a shame we don't have time.'

'Another night, perhaps.'

The bench was narrow. His arm was clasped loosely around her waist. The night air was salty, fresh. Aleksei was warm, one leg pressed against hers, the other braced on one of the rowing boat's ribs. 'I used to negotiate the many canals with ease. I'd probably get lost now, there has been so much building since I was last here.'

She turned slightly, the better to see his face. 'Don't you miss it at all?'

'I miss this. It feels so familiar, as if I was born with a map of it engraved on my heart. Despite what I said, I don't for a moment think I'd ever get lost. I expect you think that sounds ridiculously fanciful.'

'No.' Allison let her head rest on his shoulder. 'I feel the same about Strachur, the village where I was raised, and the whole network of drovers' roads and ferries around that part of Argyll. I could find my way through the forests with my eyes closed, even after seven years away. It is in my blood.'

Aleksei pulled her closer, resting his chin on her head. 'Don't you ever think of returning?'

'There is nothing for me there now that Seanmhair has gone.'

'Shen-a-vair,' Aleksei pronounced carefully. 'Is this Scottish?'

'Gaelic.'

'In Russian we say *babushka*. I never knew any of my grandparents. Your *babushka* sounds like a very wise woman.'

'You must not be imagining some fluffy, white-haired, apple-cheeked old lady, you know.'

'Nor a witch, even?'

Allison chuckled. 'No, though my grandmother would most likely have found that description flattering. She was, as the saying goes, as hard as the stag's horn and as prickly as a thistle. She had a heart of gold too, but she kept it very much hidden from view.'

'And was there never anyone in this little Scottish village, who wished to claim you from this dragon of a grandmother?'

She lifted her head to meet his eyes. 'An admirer, you mean? Youthful flirtations, nothing more. Though in London, there was a man.'

She turned away from him to stare out at the water. She had never discussed Robert with anyone, rarely thought of him at all, once she had cut him from her life. She had no obligation to explain herself to Aleksei, but she wanted to. She had not permitted herself to imagine that their liaison would lead to making love but the possibility was there, and now she did think about it...

'When I first came to London, after my grandmother died, I was very lonely,' Allison said. 'This man and I, we became friends. And then…' She forced herself to turn back to Aleksei, hoping that the darkness would hide her blushes. 'You see I thought he felt as I did,' she continued awkwardly, 'that when we became lovers, it was simply a—a natural progression, though not one I wished to take further.'

'But he did not think the same way, I take it?'

'No,' she agreed sadly. She hated herself for having, albeit inadvertently, caused such hurt. 'He wanted us to marry, but for me that was out of the question. I was but a year in London, my list of patients expanding, but I was still nowhere near established. In the end it was an easy choice for me, but he took it badly, and I regret that.'

'Though not the decision.'

'No. He told me I was cold-hearted, but it's not that. I have a heart, but it is reserved for my patients, there is nothing left over for anyone else. My vocation means everything to me, Aleksei. And for a woman, a calling and a family are quite incompatible.'

'For a soldier too.'

'I hadn't thought of that. Is that why you have never married?'

'Because I'm married to the army, that old chestnut?'

'Well, is it true? There has never been anyone—you've never been in love?'

'I've never been in one place long enough.'

'So you don't believe in love at first sight, then?'

'A *coup de foudre*? The only fatal blows I am familiar with come from a sabre or a cannon ball. As to love—I've enjoyed numerous affaires.' Aleksei frowned down at the river. 'Lovemaking is the perfect antidote to making war—an unpalatable thought perhaps, though true none the less. But for me that's all it has ever been, an idyll between battles, I've never wanted more. Like you,' he said, 'my passion has been for my vocation, to serve my country.'

'And now?'

'I have no idea, and until we have resolved the mystery—but there you see, I've brought the conversation back round to the subject we said we would avoid.'

'Then we'll stop talking, and simply enjoy the view.'

'It is a very enjoyable view,' Aleksei said, angling himself towards her.

'I was thinking the very same myself,' Allison agreed with a teasing smile, 'when I was watching you clamber into the boat.'

'Miss Galbraith, were you admiring my rear?' He pulled her into his arms. 'If so, I should confess that I have, from the moment I first set eyes upon you, been very much an admirer of yours.'

'Aleksei!'

'Allison.' The way he said her name made her mouth go dry. 'You can have no idea how very, very worthy of admiration your rear is since it is quite literally behind you,' he said, sliding one hand down her back to cup her bottom, 'but believe me, it is.'

'If that is an attempt at a compliment, it is a novel one.'

She felt the rumble of his laughter. She felt the soft whisper of his breath on her face. 'It is not a compliment, it is the truth.'

Her heart began to pound. He was going to kiss her. She wanted him to kiss her. Ached for him to kiss her. She slipped her arms around his neck and angled her head in mute invitation. And he accepted it with alacrity.

The taste of him made her head spin. A hunger she had never experienced before ravened her as their lips met. She wanted to savour him, and at the same time to devour him. She felt torn, her body clamouring for release, but at the same time demanding deliciously protracted pleasure. She had never felt like this. She didn't want to feel like this. She wanted nothing more.

They clung to each other, their mouths locked, tongues touching, darting, thrusting, and hands, feverish hands seeking skin where there was only clothing. Aleksei's breathing was ragged. Hers was shallow. His cheeks were flushed, his eyes heavy-lidded. She didn't doubt his desire was as strong as her own as he cupped her breasts, stroked her back, the curve of her bottom.

Only when he tried to lift her closer, and the boat rocked wildly, one of the oars falling into the water, did they come to their senses. Flailing for the oar, Allison would have toppled in, had Aleksei not caught her.

'I think,' he said ruefully, pulling her back to safety before reaching for the oar, 'that someone somewhere is trying to tell us something.'

'By dousing us with cold water, you mean?'

A clock chimed in the distance. 'Or reminding us that tomorrow is rapidly approaching, and that our sightseeing expedition must end, for the time being.'

'You're right.' She settled herself reluctantly on the rear bench.

He leaned over, cupping her face and their cold lips met once more. 'I earnestly wish I was not.'

'So do I.' She pulled him closer, kissing him fiercely. 'So do I.'

Morning broke too quickly for Allison. Having lain awake for hours reliving their kisses, her body thrumming with frustrated anticipation, she had fallen into a deep sleep just as the sun rose, only to be awakened what seemed like a mere five minutes later, by Natalya bringing her tea.

The children were fretful, Catiche sullen, Elena determined upon mischief, finally succeeding when she deliberately tore the ear from Nikki's favourite knitted rabbit, resulting in an epic tantrum and a storm of tears which summoned the almost-deaf nanny from her room.

By now extremely relieved to surrender her charges to the old woman's care, Allison resisted the temptation to return to her chamber and, with more than two hours to spare before she was due to open up her dispensary, decided to explore the succession houses again. She was in the first of the glasshouses, a fernery, eyeing the incongruous statue of a completely naked Aphrodite set under a palm tree, when the creak of the door alerted her to another presence.

'I saw you from the study window, and followed you here.' Aleksei was dressed in his formal uniform, freshly shaved, and looking ridiculously, sinfully attractive.

'Good morning. The children were...' She bit her tongue. He wasn't in the least bit interested in the children's mood. 'I thought I'd take another look to see if I've missed anything.'

'I am going to miss you.' He took her hand, made to kiss it, then changed his mind, pulling her suddenly into his arms and kissing her lips instead.

'Aleksei! You must not—what do you mean, you will miss me? Where are you going?'

'I've been thinking. Since I couldn't sleep last night, my—my mind being over-stimulated...'

'Aleksei!'

He held up his hands in mock surrender. 'I was thinking about my next move, and I came back to the question of possible motive. It is a long shot, but I thought it was worth trying to find out a bit more of Michael's activities in the period before he died. I thought I could take up some of those invitations I keep receiving, attend the court, ask a few pertinent questions, reconnoitre the lay of the land, so to speak. If I'm very, very lucky, I might even find someone who knows where the Orlova woman might be hiding.'

'That's an excellent idea.'

'Yes, it's brilliant,' Aleksei agreed sardonically. 'Endless meetings and dinners and parties fuelled by gossip and speculation. All my favourite activities.'

'But well worth it if it flushes out a new suspect, or more importantly, helps you to flush out our prime suspect.'

'Indeed. I will be paying a call on my cousin, our only available suspect too. So I should warn you that I will require to be away from the palace a good deal in the next week or so.' He took her hand again, saluting over it and pressing the lightest of kisses to her fingertips. 'I hope it will not be too long before Aleksei and Allison can meet in more congenial circumstances.'

Watching him walk purposefully away, and hoping that the congenial circumstances were not too many days away, Allison reminded herself that Miss Galbraith had a fee to earn.

She began to wander through the fernery, enjoying the rich, loamy aroma of the compost, the slightly bitter scent of the larger ferns, testing herself to see if she could name them all. A fish pond lay at the centre of the succession house, stocked with colourful carp. A little woodland grove planted along one wall caught her attention. Here was yellow-leaved meadowsweet, which was good for the digestion. A late-flowering knotweed. Blowsy chrysanthemum in autumn gold and copper. The dried crimson spikes on this one suggested it was the lily known as red-hot pokers. This one, with its plumes of tall white flowers, she didn't recognise, but beside it was a clump of delphiniums, one of the flowers Lady Hunter favoured for her vases. Allison had fond memories of trailing through the garden in her ladyship's wake, carrying the trug.

Suddenly, she recalled the salutary lesson Grandmother had taught her when she had brought back a bunch of the blowsy blooms to the cottage as a surprise.

'By all that is sacred!' Allison exclaimed.

The drawing in the book which Seanmhair

had shown her had looked, to Allison's un-initiated eyes, exactly like the flowers Lady Hunter had given her to take home. It had the same shape and stature. But the stem and the leaves depicted in the drawing were a much darker green and, her grandmother told her, rough to the touch. Where the delphinium had bell-shaped flowers, the other plant had sinis-ter, cowl-like hoods, a vivid blue in colour, the stamen almost black, glinting with moisture and, to Allison's childish eye, malignant.

'Wolf's Bane. Monkshood. Devil's Hel-met. Aconite.' She remembered pronouncing the strange words carefully. There were many names for this darkly beautiful and deadly plant, for every single component, from petal, to seed, to root, was poisonous. The roots and seeds were especially dangerous if ingested, but equally lethal if the skin was pierced by an arrow or a dart or a knife.

Allison stared at the delphiniums mes-merised, trying to recall everything she knew about its lethal lookalike. Death could be speedy. A racing heart, a squeezing of the chest or gripe of the stomach, then it was over. But sometimes it took longer. There could be violent sickness. Some victims complained of numbness spreading across their body, some claimed that their bellies were on fire, or that they felt as if ants were crawling under their skin. Some sweated, some shivered, became delirious. Ultimately, breathing became more and more laboured, and always death, when it came, left the victim struggling frantically for air as if they were drowning, or being smothered. Or having an apoplexy.

Could Wolf's Bane have killed Michael? Without question. But it was the next question Allison asked herself which made her stop in her tracks. She needed to consult her Culpeper's *Herbal Guide*. She needed to inform Aleksei…

No! For what she was contemplating was so radical, she had to be certain of her facts. She would bide her time, do some further research. And in the meantime, she thought, hearing the distant clang of the midday bell, dispense her lotions and potions to the waiting sick.

Chapter Seven

Allison awoke with a start, her heart pounding, bathed in sweat. Completely disorientated, she lay staring up at the ceiling, trying to calm her breathing, but the image remained with her, the child's waxen face, his hands curled tightly around the sheets, his mother staring at him in utter disbelief. There had been the oddest silence for what seemed like eons, before a series of horribly rhythmic high-pitched screams started.

It was the lady's maid who stopped them by striking her mistress across the cheek. It was she who helped the broken woman to a chair, ringing the bell to summon a manservant, demanding brandy be brought, the whole time looking at Allison, who was standing stock still in the middle of the room. It had been the lady's maid who heard Dr Anthony Merchmont's accusations, who had witnessed Allison flinch at them, bow her head abjectly, visibly wilt under them. She might as well have held up a placard proclaiming herself guilty. Even now, forcing herself to sit up in the bed, pushing aside the tangle of sheets and blankets, she felt a surge of guilt. What had she done? What should she have done?

Staggering out of bed, she drank thirstily from the jug of water left on her night stand. Why had the dream returned to torture her now? She had not forgotten, she would never, ever forget that tragic night, but she was in the process of putting it behind her. She was once again practising her skills, helping people, easing suffering which had been borne stoically, in some cases, for years. Ironically, the free dispensary, which was growing in popularity by the day, was proving more rewarding than her lucrative practice in London.

She pulled back the curtains, leaning her forehead against the cool window pane. For six long months she had withdrawn from society, punishing herself by giving up the thing most precious to her. For six months she had tortured herself by constantly reliving the tragic events of that day, doubting herself, berating herself, making the slurs thrown at her by the medical establishment seem trivial in comparison. She had even managed to convince herself that she deserved the scandalous accusations spread by the press.

She had paid a heavy price. And now she was atoning, through her charitable dispensary. A spark of anger flared inside her. 'It was not my fault,' she muttered. 'It was *not* my doing,' she said again, with a new certainty. 'It was not.'

She could not envisage returning to London, but the fee she would earn here would give her the freedom to go anywhere she wished. Edinburgh, York, Bristol, even Paris. She could start afresh, and on her own terms.

And as for physician Anthony Merchmont! At the end of the day, all he'd wanted was to protect his exalted status with his privileged clientele. Well, she'd conceded him that, quite uncontested. Foolishly, she could almost hear The Procurer say in her lilting tone, and could easily imagine her grandmother nodding in agreement.

Allison reached for the locket under her pillow and opened it up to look at the miniature portrait. 'He's welcome to it, Seanmhair,' she whispered in Gaelic. 'I will start again somewhere else.'

She closed the locket, kissing the gold casing. Her heartbeat was back to its usual steady thump. The last horrible remnants of the dream faded. She was ready to face the new day, and to make a fresh start with her charges.

She'd been hiding behind the excuse she'd given Aleksei, that it was for the best that they didn't care for her. The children had no one else but her for the time being, and they needed someone. She'd been too reserved with them, following their lead, and fretting about the shadow of the much-loved Anna Orlova. It was time she tried to build bridges her own way, with stories and cuddles and entertaining games. She couldn't bring herself to like that blasted dog of theirs, but if she could find a way of making him less noxious? He was a greedy thing, which was part of his problem, for he ate anything and everything. If only he could be persuaded to eat something that was good for him, and good for his closest companions too! Allison smiled to herself. Yes, she was pretty certain it could be done, and she was pretty certain the children would like to help her too.

* * *

Aleksei wearily pushed aside the sheaf of papers that he had been working on, and rolled his aching shoulders. He'd been hunched over the desk for hours working on his suggested reforms. The only positive thing to come out of the effort he'd been forced to put in to oversee the Derevenko estates these last few months had been his ideas for change. Working through them with the extremely enthusiastic and supportive man of business, who produced a suspiciously complete set of his own proposals, Aleksei got the impression that Michael had been even more of a traditionalist than he'd thought. Now, the whole antiquated system would be made more efficient, and brought into the nineteenth century. Aleksei had been forced to learn a great deal more about estate management than he'd ever wished to know, and he'd had a surfeit of it for today.

The study looked out over the formal gardens at the rear of the palace. It was a lovely day outside, the early autumn sunshine giving no hint of the harsh winter to come. He opened the window, and a burst of laughter alerted him to the presence of his wards. They were throwing a stick for that dog of theirs, and the rotund animal was lumbering after it. They probably fed it sweetmeats. He should have a word with them, put an end to that.

Elena was wrestling the stick from the dog now, falling on her bottom when it wouldn't let go. Aleksei waited for the wail which routinely preceded her tears, but instead the little girl laughed as the bulldog licked her face and Nikki started to tickle her. There was such sheer joy in the sound of their unbridled laughter, he couldn't help but smile.

Allison, who must have been watching on from one of the benches just out of view, now appeared, engaged in conversation with Catiche. What were they talking about? Aleksei felt oddly left out, like a stranger looking down on a tableau which he was permitted to view, but not to participate in. There had been a dog when he was Nikki's age, he recalled suddenly. Not a bulldog, something much larger and long-haired, a hunting hound big enough to carry him on its back—or so he'd thought. Michael had acted as the mounting block, crouched down on all fours when he had failed to help Aleksei up using his cupped hands as he'd seen the stable hands do. He couldn't recall the dog's name or what had become of it.

Were the children unhappy, as Allison alleged? They didn't seem to be. A week ago, she'd claimed they hadn't warmed to her either, but either her expectations were high, or there had been a recent thawing, for there were Nikki and Elena shouting to her now to throw the stick for the dog, laughing at her paltry attempt to do so. Catiche, who had been hanging back, had decided that the game of tickling wasn't beneath her dignity after all, and was now joining in.

Thirteen, an age which hovered between childhood and adulthood. She'd be expected to embrace society soon. Catiche and Elena were destined to follow in their mother's footsteps, just as Nikki couldn't escape following in Michael's. It was how it was, how it had always been. Aleksei couldn't change that.

His own solution had been to join the army to escape his predetermined fate. 'And look where that has got me,' he muttered to no one in particular. Ought he to stay here, sacrifice his freedom for those three children out there? Was that what Michael expected of him, when he wrote that damned will? And if so, why the devil hadn't he discussed it with him?

Outside, Allison was attempting to restore order. He smiled, remembering their midnight row. A whole week ago, and they had barely spoken since, while he endured seven days and nights of tedium playing the aristocrat. How Michael put up with it was beyond him. Tonight he was engaged to dine at the Winter Palace again, but he could see it far enough.

As he watched Allison swoop down to catch Nikki up, swinging him around in the air, Aleksei felt something approaching a physical shifting inside him. Elena was pleading to be swung too. Catiche tried to pick her up, staggering backwards with her sister's weight until they both fell on to the grass. They rolled over, leaning on their elbows, looking expectantly at Allison, who set Nikki down and joined them. What was she saying? Her hands were clasped together. He remembered the way she'd recounted the tale of the seal husband, that same teasing, smile on her face. She must be telling them a fairy tale. The only tale he could recall being told as a child was the legend of the Derevenko dynasty, and a more tedious tale he could not imagine. Whatever tale Allison was telling, judging from his wards' entranced faces, it was not tedious.

To hell with it, he deserved a break. Closing the window, he gathered the papers together and stuffed them into a drawer of the desk. He locked it and put the key in his pocket, before making his way out into the gardens.

To his consternation, his arrival made all three of his wards jump up into awkward curtsies and bows. Strange to feel uncomfortable with this formality, when it was what he'd required of them.

'Miss Galbraith was telling us a story,' Elena informed him, 'but it's finished now. You are too late.'

'Not too late to help you exercise that dog of yours though, I hope. He is too fat.' Aleksei picked up the stick. 'You need to make him run a bit further than the end of his nose.' He bent down, putting the stick in the little girl's hand, gently angling her arm to maximise the throw. 'Now, you take first turn, and then we'll see which of the three of you can make Ortipo run the furthest.'

'So, while I could now write a thesis on who is bedding who,' Aleksei concluded some time later, as he sat with Allison in the herb garden, 'I have been unable to uncover any plausible motive for Michael's murder. Which, ironically, is the one thing people are not speculating about.'

Allison studied him from under her lashes. He looked tired and unusually despondent. 'Did you encounter your cousin Felix during any of your socialising?'

Aleksei rolled his eyes. 'It has been four months since Michael died, yet Felix still avoids company.'

'I know. The children have been asking for him. It seems he used to be a regular visitor here.'

'I called on him at home. He all but fell on my shoulder and wept like a widow when I tried to talk of Michael. Of course they could be crocodile tears, but I really don't think so.' Aleksei cursed under his breath in Russian. 'In all honesty, I can't believe Felix is guilty of anything more serious than a predilection for mawkishness.'

'That is rather uncharitable.'

'I don't feel like being charitable! What possessed Michael to leave his progeny in my charge? Why he imagined that *I* was in any way suitable to do what he'd expect by his children…' He shook his head wearily. 'He should have stuck with Felix. The man lives and breathes St Petersburg, he could care for them in a way that I cannot. I wish to hell I could prove him as innocent as I believe him to be, but we are no closer to the truth than we were a week ago.'

He dropped his head on to his hands, rubbing the frown which was etched on his forehead. Allison put her hand on his knee. 'Not necessarily. I might have made a significant discovery. I hadn't planned on telling you, because I'm not absolutely certain yet, but...'

His eyes lit up. 'What have you found? Tell me.'

And so she did, explaining how the delphiniums triggered her memory of the existence of Wolf's Bane. 'I need to pay another visit to the Apothecary's Garden to confirm, as I would expect in such an extensive collection, that it is grown there.'

'Sweet heaven! So it is what you have been looking for, lethal and simple to use?'

'Wolf's Bane is unusual in that every component of the plant is poisonous.'

'And the symptoms?'

'It very much depends on the dosage, and which part of the plant was used, but if Michael ingested the root in any quantity, he would have died almost immediately.'

'And it would have appeared to have been an apoplexy?'

'With a high dosage, the symptoms would have seemed very similar. It would have been very quick-acting.'

'Then we must be thankful for small mercies,' Aleksei said grimly.

'Yes.' Allison bit her lip. 'I'm afraid there's more.'

'What? For the love of—spit it out.'

'It is Elizaveta. I don't think she died of natural causes either.'

His brows snapped together. 'Elizaveta fell ill after suffering a severe reaction to a fish she should have known better than to eat.'

'That may be what she thought happened, and it is certainly what she told the doctor, but I don't necessarily believe it is true. You remember what I said, about the symptoms of Wolf's Bane poison varying depending on the dosage…'

Aleksei's jaw dropped. 'You believe—are you really telling me that we are dealing with not only one murder but two?'

'Yes.' The more she thought about it, the

more certain she became. 'Elizaveta was very sick, with severe stomach pains. The symptoms appeared to ease after a day and the sickness stopped, as one would expect in such cases of food intolerance, but then, as they do sometimes, they returned in a different form, and Elizaveta went into a rapid decline. Her pulse grew weaker, her breathing became laboured, until she could breathe no more. It could have been an extreme case of intolerance, as the doctor concluded. But the same effect could have been achieved with a small dosage of Wolf's Bane.'

'Not a tragic coincidence after all, but simply too much of a coincidence.' Aleksei looked every bit as dumbfounded as Allison had been when she had first made her discovery. 'By all the stars in heaven! This puts Michael's murder in a very different light. But why would anyone kill Elizaveta? I know nothing of the woman.'

His brow cleared. 'Though I know someone who does. Her brother has been in Finland on some errand for the Emperor, but I think he is due back in St Petersburg soon. Grigory Fyodorovksi is a charmer, a rake and a rogue, but a likeable one, welcomed everywhere because the currency he deals in is what St Petersburg thrives on.'

'Gossip?'

'And scandal. A more contrasting pair of siblings you could not find, for my sister-in-law was, as they say here in St Petersburg, as straight as the Kryukova Canal while they say that if Grigory Fyodorovski doesn't know a secret, then that's because it doesn't exist. Perhaps he'll be able to shed some light on the situation.'

Aleksei got to his feet, looking a very different man than the one who had joined her in the garden an hour before. 'I'm going to spend a few hours going through Elizaveta's papers. And I'm going to excuse myself from tonight's dinner at the Winter Palace. I think we both deserve some time off. Would you do me the honour of dining with me?'

Allison pursed her lips. 'I will have to consult my diary, it is very short notice.'

'May I hope that if you do have a prior engagement, you will cancel it?'

She laughed. 'You may. I look forward to it.'

Aleksei smiled, bowing over her hand, and pressing a fluttering kiss to her fingertips. 'As do I.'

* * *

They dined as before, *à deux*, in the Green Dining Room, and as before, Allison wore her green evening gown. Though he needed some tactful encouragement, she persuaded Aleksei to tell her something of his life in the army. An itinerant life, it seemed to her, where the excitement and terror of battle were intermingled with long periods of tedium, waiting out winters or waiting for new orders.

'I'm making it sound as if I've spent my life doing other's bidding,' he said, frowning. 'In a way, I suppose I have, though it did not seem so at the time.'

'But you cannot remain in the army and be a law unto yourself, unless you have set your sights on General Arakcheev's job,' Allison said.

Aleksei shuddered. 'Heaven forbid. Besides, ultimately Arakcheev dances to our Emperor's tune.'

'Then you must set your sights even higher,' Allison teased.

'If I wished to do that, I'd stay in St Petersburg. I'd find a couple of European princes to marry Catiche and Elena off to. I'd abandon my plan to employ some of my former comrades as estate managers and keep Nikki's empire in my own iron grip. And I grow weary of talking about myself.'

Allison pushed her empty plate to one side and leaned on the table, resting her chin in her hand. 'Then let us talk of other things.'

Aleksei pushed back his chair, pulling her to her feet. 'Or we could stop talking altogether.'

There was a gleam in his eye that made her stomach flip. 'We could. We are off duty after all.'

His hands smoothed up her evening gloves to rest on her shoulders. She stepped closer, reaching up to touch the white-blond kink in his hair. He dipped his head, nipping her earlobe, then kissing the column of her neck. She moaned softly, flattening her hands over the expanse of his shoulders. He slid his hands down her back, cupping her bottom to pull her up against him, and then their mouths met.

Such a kiss. Sweet and deep, a long, slow slaking of a thirst. Enough, just this meeting of lips and this tangling of tongues, it was more than enough for now. Allison closed her eyes, surrendering to the sensations, drowning in their kisses, sinking slowly, into the dark folds of their passion. His hands swept over her body, her bottom, her breasts, the curve of her hip, the dip of her waist, sensing her, mapping her, learning her, rousing her. More kisses, and she touched him too, learning his body as he did, not yet frustrated by their clothing, wanting only to kiss and to touch and to kiss, and to lose herself, to forget herself, to submerge herself in the languorous, melting sensations of their kisses, more and more kisses.

And then the nature of the kisses changed, became more urgent, and their hands became more demanding, and their clothes became a barrier, and Allison pressed herself against Aleksei, and he staggered back, and a large serving tureen crashed on to the floor, and they both leapt apart as the door opened, and a sheepish footman asked if they required him to clear the table.

'No!' Aleksei cursed under his breath as the servant retreated hastily. 'Do not tell me he was simply doing his job, I am perfectly well aware of that.'

'I wasn't going to say any such thing.' Allison stared in dismay at the shattered, no doubt priceless, Derevenko china. 'I can't think how we came to…'

Aleksei grinned. 'We were not thinking.'

'No. But we can't possibly—at least, not here.'

Her words, the product of her thrumming body, spoken without thinking, seemed to crackle in the air. 'Do you mean that?' Aleksei asked. 'That you would, if...'

Her mouth went dry. She could deny it, but it would be a lie, and who was to say when there would be another chance? 'Yes.'

Yet he did not move. 'Are you sure?'

'Yes, but not...'

'Not here.' He kissed her. 'We will go where we will not be disturbed.' He kissed her again. 'Not your chamber. Nor mine. Not any room in this damned palace where a servant is a bell-pull away.'

'The barge?' Allison suggested, half-teasing.

'Too far away, but if you are in the mood to be transported, I have just thought of the perfect venue.'

Ten minutes later, after traversing a bewildering maze of corridors and staircases, Aleksei pushed open a huge wooden door. 'Don't worry,' he said, as he held the door open, 'the stables and the grooms' quarters are in quite another part of the grounds. This is the carriage block, and no one will come here unless summoned, but just to make sure we are not disturbed...' He turned the key in the lock, then held the lamp high. 'What do you think? Are you transported?'

'Good heavens.' Allison stared around her in astonishment. 'How can one family possibly require so many sleighs?'

'The rivers and canals of the city are generally frozen from December until March. A sled is the quickest and safest way to get around. Here,' Aleksei said, pointing, 'are the small ones used by servants, which can be drawn by a pony or dogs.'

There were several simply constructed sleds, the main body a basket-like structure, balanced on wooden runners. 'They are compact enough to be used on the narrowest waterways,' Aleksei told her. 'Michael and I had our own sleighs when we were children. Mine was just exactly like this one, but Michael, naturally, had his livery painted on it. It will be Nikki's now.'

'And will you teach him to use it?'

'That is for one of the grooms to do.'

Allison said nothing. Sometimes it was best, she had discovered, to allow her silence to ask the question. And she was rewarded this time.

'Though the grooms likely have more than

enough to occupy them, and if I do say so myself, I reckon I'll be able to pass on a few winning tips to my nephew.'

'I hope not a few neck-breaking tips.'

He laughed. 'No, he'll discover those for himself. I shall teach him how to sled at a nice sedate pace.'

'Something tells me that a nice sedate pace is anathema to you.'

'No option, in one of those, but if you come over here—here is a troika. Now this,' Aleksei said, running his hand over the sleek little sled, 'is built for speed. Three horses, harnessed abreast, so it can only be used on the widest of the rivers or in the open country. The middle horse wears this larger collar, see. The trick when driving, is to keep him at a slower pace than the two outsiders.'

'That sounds challenging,' Allison said, eyeing the narrow seat doubtfully. 'And extremely dangerous.'

'This is a racing sled. This one,' Aleksei said, taking her a few paces on, 'is the Duke's official troika. Still tricky to drive mind you, but as you can see, designed for show rather than pace.'

'Good grief! It looks like a throne balanced inside a crown.' The troika was curlicued and gilded, the velvet-lined seat seemingly held aloft by four burnished angels, an elaborate construction of mystical creatures rising to a peak at the front of it, topped with the birds which adorned the portico of the palace.

'Magnificently monstrous, isn't that how you described the barge? Wait until you see the *pièce de résistance.*'

Aleksei led her through a maze of smaller sleds designed to seat one or two. Some were stacked with wicker baskets, some bore the ducal crown and the bird symbol. Some had no covers, some had leather hoods.

'Miss Galbraith, I present to you, the ducal sleigh.'

She burst out laughing. The so-called sleigh was actually a full-size carriage on runners, painted, predictably, in crimson and gold, the Derevenko coat of arms emblazoned on the central panel, which also served as the door. There were four windows on each side. 'It looks big enough to hold—what six people?'

'Eight, at a push.' Aleksei opened the door and pulled down the step. Inside there was a throne-like seat at each end, and wide benches lining each side, all upholstered in velvet. 'Like the barge, it's ridiculously heavy and is rarely used. Six horses struggle to get it moving. I've only been in it once. I can't remember the occasion, it was at the Winter Palace, I think. I was very young, and forced into wearing some ridiculous robe.'

'I can't imagine what the Imperial carriage must be like, if this is for a mere duke. The ice on the river must be very thick, to support such a contraption.' Allison sat down on one of the benches. The ceiling of the sleigh coach depicted the heavens, complete with puffy clouds, putti and winged horses. 'This reminds me of the Winter Palace.'

Aleksei sat down beside her. 'Most likely by the same artist.'

His leg brushed her gown, and excitement flickered low in her belly. It had been possible, while engrossed in this display of sleds, to forget the purpose of this tryst. No, that was not true, but she had pretended to forget.

'Allison.'

She jumped as Aleksei took her hand. Butterflies fluttered wildly in her belly. His thumb stroked circles on her palm. He smiled at her quizzically. 'If you have changed your mind I will understand perfectly.'

Her heart was racing. Though she was flustered, terrified of making a fool of herself, and feeling irrationally gauche, she was also… 'No. I mean, no, I have not changed my mind.' And she was blushing furiously. 'It was different, in the heat of the moment. If you would just kiss me or—or something, then I would be able to stop thinking and…'

'I want nothing more, but I can't, not while you are uncertain.'

'I'm not!' She grimaced. 'I know, it sounds as if I am but I'm not. I'm nervous. What if you are disappointed?'

'That is simply not possible.' Aleksei turned her hand over, pressing a kiss to her palm. 'I have wanted you so much from the moment I met you.'

'Have you?' Her voice no longer sounded strident, but breathy. Her pulses were still fluttering, but in a very different manner.

'You know I have.' He touched her hair lightly. 'I want to see your hair tumbling down over your back. I want to find out if your skin is the colour of cream, as I imagine it to be. I want to kiss you, not just on the mouth,' he said, pushing back an escaped curl to kiss her cheek, then the sensitive spot behind her ear. 'I want to kiss every inch of you. Here,' he said, cupping the swell of her breast through her gown. 'And here,' he said, sweeping down the dip in her waist to the curve of her bottom.

'Aleksei. Yes.'

The taste of her sent his senses spinning. He eased himself on top of her, kissing her all the while. She returned his kisses eagerly, and he lost himself in the sweet, drugging taste of her, in his own aching response as he cupped her breasts, as she ran her hands over his back.

Why were there still so many layers of clothes between them? He shrugged himself out of his coat. He had not allowed himself to believe this could happen, though he had imagined it many times. The reality was so different, nothing like anything he had felt before, infinitely superior. Her kisses. Her mouth. Her tongue touching his, her hands on him, her hot, sweet breath. He wanted to devour her. He wanted to lose himself in her. Blood surged to his groin, making his shaft pulse. Aleksei groaned. If he was not careful, he'd lose himself far too quickly.

Her hair was spread over the velvet of the carriage upholstery, the copper and auburn putting the crimson cushions to shame. Her lids were heavy with desire, her cheeks flushed. Breathing raggedly, he dragged his mouth from hers to concentrate on loosening the fastenings of her gown. Her hands fumbled with his waistcoat buttons. He tore himself free of it, and his shirt at the same time.

'Aleksei,' she whispered, in that tone that sent his pulse rocketing. 'Aleksei.' He adored the way she said his name. Her hands were on his chest, flat over his nipples, making his throat constrict. He eased her gown over her shoulders. He loosened her corset enough to free her breasts, now covered only by a white chemise. He could see the dark, peaked outline of her nipples through the linen.

He untied the ribbon of her chemise. Her skin was like cream and silk, just as he had envisaged. He dipped his head, kissing the warm valley between her breasts, then licked his way around the contours before taking one dark pink nipple into his mouth, sucking hard. Allison arched her back, moaning her pleasure. He was so hard he ached. He sucked on her other nipple. Her nails dug into his back.

He wanted to take his time. He wanted to savour her. But her kisses were fervent, her hands urging him to hurry, and his own body was clamouring for fulfilment in a way that was impossible to resist. When he slid his hand beneath her gown, he forgot all about the kisses he had dreamed of bestowing over her shapely, stocking-clad legs, drawn irresistibly to the heat of her thighs, the musky, damp, feminine core of her. She was so wet, his fingers slid easily into her, the harsh, yet sensuously female cry his touch elicited making his shaft pulse in response. Their kisses were feral now, their tongues thrusting and clashing. He wanted to pleasure her, to linger over the readying of her, but she was more than ready, saying his name over and over and over, a plea he could not resist.

He would curse his lack of his usual finesse later, he knew that as he struggled to unfasten his breaches, to kick off his damned boots at the same time, but Allison didn't want to wait, and he wasn't sure that he could.

At last he was free. His shaft sprang to attention. He wanted her to wrap her hands around it, but he couldn't wait for that either. 'Are you sure?' he asked, clinging desperately to the last vestiges of self-control.

'You really need to ask?' she replied, pulling him down on top of her. 'You need not worry, if that is what concerns you, I have the skills to ensure…'

But this was too much to take for granted. It was a matter of honour with him that he always took care. A kiss, the deepest of kisses, the most sensual of kisses. His hands under her full buttocks, lifting her. Slowly, slowly, he entered her. Slowly, he told himself, but as soon as his tip nudged the slick heat of her he was lost, and as soon as he sank into her, her climax took her, strong, pulsing waves that he could not resist. She was crying out, shaking and shuddering under him, and he thrust wildly, hard, driven by a primal need he had never felt before, falling suddenly, fast, to his own completion, only just managing to spend himself safely, in a shuddering climax that felt like it would never end.

She was sprawled semi-naked on the bench of the Derevenko state sleigh, with the completely naked *His Illustrious Highness* Count of Derevenko on top of her. 'I think we may just have committed treason,' Allison quipped, because the situation was so unreal, she felt she had to say something.

Aleksei's laugh seemed very slightly forced. 'Desecration, perhaps.' He sat up. His colour was high. His torso seemed tanned. She hadn't expected that. His chest was smooth. She hadn't expected that either. The ripple of his hard-packed muscles had had a very unexpected effect on her senses too. In the heat of passion, she hadn't even been able to look at or to touch the rest of his body, and now she was too embarrassed, in the aftermath, to do anything but look the other way as he grabbed his breeches and pulled them on.

She had behaved like a wild animal. Her one lover had been accomplished and selfless, but had never kissed with the wild abandon of Aleksei's kisses, had never lost himself totally in passion as Aleksei had. Her response tonight had been visceral, her climax sudden, violent, unstoppable.

Belatedly realising that she was still supine, Allison sat up in a tangle of skirts and petticoats. Her fingers fumbled with her various hooks and fastenings. How did there come to be so many! Her hair most likely looked like a bird's nest.

'I'm sorry.'

Startled, she looked up from her attempt to straighten her attire. Aleksei had pulled his shirt on. He was sitting beside her, but they were no longer touching. 'What for?' Allison asked, confused.

'My lack of finesse.'

The white-blond streak in his hair was standing up like a comma. A cow's lick, her grandmother would call it. '*Your* lack of finesse. I behaved like—like a wanton.'

'Allison!' He pulled her into his arms. It was so very, very good, to be able to burrow her head into his shoulder, but Aleksei gently forced her to look up, to meet his eyes. He laughed awkwardly. 'I wanted it to be perfect but I lost control.'

I lost control. Was it wrong of her, to take delight from those words? 'We both did.'

His eyes darkened. His smile became sinful. 'Perfectly so.'

He kissed her, a sated, deep kiss, that gave her confidence. And to her astonishment, made her realise that she was not so sated as she had thought. 'True perfection,' Allison said wickedly, 'is something which requires diligence. There is a saying—if at first you don't succeed...'

'Try again?' Aleksei pulled her to her feet, pulling the back of her gown together, and managing to deal efficiently with the tiny buttons. 'I look forward to that. But in the meantime...'

'Is it very late?'

'I don't know. I was going to suggest a riverside stroll, but if you are tired…'

'No,' Allison said hurriedly, 'I'm not tired. Not a whit.'

Aleksei found a thick cloak belonging to one of the coachmen for her, and they walked along the embankment of the Moyka River, following the same route they had taken in the rowing boat. 'I can't believe I've been in St Petersburg less than a month,' Allison said.

'I know, time is flowing faster than the Neva.'

He pulled her closer, wrapping his arm around her waist. It was another clear night, the stars pinpoints of light in the canopy of the sky. Though the buildings varied in size and height, in colour too, the façades painted gold and white, terracotta and blue, at night they formed one solid, dark mass on the narrow towpath of the embankment. The lights from some of the windows reflected in shimmering gold in the water. Allison shivered. There was a marked autumnal bite in the air that made her grateful for the heavy cloak.

'The season is changing,' Aleksei said, as if

he had read her mind. 'We will not see many more days such as this one. You brought the sunshine with you from England. It has been unseasonably warm since you arrived. Soon, the temperature will plummet, and the rain will set in. St Petersburg in the rain is not such a beautiful place.'

'In Scotland, we had rain in the winter, the spring and the summer as well as the autumn,' Allison said. 'Freezing rain in the winter, soft in the summer, but it soaks right through you all the same. It makes everything very green, mind you. It's a different kind of climate in London, much warmer and drier. You'd be astonished at the difference five hundred miles can make—and at the variety of plants which can be cultivated as a result.'

'You have your own garden?'

'Of course I do, and grow many of the same herbs as are grown in the palace garden. Would that I had a little succession house though, I'd grow a lot more than orchids.'

'Is that what we have in our succession houses, beside deadly poison?'

'Ours, is it now?' Allison teased. 'Don't you mean Nikki's? There's a grape vine in one of them, and lemons and oranges in another, and then of course there is the fern house, but it's all very—very ornamental.'

'You don't approve of ornamental plants?'

'Only if they also have a practical application.'

'Well you'll have the luxury of being able to afford both, once you have completed your work here.'

They had arrived at the Red Bridge, and of one accord stopped to lean on the railings, to watch the faint ripple of the Moyka as it flowed out towards the Neva and then on, out into the Baltic Sea. The journey she'd be taking, when this adventure was over.

Her stomach lurched. How soon would it be over? How many more days and nights did they have together? Surely she should be counting down the time with anticipation, for when she left, her new life would begin. And this interlude would be over. No more St Petersburg. No more Catiche and Elena and Nikki. Though there were times, especially with Catiche, when her ingenuity and her patience were stretched, her efforts to engage with them on her own terms, without trying to emulate the saintly Madame Orlova, were increasingly paying off. The dread she'd felt every morning at the schoolroom door was a thing of the past. She relished their company now, delighted in stretching her always vivid imagination to invent new stories to tell them, new ways to entertain them. She was beginning to enjoy their company far too much for her own good.

But worse, much worse than no more children, would be no more Aleksei.

'I'm glad,' Allison said, surprising him by throwing her arms around him. 'Tonight. I'm glad we did not wait.'

He pulled her tight against him. His lips were cold, but his kiss was warm, sensual, a promise. 'I'm glad too,' he said. 'Very glad.'

Only afterwards, lying alone in her bed, unable to sleep, watching the dawn light filter through the curtains, did Allison finally concede to herself that she was in far deeper waters with Aleksei than she ever intended.

It was not their lovemaking but the aftermath, the intimacy of their stroll, the recognition that time was against them and all that implied about their feelings. For the first time in her life, she had an inkling of what it would feel like to fall in love. Not that she would allow herself to do such a thing. She was only *envi-*

sioning it, because Aleksei was—yes, she could admit that much—he was like no other man she had ever met. Though they were polar opposites in many ways, they were also in many ways soul mates. As for the unbridled passion that had flared between them—didn't opposites attract? Particularly when the situation encouraged them to surrender to that attraction without fear of consequences.

That was it. Nothing more. She was not falling in love with Aleksei. She was immune to love. And even if it turned out that she was not, the antidote was there, waiting for her, in the form of a ship which would transport her back to England at the end of her assignment, where her future awaited her.

Chapter Eight

Allison had forgotten all about the footman's ill-timed arrival until the next day, when she left the children with their nanny, and was in her chamber, preparing for her daily dispensary. If the servant had talked—and why wouldn't he?—the entire servants' hall would know what she and Aleksei had been up to last night. All very well to tell herself that they must have guessed at the liaison after their first illicit dinner together, but that night no one had witnessed anything untoward. Now, there was tangible proof. The occupants of Derevenko Palace would brand her a harlot, and this time, it would be the truth.

No! Allison glowered down at the scarf she was about to use to tie back her hair. She was not a harlot, any more than Aleksei was a—

whatever the male term might be. Though of course, she thought bitterly, rather tellingly there was no male equivalent.

But it was with a sinking heart that she made her way to the garden room, where she was surprised to find the crowd of patients awaiting her was no smaller than usual. And as the consultation progressed, and not a word or a hint of anything other than gratitude was spoken, Allison's spirits lifted considerably. As she tidied away the detritus of her work and checked the contents of her herb chest, she was singing lustily to herself in the Gaelic.

'I think that is a happy noise, but I'm not absolutely sure.'

She whirled round to find Aleksei standing in the doorway. 'It is a song about the cutting of the peats—that is the turf that is burned in the Highlands instead of coal. The peat is thick and dark and moist, and it wobbles as you cut it, and the cutting of it makes your shoulders burn, and the burning of it when it is dried fills your croft with an unmistakable aroma.'

He laughed. 'A very happy song, then.'

'Oh, aye,' Allison said, deliberately broadening her accent, 'for when it is done you have fuel to last the whole winter.'

'Are you finished consulting for the day?'

When she nodded, he came into the garden room, closing the door behind him. 'Good,' he said, taking her into his arms and kissing her.

'Aleksei, we must not—not here.' But even as she protested, she was standing on tiptoe and claiming another kiss, and then another, and another, until they dragged themselves apart, breathless.

'If someone came in…' Allison said, then stopped short. It would make no difference if they did, if this morning was anything to go by. She locked her herb chest and slipped the key into her locket.

Aleksei was idly turning a pestle in an empty mortar. 'Do you think that a permanent dispensary here would be worth considering? I was thinking about what you said, about the servants having nowhere else to turn. Obviously if they were seriously ill, a doctor would be summoned—at least I'd like to think so—but from all you've told me, the complaints you treat, they are not life-threatening, are they?'

'Only painful and often very debilitating. Are you serious?'

'Yes.' He smiled at her. 'Michael's valet has been singing your praises, and so too has the butler. All of the staff are much happier, I'm told. And what's more, we've had any number of servants from other palaces enquiring about employment here. Thanks to you.'

'Oh.' A lump rose in her throat. 'That is most—most gratifying. Thank you.'

He laughed, catching her hands in his. 'It is I who am grateful. Do you think it's something I should pursue?'

'Absolutely, but do not underestimate the effort required to establish a dispensary, Aleksei. You would need to find a herbalist, for a start.'

'Wouldn't you be able to train someone?'

'Yes, but it would take months, if not years, and I…'

'Won't be here for much longer.' He let go her hand, turning away. 'Nor will I. I shall simply have to make the suggestion to whomever I find to replace me.'

His shoulders lifted in a shrug. She had not seen that shrug of his for some time. I won't let it bother me, that shrug said, which meant it did.

If only she could help. Allison caught herself just in time. She picked up the mortar and pestle Aleksei had been toying with, and placed them on a shelf. 'Was there something you wanted from me?' she asked, keeping her voice light. 'Apart from a kiss that is?'

'Yes.' He turned back to face her, keeping his own voice light too. 'There is to be a grand picnic to celebrate peace in Europe at the Peterhof Palace in a couple of days' time. The Emperor wants to reward all the men who fought for Mother Russia—though of course, he means only the officers. I thought that the children might enjoy it.'

'Did you indeed? You are in danger of concerning yourself with their welfare.'

'It will be good for them to get out a bit more, now that the mourning period is over.'

'That is true.'

'And I was thinking that Nikki would enjoy the spectacle, for there will be every uniform in the country on display.'

'That is a nice thought, Aleksei.'

He drew her a wry look. 'I am not entirely indifferent to them, you know. There will be a fair, puppet shows, that kind of thing. Plenty to entertain them all.'

'And time for them to get to know their Uncle Aleksei a little better?'

He shrugged again, but he also smiled. 'Do not push your luck, Miss Galbraith. I am hoping that it will also present the opportunity for me to do a little more digging, hopefully finally track Grigory down, but with the pleasure of your company to take the edge off the tedium. What do you say?'

She wanted to say that if he tried to get to know the children better he'd find them eager to reciprocate. She wanted to say that it would not take much for them to overcome their awe of him, if he could overcome his reserve. But she did not want, as he had warned her, to push her luck. He was reserved for very good reasons. So she smiled up at him, dropping a curtsy. 'I say thank you very much, Count Derevenko. The children and their governess will all look forward to it with great anticipation.'

The day of the picnic at Peterhof dawned unseasonably warm for late September, with the sun splitting a clear blue sky in which no cloud dared to trespass. Most likely, Allison thought, on orders from Tsar Alexander himself, who was nominally the host, even though he was still abroad and would not attend in person.

It was to be a simple, rustic affair, Aleksei had informed her, information which she took with a very large pinch of salt, having a fair idea by now of what the Romanov court considered understated. Her gown was white, the skirts consisting of layers of plain muslin, but the bodice was intricately pleated and trimmed with pretty white lace. The long sleeves were full, like a man's shirt, but gathered and tucked into the same lace at the shoulder, elbow and wrist, ending in a wide flounce. A blue sash the colour of the sky overhead formed the only other decoration, the same colour as her reticule, and the trimming on her bonnet. With Natalya's help, Allison had purchased a sky-blue silk wrap to drape around her shoulders, although in the growing heat of the day, she had little need of it.

Catiche and Elena, also thanks to Natalya, were dressed in matching white trimmed with sky blue. 'Though our dresses are far nicer,' Elena announced guilelessly, 'I think you look very pretty.'

'Elegant,' Catiche corrected her. 'Miss Galbraith is too old to be pretty.'

Which backhanded compliment, Allison decided, biting her lip to hide her smile, was progress of a sort.

'Good morning.' Aleksei appeared, wearing his dress uniform. There really was something quite shockingly appealing about him in that uniform, the way it drew attention to his physique, the fit so perfect as to be almost breathtakingly tight. Allison could almost *see* the flexing of his thigh muscles as he moved. And she should most decidedly *not* be looking at his thigh muscles. His shoulders instead then…

'Uncle Aleksei, I have a uniform too,' Nikki said, thankfully distracting her. 'Papa had it made for me specially, so I could be one of your soldiers.'

The little boy saluted then stood to attention. *Return the salute*, Allison begged Aleksei silently, but there was no need. He did so in all seriousness, before telling the child, much to his delight, to stand at ease. 'You will meet a great many soldiers today. I hope you will salute them all as smartly. Now, shall we show these lovely young ladies the way?' he said, sweeping Nikki up on to his shoulders and heading for the boathouse.

The jetty where the boat moored at the end of their brief river journey was at the mouth of a long narrow channel of water which led the eye naturally up to the Peterhof Palace, sitting atop a small rise. Painted straw and white, the palace was gracefully symmetrical and extremely beautiful.

'They say it is modelled on the French palace of Versailles,' Catiche informed Allison as they docked, 'but naturally, Peterhof is superior.'

'How so?' Allison asked.

The girl looked somewhat surprised at this question. 'Because it is Russian,' she said, as if this was self-evident.

'I have visited Versailles,' Aleksei said. 'It is vast. The courtiers are forever getting lost, and have to climb out of windows into the gardens, simply to get their bearings.'

'That is preposterous.' Catiche eyed her uncle uncertainly. 'Are you teasing me?'

He looked at her blandly. 'Why would I do that?'

'I don't know. You have never done so before, but I think—when Papa teased us, his eyes crinkled at the corner just as yours have just done, so I think you must be.'

Though the girl turned quickly away, she failed to hide the sheen of tears which welled up in her eyes. 'I don't look at all like Michael,' Aleksei whispered to Allison, looking rather dumbstruck.

'Actually, you do a little. Catiche has a miniature portrait of him, and there is as she said, a strong similarity about the eyes.'

'What is Catiche doing with a miniature?'

'It belonged to her mother. I believe she took it from her room.'

'Why on earth would she do that?'

'Honestly Aleksei, isn't it obvious? She has a miniature of her mother, too. They are keepsakes, to have something close at hand to remind her of her parents.'

'She ought to have asked permission.'

'Please don't even think of chastising her,' Allison whispered urgently under her breath. 'She trusted me enough to show them to me and I don't want to risk betraying that trust. You have to appreciate that she's at that awkward age for a girl, laughing one minute and in floods of tears the next. She is even ambivalent about her debut children's ball, which is fast approaching, occasionally excited but mostly adamant she does not want to attend. And on top of all these emotional dramas every girl her age goes through, Catiche has recently lost her parents. She misses them dreadfully, Aleksei, they all do. I know you don't want to hear this, but like it or not, you are all they have now. You are their closest relative in the world, and you are their father's brother.'

'But I am not their father. And they won't have me for much longer. Weren't you the one who told me that it might be for the best not to get too close to them? You know that this arrangement is not permanent.'

Allison flushed. 'I was referring to myself.'

'Are you implying that it would be best if I remained here as their permanent guardian?'

'No. Yes. I don't know. For the time being perhaps. You said yourself, the army in peace time is not for you.'

'Quitting the army is one thing, deciding to dedicate my life to raising my brother's children quite another,' he snapped. 'If I wanted to be a father, I'd have married and had children of my own.'

'Haven't you ever wanted to do either?'

Her question clearly took him aback. It had surprised her just as much that she had asked it, and she found herself, for some odd reason, holding her breath. 'My career has always taken precedence,' Aleksei replied, eyeing her askance. 'As has yours. I believe we discussed this.'

They had. Allison tried to replicate one of his dismissive shrugs. 'I just wondered...'

'Playing the guardian to those three has not changed my mind, but I wonder if it has affected you more than you realise. I think you are in danger of taking your role as governess too seriously.'

And he was horribly right. She could feel a flush creeping up her throat. 'I cannot afford to do so.'

'While I, on the other hand, must take my role as guardian very seriously indeed. Which is why I will revoke it, in due course.'

'I know that, Aleksei.'

He raised a haughty eyebrow. 'Do you?'

'I do. I should apologise. The children's future is none of my business.'

To her surprise, his expression softened. 'Yet you cannot help caring. It is in your blood, Madame Herbalist. Just be careful you do not come to care too much.'

Aleksei and Allison walked on together in a silence which grew more comfortable as they progressed, and found them both fully restored by the time they reached the top of the walkway where the children waited impatiently for them.

From a distance, Peterhof's famous grand cascade had looked simply like two sets of steps built around a grotto leading up to the central portico, but as the Derevenko party approached, the fountains suddenly spouted, and even the children, who had seen the spectacle before, stopped to gaze in wonder.

'Do you know how many fountains there are?' Allison asked Nikki.

The little boy shook his head. 'But when I am big, I am going to build even more at my palace.'

'I thought you wanted to be a soldier like Uncle Aleksei, Nikki,' Elena said.

'He can't be a soldier, he is a duke,' Catiche said.

'Yes, I can,' Nikki said, his lip trembling. 'I can be a soldier as well, can't I, Uncle Aleksei?'

It would be tempting to lie, and so much easier, Allison thought, watching as Aleksei hesitated, though she was unsurprised by his answer. 'No,' he said firmly. 'It is as your sister says, I'm afraid. You are a duke and, more importantly, will be head of the Derevenko family. That is your destiny.'

'But...'

'Aleksei! And accompanied by my favourite nieces and nephew. It is very good to see you all out and about on this most auspicious day.'

'Uncle Grigory!'

The appearance of the large, red-faced man averted Nikki's tears. All three children clustered around their uncle, who hunkered down, his pantaloons straining at the seams, to envelop them in a communal bear hug.

Grigory Fyodorovski looked to be in his early forties. A man whose figure and florid complexion reflected his appetites and, Allison thought, made longevity a remote prospect. There was an exuberance to that moustache, and despite his size, a flamboyant style to his attire that indicated the dandy. The twinkle in his currant-like eyes, lost in the creases of his chubby cheeks, spoke of a jovial nature. It was clear that the children loved him, and equally clear, from the familiar way he spoke to them, that he was very fond of them too.

'I have missed these little ones very much. It does my soul good to see them. And Elena, looking so like her mama, my dear late sister. I still find it hard to believe that she has gone. Forgive me,' he said, creaking to his feet a few moments later, turning his attention to Allison, 'I am, as you may have surmised, their uncle, Grigory Fyodorovski, and you must be the new English governess everyone is talking about.'

The man made a sweeping bow, pressing a rather wet kiss to the tips of her fingers, before studying her quite unashamedly through his quizzing glass. 'Well,' he said, his busy brows waggling, 'for once the gossipmongers did not exaggerate. Not an English rose, certainly not, but—ah, I will say no more. I have no wish to embarrass you.'

'Then it is as well that I require a private word with you,' Aleksei said, drawing him to one side.

'It has been too long since I saw these little ones. My time is not my own these days, but our Emperor's to command. How are you, Aleksei? Such a tragic business,' Grigory said with an immense sigh. 'One minute, to be in the peak of health, and the next—an appalling stroke of fate for the little ones especially, to be deprived of both Mama and Papa. But they are looking very well, rosy of cheek and bright of eye. That governess of yours is doing something right.'

'Miss Galbraith has persuaded them to share her love of fresh air and life outdoors,' Aleksei said, realising with a start that this was true.

'Ha! Unlike the previous governess, what

was her name—Orlova? She left rather abruptly, I believe. I wonder why?'

'I was rather hoping you might be able to enlighten me.'

'Really? I'm afraid I cannot. I suppose it's possible my sister dismissed her.' Grigory frowned. 'But I had the distinct impression that Elizaveta thought the world of the woman, so I must assume that she left of her own accord.'

'I don't suppose you have heard where she may be now?'

'You wish to reappoint her and replace that rather sumptuous Englishwoman? Are you sure?' Grigory shook his head. 'Well, I'm afraid I can't help you, though I can say with certainty she has not taken up another position in St Petersburg,' he added, puffing out his chest. 'If a pantry mouse steals a piece of cheese in this city, I will know of it.'

Aleksei grinned. 'And no doubt the name of the cheesemaker who made the cheese.'

Grigory opened his palms in a self-deprecatory manner. 'You can't really be wanting her back though, surely? Unless all is not well between you and that charming redhead? Forgive my bluntness, but I take it you know that the *on dit* is that she is your mistress?'

'And I take it, Grigory, that you know I would not stoop to comment on scurrilous rumour?' Aleksei retorted. 'Tell me, how did you find your sister in the weeks before she died?'

'Same as ever, dear boy. Doing her good works, minding her children, standing virtuously by Michael's side when the occasion demanded. Our paths crossed less than you seem to think. My sister made great store of holding a very low opinion of me and my profligate ways.' Grigory pursed his lips. 'Very fond of taking the moral high ground, was our Elizaveta, and very proud of her position at its zenith.'

'Straight as the Kryukova Canal.'

'That is what they said.' Grigory frowned, looking unusually serious. 'But now she is gone, and life is for the living. It's a damned difficult position circumstances have placed you in. A military man, without a wife, landed with three orphans. I know you cannot have welcomed the role, but it occurs to me that your brother might just have been thinking along the right lines in appointing you. Like Michael, you are that rare creature in St Petersburg, a man of honour and integrity. Although at the risk of causing offence, I have to tell you that

I personally found your brother something of a bore. There is nothing more tedious than a paragon of virtue.'

He slapped Aleksei on the shoulder. 'Not a charge that could be levelled at you. I'll wager there's a bit more devilment in you. And talking of devilment, why don't I take the children off your hands for an hour or so, and allow you to enjoy the company of your feisty redhead instead.'

Allison, who had been watching the encounter through her lashes, had been unable to determine anything from Aleksei's countenance. As soon as their uncle swept the three children away in search of ices and lemonade, he brought her up to date succinctly. 'I drew a complete blank,' he said. 'He has no idea why Madame Orlova left and he doesn't know where she might be. He could tell me nothing of interest about Elizaveta. And he confirmed what we already know, that my brother was as white as the driven snow.'

'Which makes it unlikely that he was murdered to silence him, prevent him revealing some dark secret, I suppose,' Allison said.

Aleksei laughed sardonically. 'Let us call that progress then, and forget about it for today.

Grigory is a very fond uncle and the children clearly adore him. It was good of him to take them off our hands. We should take advantage of the rare opportunity to spend time alone in public together.'

They walked arm in arm, making their way beyond the façade of the palace to where the main gardens were situated. Cavalry officers in full dress uniform were allowing children to sit up beside them on their horses. They waved at Nikki, sitting astride a large black stallion in front of a very young ensign. A puppet theatre had been set up in one of the many pavilions. In the centre of one large lawn, was a strange contraption, a tall pole, in the centre of which a complicated set of wires and struts formed a hexagonal frame. At each point, suspended on a wire, hung a carved dragon painted in garish colours, and on the back of each dragon, clinging for dear life, sat a rider, including two ladies sitting precariously side-saddle.

'It is a French design,' Aleksei told her, 'I saw one in the Tuileries Garden in Paris, they call it a *jeu de bague*. Watch, it is about to begin revolving.'

A muscular man in a leather waistcoat with the look of a Smiddy, approached the machine, and began to crank a long handle. With the creaking sound of sturdy oaks being blown in the wind, the hexagonal frame began to turn, sending the dragons and their riders spinning, slowly at first, but as they gained momentum the wires stretched taut and the dragons flew out, making everyone, riders and spectators, shriek with slightly hysterical delight.

A knot of men lolled on the grass in the lee of a tall hedge. Officers, Allison deduced from their uniforms, though they incongruously sported long, straggly beards, and were talking loudly in Russian. They were all somewhat the worse for wear, as evidenced by the many empty bottles, and she was not unduly surprised when two of them got to their feet and began to brawl, much to the delight of their comrades, who formed a jeering circle.

'Followers of Volkonsky,' Aleksei said, eyeing the group with distaste. 'They eschew all things French, since Napoleon invaded Moscow. They drink the peasant gut-rot spirit, vodka, they grow beards and dress like serfs, and as a result all are banned from court. They claim to espouse the cause of the common man, though to no practical purpose.'

'At least,' Allison said, eyeing the rabble doubtfully, 'they are speaking up.'

'And laying themselves wide open to arrest in the process.' Aleksei watched the group through narrowed eyes. 'It is not that I don't sympathise. Our peasant army proved themselves and their love for Mother Russia at Borodino, and for reward they were sent back to the land, made serfs once more as if nothing had changed.'

'In England, the hope is that the victory at Waterloo will put an end to the years of poverty which the war has caused,' Allison said, 'but I confess, I have my doubts. It will be the same as here—a return to what was before, and the men who fought—peasants too, many of them—their campaign medals will not put food on their tables.'

The distinctive sound of a fist slamming into a nose was succeeded by a roar of approval, and Aleksei turned away, his face wrinkling with distaste. 'Perhaps I underestimate them, but it seems to me they are interested only in spilling more blood, and I want no part of that.'

'Even if they succeed?'

'They will not. Nothing will change here unless our Emperor decrees it. Those men over there—their protests will be ignored or forcefully stifled, and that is the simple truth of it.'

'If you chose to remain here, use the Derevenko influence...'

He shook his head. 'I'm not the political animal Michael was and that power is not mine to wield. Besides, Michael would turn in his grave if I used his influence in support of what he would see as a truly subversive cause.' He looked over his shoulder at the officers, now lolling on their backs and singing what sounded like a folk song. 'Look at them, the future of the Russian army. It is not my future.'

'You are set on leaving the army, then?'

He smiled sadly. 'I have no choice. All my life, I have served my country but now—no, I am done with it, there is no place for me any more. I am not one of those young hotheads, and I am certainly not one of the old guard, like Arakcheev. Besides, I'm done with killing and I am done with taking orders—and for that startling realisation, I lay the blame at your door.'

'How so?'

'Independence, isn't that the flag you have been waving?'

'For myself, yes.'

'Well, it is a banner I like the idea of marching under myself. Though I'll have to wait until I'm free of my charges first.'

Which left her in no doubt that he was still determined to be free of them. Allison understood Aleksei well enough to know that he would very quickly find the responsibility of permanent guardianship too heavy a burden to bear. And who was she to wish him shackled, when she herself was so desperate to claim her freedom? 'Well, we are free of them for at least another half-hour,' she said, smiling brightly, 'that is something.'

'Something delightful,' he agreed, happily taking his cue from her. 'I don't often get the opportunity to enjoy your company alone, and in broad daylight.'

And then he smiled, the smile that sent a *frisson* shivering down her spine and made her forget everything and everyone, save him. 'We are hardly alone,' Allison said, for her own sake as much as his. 'There must be hundreds here.'

'Thousands, more likely. Sadly, Peterhof gardens during an Emperor's picnic is an even poorer choice of location for a kiss than a rowing boat.'

Desire flickered in her belly, a curling, tingling, unfurling sensation. 'Yet you found no difficulty in kissing me in a sleigh. Are we to confine our kisses to ducal carriages?'

'If so, then I regret the missed opportunity in the state barge. But if you recall, we have also kissed in the dining room, in your dispensary, and in the garden several times.'

'You forgot the succession house. Really, when you put it like that,' Allison replied, trying not to smile, 'there are few locations where we have not kissed. We have been uncommonly adventurous.'

'You think so?' He eyed her speculatively. 'I wonder, would it be wrong of me to take that as a challenge?'

'Can one be delightfully wrong?'

His laughter was a low rumble that set butterflies dancing in her stomach. 'I hope so, Miss Galbraith. May I dare to ask if you are available to judge for yourself tonight?'

'You do not have another engagement?'

'I will have done my duty by the end of today.'

'Then I accept.' Smiling saucily, she dropped him a curtsy. 'But for now, I think we should resume our duties and seek out our charges.'

Chapter Nine

'The State Bedchamber,' Aleksei announced later that night, throwing open the door theatrically. 'Created for my grandfather in the days when the Duke and Duchess gave formal audiences from the comfort of their bed.'

She understood now why he had kept her waiting in the corridor, for he had been busy lighting the candles, allowing her to see the stage he had set in all its glory. And it was a glorious sight. 'You omitted to show me this room when you gave me the grand tour,' Allison said, gazing around her, eyes wide.

'I didn't show you any of the bedchambers, actually. Frankly, I didn't trust myself!'

The chamber was almost entirely decorated in blue and gold. Blue-silk wall hangings were framed by blue-painted pilasters topped with gold acanthus leaves. Blue upholstery adorned the gilded chairs and *chaise longue* grouped at the foot of the bed. A golden guard rail forming a semi-circle around the bed itself. A duck-egg-blue-and-gold canopy stretched over the head of the bed, surmounted by the Derevenko insignia painted in gold. The white marble fireplace was inset with shards of peacock blue.

And above, the ceiling depicted a celestial-blue sky. 'Psyche's wedding,' Aleksei informed her. 'The whole chamber is a copy of the Imperial bedchamber of the Gatchina Palace, which was built by Catherine the Great for her favourite lover, Count Orlov—and yes, he is a distant relation of our missing governess, I believe.'

Aleksei released a hidden catch to open a gate in the railing. He sat on the bed, holding his hand out to indicate she join him on the embroidered silk coverlet. Light from the candles reflected from two huge mirrors which flanked the bed.

'If you think it's too bright I can snuff out some of the candles,' Aleksei said, kissing the nape of her neck, his fingers tugging her hair free of pins, 'But frankly I would prefer to see you in all your glory.' More kisses, down the column of her throat.

Until Aleksei, Allison's previous experience of lovemaking had been under the covers and in the dark. Now she relished the contrast, relished the edge of daring, which racked up her already high level of anticipation. 'Let the candles burn,' she said, 'I want to look at you too.'

She did so brazenly, running her hands over the endearing kink in his hair, down his back, while her eyes travelled down past the open neck of his shirt, the falls of his breeches.

She smoothed her hand over his shaved chin and he exhaled sharply. His hair was so closely cut to his head at the back, it was prickly, and yet silky smooth where it was longer. 'Your eyes match the colour of this room,' she said.

He laughed. 'As does your gown. It is almost exactly the same colour as this bed. I think we should remove it, lest you disappear entirely.'

Her cornflower-blue day dress laced at the back. Aleksei turned her around and began to deal efficiently with the fastenings, distracting her with kisses while he worked, focusing his efforts on rousing sensations in every part of her body. His lips were warm on her bare skin, kissing her nape and her shoulders as he loosened her gown, slipping his hands inside to cup her breasts through her chemise, his thumbs circling her nipples, sending little *frissons* of pleasure rippling through her. Gently, he eased her arms free, pressing kisses on to the pulse points in the crook of her elbow, on her wrist.

Easing her to her feet, he removed the gown before wrapping his arms around her, cupping her bottom through her petticoats. She twined her arms around his neck, pressing herself closer, feeling the hard length of him against her belly. Their kisses became deeper, their tongues touching and tasting, but there was still a restraint, their eyes open, watching, desire reflecting desire. His mouth drifted down to the neckline of her chemise. He kissed the swell of her breasts, the valley between them, cupping, stroking, making her pulse with pleasure. This was not to be like the last time. This was no urgent sating, but a slow savouring.

She tugged his shirt free from his breeches. She slid her hands up, under the soft cambric, flattening her palms over the taut skin of his back, feeling the knots of his spine then moving her hands to the front, to caress the ripple of his abdomen, the breadth of his chest, the hard nubs of his nipples. His breathing was fast, like hers. Colour slashed his cheeks. His eyes were ablaze with passion. It stoked the flame of hers, the way he looked at her, the way he breathed her name. It made her feel powerful. Confident. When he pulled his shirt over his head, she pressed herself against him, kissing the hard wall of his chest, daring to lick his nipple, and when he moaned softly, further daring to suck on it.

He muttered something under his breath in Russian. Then he picked her up, laying her on her back on the bed. Her slippers were removed. Her garters undone. There were kisses where she had never experienced kisses before, arousing kisses on her toes, her ankle, on her calf, behind her knee. First one leg, as he slowly removed her stockings, and then the other. As she held her breath, expecting for him to move higher, instead he lay down beside her, and there were more kisses. On her breasts, as he undid the ribbons at the neckline of her chemise. And then his mouth sucking on her nipples in a way that almost overset her, that made her curl her toes to regain control, and when that did not work, she pushed him away, taking him by surprise and rolling him on to his back, straddling him, her hair a curtain over them, sensing the barely leashed passion in his kiss and relishing it, wanting him to lose control, but wanting him not to.

'Wait,' she said, still kissing him, feeling the rigid shape of his erection through his breeches, between her legs, and wondering if she could follow her own advice.

'I will,' he said, 'but you—no, I think not.'

Catching her by the waist, he rolled her over, managing to remove her chemise at the same time. She lay naked, spread out on the blue-silk coverlet of the state bed, but the way he feasted his eyes on her prevented her from feeling any sort of embarrassment. She did not need him to tell her he thought her beautiful, but he did anyway, and she believed him. She did not need to tell him to remove the rest of his clothes. Her eyes spoke volumes, and he did her bidding, and she feasted her eyes on him, as he had done on her, relishing, unashamed. Tanned torso, narrow waist, long, muscular legs, and the thick erection jutting between them. She sat up, tentatively touching. Another new and unfamiliar act. Her fingers fluttered over the length of him, so hard and yet so silky smooth. When she curled her hand around his girth, he moaned and he pulsed and his jaw worked in the effort to control himself, and she felt herself unravel, just watching it. A careful stroke, up and down, and he moaned again, and another, and he breathed out her name, and another, and she was on her back.

'You test me,' he said, 'and now I will test you.'

And before she could guess what he was going to do, he parted her legs, and knelt between them, and he licked into her, and Allison cried out, partly in shock, because this was completely new experience, but mostly with pleasure.

Kisses. Were those kisses? Stroking. Or was it licking? She couldn't tell. She didn't care. She was slipping and sliding into oblivion, now climbing and tensing and pulsing and whatever he was doing, she didn't want him to stop, not ever, not ever, and oh, dear heavens…

Her climax shook her to the core, ripping through her, tossing her high on to a throbbing, pulsing cloud of sensation. She could hear herself crying out, hear herself begging, don't stop, more, again, her hands clutching at the silk bedcovering, her back sliding on it, as she arched and tilted towards the delicious, delightful source of unadulterated pleasure.

'Aleksei,' she breathed, when she could finally breathe. 'Aleksei.' More of a command this time, half-sitting up so that she could reach him, her hands on his shoulders, and then she was on top of him, skin on skin, a tangle of limbs and heat. She sat astride him, his face, skin stretched taut, eyes dark, pupils dilated. She was so glad of the candlelight, so that she could witness the desire etched in his face, and all for her.

The tip of his shaft nudged at her. Inch by inch, she guided him inside her, shuddering as he pushed deeper, entranced by the rapid rise and fall of his chest as he thrust, so slowly, so carefully, until he was there, all there, and his eyes drifted closed as she held him, tightening around him. And then she moved, and he moved, a small thrust and then another one, and then his hands on her waist. More thrusts, wilder now, and finally his passion was unleashed, and he rolled her on to her back, her legs around his waist now, thrusting harder, oh, so deliciously, delightfully harder and harder, until she felt the thrumming pulse of her climax crescendo and, as she toppled over into the abyss again, he cried out his own release, pulling himself free with a loud guttural groan.

* * *

They lay on top of the silk coverlet. The candles were burning down, making the light reflected in the mirrors flicker gold, which made the room feel like an underwater cavern. Aleksei's heartbeat was finally beginning to slow. Allison's hair was spread out on the pillows, exactly as he had imagined it. He buried his face in the silken mass, breathing in a spicy perfume, maybe cinnamon, and the unmistakable scent of their lovemaking. She was lying on her side, her back to him, her delightfully curvaceous bottom tucked against his groin. He cupped her breast with one hand, his other lay flat on her flank. They had not spoken. He couldn't think of any words.

Perfect? No, for that would be to imply that it couldn't get any better, and he knew, he was certain, that it could. Would. He pushed aside a thick silky handful of Allison's tresses to nuzzle into her neck. She wriggled her bottom against him, and he felt himself stir, and she chuckled, a throaty sound that made him thicken instantly.

'Aleksei,' she said, turning around, her eyes alight with laughter and desire. 'So soon?'

He kissed her. 'What is it they say about practice?'

'Makes perfect.' She cupped his buttocks, pulling him up against her. 'Who would have thought that repetition could be such fun?'

Autumn arrived in St Petersburg the next morning, a stark contrast to the previous day. The sky was heavy with the promise of rain, iron-grey clouds skidding briskly across a lowering sky. The children seemed not to notice the change in the weather, happily playing their customary game of catch with a considerably less noxious Ortipo. A simple concoction of fennel seed and peppermint mixed with flour and beef tea prepared by Allison, and administered daily by the children in the form of a biscuit, had cured the dog of the worst of his emissions and earned Allison the unexpected gratitude of Nyanya. The bulldog was considerably less rotund too, thanks to the daily outing to the gardens which all three children now looked forward to every morning.

Though it wouldn't be long now before they would have to confine their play to indoors. She must ask Aleksei which room they might appropriate—though that was probably unnecessary. By the time the weather became too cold, she'd likely be on her way back to England.

Time was, as Aleksei said, flowing faster than the Neva River. She couldn't possibly want it to stop, that would be quite wrong of her.

The stone bench she favoured while watching the children play was cold, but Allison, huddling her cloak around her, did not notice as she sat down, closing her eyes as her mind drifted back to last night.

Last night had been—she didn't think there was a single word that encapsulated it. Exciting. Passionate. Wildly, ecstatically satisfying. She had never imagined that lovemaking could be so utterly enthralling, so all-consuming. And so liberating. She had forgotten herself last night, entranced by Aleksei's touch, by the strength of his reaction to her. She had forgotten who she was and had discovered some other, sensual, powerful being, who cared not where she ended and where Aleksei began. As if their borders had become blurred. As if they had somehow been transformed into...

Allison sat up abruptly, opening her eyes. What nonsense was this! Certainly no way to be thinking about a man who was destined to become part of her past in the not-too-distant future. Independence was what she had come here to achieve, freedom to be herself, to make her own life. She had not come here to entangle herself in someone else's life, to think herself only half a person without him.

She frowned at this notion. Since coming to St Petersburg, she had not only regained her shattered confidence, she had become ever more sure of herself. Increasingly certain, in fact, that she would and could make a new, better life for herself, and she didn't need Aleksei for that. So it was this other creature then, who craved him?

She rolled her eyes. This fanciful piece of imagining was not at all like her. But last night—oh, last night had been so very different from anything…

Which brought her back full circle, just as the object of her thoughts appeared, making his way towards her at a run. 'You will never believe this,' he said, waving a letter at her. 'Look what Catiche has just shown me.'

The next day, Allison paced the floor of the chamber she now knew as the Square Room, awaiting Aleksei's return. What was keeping him?

She considered making herself a cup of tea but, daunted by the complicated process, she instead pulled the letter from her pocket and scanned the contents one more time. With every reading—and this was at least the seventh—she became more convinced that she was not looking at the words of a murderer. Anna Orlova's script was elegant, flowing across the page in impeccably straight lines. The hand of an educated woman. A well-born woman, who wrote in grammatically perfect English. A woman whose care and love for the recipient shone through in every gentle reminder to Catiche to tend to her lessons, in every entreaty that she look after her little brother and sister.

Very soon you will be attending your first children's ball, little one. Have you chosen the fabric for your gown? Gold, the colour of your hair, or blue the colour of your eyes would suit you best. I hope that my replacement will guide you wisely.

You will have a dancing master, I expect. I wish that I could be with you to practise your steps.

Catiche had however, in her own inimitably contrary fashion, insisted on a pink gown. She had been a very unwilling pupil for the dancing master too, though Allison had put this down to a natural reluctance to attend the event after the tragic turn in her fortunes. Or perhaps she simply didn't want to attend with Allison.

Though the question of the upcoming ball was hardly the most important point of the letter she was holding. Catiche had sought Aleksei out, so excited had she been to finally receive word from her beloved governess, the missive having been delivered by some unknown intermediary to Nyanya.

'May I write back, as Madame Orlova requests, Uncle Aleksei,' she had asked, utterly unaware of the potentially life-changing nature of the letter she held. It was to Aleksei's credit, Allison thought, that he had refrained from snatching it from her. Instead, containing his excitement, he calmly informed Catiche that he was honoured she'd consulted him, and that he wished to do justice to her request by reading the letter carefully. He promised her an answer on his return from urgent business.

Which he had not returned from. Where on earth was he? Allison was consulting one of the three clocks in the Square Room yet again, when the doors were thrown open, and Aleksei appeared, a petite, cloaked figure in his wake.

'Ensure we are not disturbed, under any circumstances,' he commanded the footman, before closing the doors firmly behind him.

The governess, Anna Orlova, looked to be somewhere between thirty-five and forty. She had the kind of gentle countenance, with brown eyes set under a mop of soft brown curls, which would have placated any fractious child, were it not for the fact that her complexion was ashen, and she was, quite clearly, terrified. She wore a white cap over her hair, the kind of everyday cap a woman would wear when she was not expecting visitors. Whatever had delayed Aleksei, it had not been waiting for the erstwhile governess to change into travelling clothes.

'We lost a wheel from the carriage, we had to wait two hours while it was repaired,' Aleksei said brusquely. 'Now, Madame Orlova,' he said, ushering the woman towards a chair, 'you will oblige me by repeating this improbable tale of yours to Miss Galbraith.'

Aleksei began to deal efficiently with the samovar, while Madame Orlova stared helplessly at Allison. 'My apologies, I am somewhat—I was not expecting His Illustrious Highness, though I should have—it was both wrong and ill judged to write to Catiche on impulse as I did, I know that. I promised Her Serene Highness I would not—and I swear, Miss Galbraith on my honour and my life, the letter is the first and only time that I have broken my solemn vow. But His Illustrious Highness has every right to be angry.'

'His Illustrious Highness is not so much angry as still trying to make sense of what you told him,' Aleksei said, handing Madame Orlova a cup of tea, 'and Miss Galbraith must be thoroughly confused already. Please start at the beginning,' he added more gently as he sat down. 'Recount to us exactly what transpired on the morning of your dismissal.'

Madame Orlova took a dainty sip of tea. 'Nikki had been sick in the night, and would not settle, he kept calling over and over for his mama. Nyanya was staying with her sister for a few days, so I took it upon myself to fetch Her Serene Highness. It was very late—or early, I suppose, about three in the morning, so I was astonished to find that she was not in her bedchamber. But at that point my only concern was Nikki, and so I returned to comfort the child.'

Madame Orlova smiled tenderly. 'Poor little mite, he had quite worn himself out with crying and was soon asleep. I slept in a truckle bed in his room to keep watch over him. When he woke, his temperature was almost back to normal, so I dressed and went to find Her Serene Highness, to reassure her...'

Here, Madame Orlova's voice faltered. Her eyes filled with tears, and she looked quite stricken. 'I said...' She cleared her throat. 'I told Her Serene Highness of how I'd found her chamber empty when I'd come to fetch her in the night, and she...' What little colour the tea had put back in the governess's cheeks disappeared. 'She was like a woman demented. Screaming at me that I lied, calling me such names, using language I would not have imagined she even understood. I thought—even now, after all these months, the memory—I barely recognised her.'

Allison, quite astonished by this revelation, cast a questioning look at Aleksei, but he shook his head, indicating that she should take the lead, while he removed Madame Orlova's empty teacup from her clasp, and set about refilling it. 'What happened next, *madame*?' Allison asked.

'She had obviously been crying,' the governess replied, her voice not much more than a whisper. 'I noticed it straight away, when I entered her bedchamber. Her eyes were rimmed with red, her hair, her beautiful hair that she was so proud of, it was a tangle. Only I was so concerned to tell her about Nikki, I did not at first ask her what had overset her so—as I should have. We were not close friends, that would not have been appropriate, for Her Serene Highness was a duchess, and I—but we shared, as you do, spending so much time together with the children, little confidences, small jokes. I thought she trusted me.'

A sob was quickly stifled. Madame Orlova's hands were shaking when she accepted her second cup of tea, and she drank it, as was Aleksei's custom, in one draught.

'You are still much affected by the events of that day,' Allison said, trying to disguise her impatience, for she had no idea, as yet, where the governess's story was leading. Save that she was by now certain that Madame Orlova was not a murderess.

'I have missed the children terribly.'

'And they you, *madame*.'

'How are they? I have been so worried about *les pauvres petites*. Such a terrible tragedy they have had to cope with.'

'Indeed,' Aleksei interjected as her mouth

trembled on the brink of another sob. 'But you will be able see for yourself that they are well, that Miss Galbraith has been taking excellent care of them, just as soon as you have finished your tale.'

'Oh!' The governess's face lit up. 'Oh, Your Illustrious Highness, I cannot thank you enough.'

'I do not want thanks, *madame*, I wish you to tell Miss Galbraith what you have already told me, as concisely as possible.'

'Yes. Of course, Your Illustrious Highness.' The governess obediently set down her cup and sat up straight. 'I asked Her Serene Highness if I could help her. Whatever had kept her from her chamber last night had obviously overset her, I said, and it was that I think, the mention of her absence, which sent her over the edge. She screamed at me that no one on earth could help her and that I was to leave. I was so shocked. I tried to reason with her, but Her Serene Highness seemed quite beyond reason. She insisted that I leave the palace at once and never return. I was not to communicate ever again with anyone from the Derevenko family, nor with any of the palace servants. I was never to mention her absence from the palace the night before or the conversation we were having to a living soul.

She said—she said that if I did there would be most dire consequences for both myself and my family. I had no option but to give her my word, and I kept it, Your Illustrious Highness, but Her Serene Highness has been dead some months, and I have been so worried about the children, so I very foolishly and impetuously wrote to Nyanya enclosing the note for Catiche. When you arrived at my cottage, I assumed that you...'

'That I was the bearer of the dire consequences Duchess Elizaveta had promised?'

'Yes.'

Aleksei frowned. 'You clearly know that both the Duke and Duchess were dead within a few days of your leaving the palace?'

'Of course. It was in all the newspapers. A terrible, terrible tragedy.'

'But still you did not break your promise? Despite being, as you have just admitted, very concerned for your former charges?'

'You can have no idea how concerned, Your Illustrious Highness, but the reach of the Derevenko family is long. I could not know what measures Her Serene Highness had taken to ensure my ongoing silence. I could not risk any harm befalling my family.'

Aleksei stared at the governess, making no attempt to disguise his scepticism. 'You honestly believed that the Duchess Elizaveta would do—what?'

'I chose not to imagine,' Madame Orlova answered with a shudder. 'Forgive me, Your Illustrious Highness, but you were not present that morning. Her Serene Highness was quite demented, clearly at her wits' end. Her desperation was obvious. I took her threats very seriously indeed.'

'What can have transpired for her to be at her wits' end, as you put it?' Allison asked.

'I would not wish to speculate, Miss Galbraith, but I will say this. Their Serene Highnesses were very, very proud of the Derevenko family's spotless reputation. At court, the Duke and Duchess were uniquely famed for their honesty and fidelity, and above all, for being above any sort of scandal. I believed that morning, and am of the same opinion now, that Her Serene Highness would do almost anything to protect that reputation.'

Aleksei paced the Square Room, his mind seething as he awaited Allison's return from the schoolroom, where she was temporarily reuniting the children with their very grateful and relieved governess. The Orlova woman was not a murderer. Her convoluted tale was so unbelievable it could only be true. But the implications…

His hands formed into tight fists. The implications were quite literally unthinkable.

One of the double doors opened just enough for Allison to slip through. She crossed the room to join him and he clasped her hands gratefully.

'The children were delighted to see Anna,' Allison said. 'Catiche was eager to thank you in person, but I told her later, tomorrow. I thought—how are you, Aleksei?'

From the way she looked at him, a mixture of sympathy and trepidation, it was obvious she had drawn the same conclusions as he. 'Never mind how I feel,' he said roughly, pulling himself free from the comfort of her touch. 'What do you make of the governess's tall tale?'

Allison was trying to decide whether or not to pull her punches. He could read her as easily as a book, and knew, from the downward quirk of her mouth, the slight slump of her shoulders, exactly when she had reached her decision. 'I don't think it was a tale, but the absolute truth.'

She sat down on one of the *chaises longue*, patting the space beside her encouragingly. Aleksei surrendered to the temptation. It was not that he needed comforting, simply that he wanted to be by her side, and why not, dammit! 'For the record,' he said, 'I believe she spoke the truth too. But you haven't answered my question.'

'No.' Allison angled herself on the sofa to face him and, pulling a pin from her hair, set about teasing it into a circle. 'Though there are still some questions which remain unanswered, I think we can conclude from what Madame Orlova told us, that—that this was a domestic matter, a crime of passion.'

'By which you mean that either my brother or his wife is a murderer,' Aleksei said brutally.

Allison dropped her hairpin. There were tears glittering in her eyes when she lifted her head. 'I'm so sorry, I wish it were otherwise.'

There he had it, the confirmation he needed and so desperately didn't want. The confirmation that his instincts had been right all along. How he wished, how he desperately wished he'd left well alone. But it was too late now. Best to lance the boil quickly and efficiently. 'Do you think it was Michael?'

Allison's hand hovered over his, but she de-cided—quite rightly—not to touch him. 'Before we leap to any conclusions,' she said gently, 'I think we need to review the few facts we can be certain of.'

Aleksei crossed his arms over his chest. 'Go on, then.'

She did not flinch from his gaze. She would not, he thought with a sick feeling in the pit of his stomach, tell him what he wanted to hear but what he needed to know. He could trust her to tell him what she really thought.

'For a start,' she began, 'I think, as Anna Or-lova clearly does, that Elizaveta must have been having an affaire.'

Exactly as he had concluded, but hearing the words aloud made it so much worse. 'I find it ut-terly unbelievable that Elizaveta would cuckold Michael!' Aleksei exclaimed. 'The only faith-ful married couple in St Petersburg, someone told me the other day.'

'But it is the only logical conclusion, Alek-sei. I'm sorry to say.'

'You're right. I know you're right. But if this got out, if it were known that Elizaveta—by the stars, Elizaveta!' Aleksei shook his head. 'The sacred Derevenko name would trailed through the mud, the family's peerless reputation be-smirched. It doesn't bear contemplating.' Which was exactly what Michael would have thought. And indeed Elizaveta. Which would lead one to conclude...

'What else?' he asked. 'Before I torture my-self with speculation, what are these other facts that you think we can be certain of?'

'We know we are dealing with two suspi-cious deaths and not one. Possibly one murder and one suicide?'

'Then it cannot have been Michael,' Aleksei said with utter certainty. 'Knowing the kind of man he was, I cannot believe he would delib-erately deprive his children of both their par-ents.' Was it wrong of him to hope that she was right, to condemn his sister-in-law to clear his brother? But with a sick feeling, he perceived the flaw in this logic. 'Though the same must be said of Elizaveta. She too was a loving par-ent. I think we must rule out suicide. Which brings us back to a double murder. Someone else must have been involved.'

Allison furrowed her brow. 'Perhaps. Though it is possible—I've been thinking, Aleksei, about the poison. It is possible that the second death was an accident. If the perpetrator cut the root with a knife, and perhaps cut his or her hand in the process, the wound could have become contaminated with poison. Or even if some trace of the root was left on the fingers which were then licked—you see, a low dosage, taken by accident—that would have done it.'

'A murder and an accident?' Aleksei nodded slowly. 'That sounds much more plausible.'

'Yes, but there is one other aspect of the poison which we have not taken account of,' she added, in a tone that sounded horribly ominous. 'To administer poison, one must first obtain it, Aleksei. Wolf's Bane grows in quantity at the Apothecary's Garden, I saw it myself on my second visit. One plant would not be missed.'

It took him a moment to realise what she was implying. 'The murder could not have been committed on impulse or in a fit of rage.'

'Only if one had already obtained the means.'

He could no longer contain himself, jumping to his feet, clutching at his hair and cursing under his breath. 'I cannot believe that my brother would do such a thing! I simply cannot. If he discovered his wife's affaire, he would be furious beyond words, and deeply hurt too. I can just about make myself believe that he might lose control and lash out, perhaps throttle her or take a knife to her. But to act in cold blood, to actually plan to kill her—no.'

'Aleksei…' He flung up his hand to quiet her, but she ignored him. 'Aleksei,' Allison said determinedly, 'I agree.'

'You do?' He sat back down abruptly. 'Why?'

'We have no evidence that Michael knew about the *affaire*. Remember, from what Anna Orlova told us, that it was Elizaveta who was at her wits' end, Elizaveta whose behaviour was completely out of character. Her absence had been noted by Anna. She took the extraordinary step of effectively banishing her, threatening her family—if Michael already knew, what would have been the point?'

'By the stars, you are right. You think then, that Elizaveta murdered Michael?' Aleksei shook his head, as if that would clear the tangle of thoughts careering around it, like a whirling cloud of starlings. 'But then why kill him? If she had banished the Orlova woman, there was no need to worry that she would be discovered.'

'Perhaps that wasn't the motive. What if she planned to kill Michael in order to be free to marry her lover?'

'Completely out of the question,' Aleksei said firmly. 'Elizaveta was Her Serene Highness,

Duchess Derevenko. She was born and raised to the position. She and Michael were betrothed as children. She dedicated her life to keeping herself and her family at the pinnacle of St Petersburg society. It is inconceivable that she would throw that away for any man, no matter how in thrall to him she may have been.'

'Whoever the man was, he *must* have held her in thrall for her even to risk an affaire, considering the risks she was taking,' Allison said drily. 'If Michael had found out, Aleksei, what do you think he would have done—assuming, as we have, that he would not kill Elizaveta, the mother of his children.'

'He'd have taken steps to ensure the scandal never saw the light of day. So the obvious step would be to silence the only other person who knew.' He clutched her hand. 'So what Elizaveta would be concerned about if he found out would not be her own safety...'

'But that of her lover!'

'Precisely. And what's more, it wasn't only Michael who would do anything to protect the Derevenko name. What was it Grigory said to me? Something about Elizaveta taking the moral high ground, and being careful to ensure that she remained there.'

'Isn't that more or less what Anna Orlova said, that the Duchess would do almost anything to protect her reputation?'

'Including go to the length of killing her husband? Is that really what we are saying?'

Allison spread her hands. 'It explains Elizaveta's insistence that a fish intolerance was the cause of her own illness. She must have realised she'd poisoned herself by mistake. She would have been desperate to prevent the doctor from making any sort of link between her illness and Michael's death because she would have been absolutely determined that no one would know what she had done. Even in the throes of death, she did all she could to avoid a scandal.'

'If she'd been so concerned about scandal, she should have refrained from taking a lover,' Aleksei exclaimed furiously. 'Can we really discount the possibility that the lover was responsible? What if he murdered them both to protect himself?'

Allison shook her head. 'That isn't likely. The poison had to be administered in situ. We have no evidence of anyone else being here at the palace on the morning Michael died. And really, Aleksei, would Elizaveta's lover consider murder the best way to protect himself?

The consequences would be an unspeakable death, if his act was discovered—and it would be likely that he would be discovered if he was so foolhardy and reckless to come anywhere near the palace. Don't you think silence on his part would be the safest route?'

'So it was almost certainly Elizaveta,' Aleksei said grimly. 'Her hand may well have been forced when the Orlova woman discovered her absence, but the fact remains, she had the poison already prepared. She was planning to kill my brother, one way or another.'

'I'm so sorry.'

He shrugged away her comforting hand. 'As to her unnamed lover, whether he was embroiled or not, he must have his suspicions, given the circumstances. When the deaths were proclaimed, he would have been terrified, knowing that he would be deemed guilty by association if his affaire was discovered. But no one knows of it, save us, of that I am sure, for there has not been even a whisper at court—nor even from the greatest of all gossips, Grigory Fyodorovski,' Aleksei said bitterly.

He sat back heavily in his chair, rubbing his temples. His head ached. Michael was murdered by his wife. Elizaveta was a murderess.

Was it really credible? That sick feeling in his gut told him it was. 'Whether Elizaveta's lover was guilty of plotting a murder, or guilty only of cuckolding my brother, we will never know. The dead cannot speak, and he has the most compelling of reasons to remain anonymous. So it seems we have an impasse. The truth, but not all of it.'

'At least now we know that your cousin is innocent,' Allison said tentatively. 'The murders were nothing to do with acquiring the Derevenko fortune.'

Aleksei sat up with a harsh bark of laughter. 'Trust you to put a positive slant on the situation. You're right. It seems like Michael's change of will was, after all, a coincidence.'

'Your brother must have known, as we all hoped, that Napoleon's defeat was imminent, that peace would follow. Perhaps he had always wished you to be his children's guardian, and only ever named Felix because you were not available?'

'I don't know. I suppose that makes sense.' Aleksei rubbed his eyes wearily. 'Perhaps.'

'I'm sorry, but it looks unlikely that you will ever know some things for certain. I am so very sorry that I can't give you the complete proof you need. I know how much you want to be sure of the facts.'

'And how sure I was, that I wanted to know them,' Aleksei said, with a twisted smile. 'We have a Russian saying, it means something along the lines of impaling oneself with one's own bayonet.'

'Shooting yourself in the foot. I prefer to say, be careful what you wish for.'

'I think I prefer that too. When you arrived here, my most fervent wish was to uncover the true circumstances surrounding my brother's death. With your help, we've done that, and though we don't have complete proof, I think we have proved what happened beyond all reasonable doubt.'

'Will that be enough for you, Aleksei?'

'It is enough for your English courts, and so must be enough for me. I need time to think. I need time to come to terms with it, but it will have to be enough. Which effectively means that you have fulfilled the primary objective of your contract. Congratulations.'

His words silenced both of them. Allison flushed red and then turned quite pale. Her eyes were stricken. 'You wish me to return to

England forthwith?' she asked, with a catch in her throat.

No! It was like a punch in the gut. Of course he had always known she would go, but—but not yet. Though he didn't have any right to detain her. And perhaps he was mistaken, and she was keen to go and get on with carving the new life she talked so passionately about. 'There is no perpetrator to be brought to justice,' Aleksei continued roughly, 'indeed no justice to be served, for I am hardly going to cause a scandal by proclaiming murder.'

'So now you can make plans to give the children into Felix's care,' Allison said, her practical words belied by the giveaway catch in her voice. 'And Anna can resume her duties, I suppose. The children adore her. Now that she can return, I won't have to worry about—they won't miss me.'

They would, but not as much as he would. And as for the children, he felt strangely resistant to releasing them into anyone's care. Timing, Aleksei told himself, that was all it was. He wasn't ready to hand them over yet. Any more than he was ready to let Allison go. Not quite yet. 'I have not decided whether to re-employ the Orlova woman yet,' he said. 'And if you recall, the terms of your contract included a secondary objective, of taking care of the children. So that duty is not fully discharged, Governess.'

His words were mere sophistry and if he knew it, so too must she. But she chose not to dispute it. With relief Aleksei noted her demeanour brighten visibly. Allison didn't want to go either. Not yet. Thank the stars she was so endearingly transparent.

'I would not like to leave so abruptly as Madame Orlova,' she said. 'The children do not love me as much, but I think they do care a little.'

'They care a great deal, as you must know,' Aleksei said, sitting back down beside her, taking her hands in his, refusing to acknowledge how relieved he was save in the tightening of his clasp. 'We will need to accustom them to the idea of your departure.' And himself too. 'Allow them to spend a bit more time enjoying your company before you leave.' And him too. Yes, that was it. 'So I'm afraid I can't release you from your contract just yet.'

'No, I don't think you can.'

She smiled at him mistily, and he felt a strange twisting in his gut. A long tress of auburn curls had been released by the hairpin which now lay discarded on the floor, shaped into an imperfect circle. He pushed her silky strands back from her cheek, twining her curls around his finger. Wanting manifested itself in an ache low in his belly. Not desire, something different. He rested his cheek against hers, breathing in her particular scent, his mouth on her hair, and closed his eyes.

Her fingers fluttered over the back of his neck, stroking, soothing. 'It has been what my grandmother would call a bit of a day,' she said softly.

Aleksei laughed silently. 'That is an understatement.'

He lifted his head, capturing her face between his hands. And kissed her.

The sweetest, achingly beautiful of kisses it was. With a soft sigh, she seemed to melt into him. Not surrender, but giving. Succour. Release. He tilted her back on the *chaise longue* and she lay pliant beneath him, her hands on his arms and his back and his buttocks, smoothing, stroking, and her tongue stroking his. He was melting with their kisses, the balm of them pushing all the trauma of the day to the back of his mind. They were not the answer, those kisses.

The questions would return. The agony of not knowing would come back to torture him.

'Allison.' He said her name, for the simple pleasure of saying it. 'Allison,' he said, between kisses. But for now, those kisses were all he needed. For now, she was all he wanted.

Chapter Ten

'I know you plan to hold your daily lunchtime dispensary, but I promise I'll have you back in plenty time,' Aleksei told Allison the next day when she joined him with the children in the reception hall just after breakfast.

'Where are we going, Uncle Aleksei?'

It was Elena who asked, but all three children eyed him expectantly. 'We are going to the food market,' he said, digging into his pockets and producing three purses, which he doled out to each of them in turn. 'You know, the place where your dinners come from?' he prompted, when the children stared at him blankly.

'But our dinners come from the kitchen,' Nikki protested.

Catiche rolled her eyes. 'Merchants deliver the food to the kitchens from the market, Nikki.'

'Most people are obliged to go and buy the food themselves,' Aleksei told them. 'Only as much as they can carry. They also have to cook it themselves.' He knelt down in front of them. 'We are very privileged. Most people in St Petersburg don't live in a palace or have servants.'

'Of course we know that, but…' Catiche bit her lip.

'What is it?'

'We are Derevenkos,' the girl said earnestly. 'Papa would not allow us to mix with ordinary people.'

'Then it's high time that you did. Think of it as an outdoor lesson, part of your education.' Aleksei got to his feet and ruffling their hair. 'But fun too.'

'What do we need this for, Uncle Aleksei?' Elena pulled out a coin from the purse, studying it as if she had never before seen such a thing. Which she might well never have, Allison thought with amusement.

'To buy whatever takes your fancy,' Aleksei said, putting his hat on. 'Now, if you are all ready?'

The three ran outside, stopping short when they discovered there was no carriage awaiting them. When Aleksei informed them that they were to walk along the river to their destination, they gazed at their uncle in astonishment. Allison waited for either Catiche or Elena to complain that walking was beneath the dignity of a Derevenko, but to her surprise, they exchanged excited glances, linked hands with Nikki between them, and set off along the wide embankment at a skip.

'I hadn't thought about it before,' Allison said, as Aleksei drew her arm into his, 'but any time they leave the palace it is either in the carriage, or in the boat.'

'Safe from contact with the great unwashed. Catiche was right, Michael would heartily disapprove of today's outing.'

'Is that why you decided upon it?'

He laughed. 'No. I meant what I said to the children. They have been far too closeted from the world, and they have far too inflated an opinion of themselves.'

'That's unfair. They are not conceited.'

'No. But they are arrogant—or they will be, if someone doesn't teach them that not everyone is as lucky as them.' He smiled down at her, and she wondered how she could ever have thought his eyes icy. 'I also thought it high time that you sampled some of our traditional Russian food.'

'Is it the same market where Elizaveta…?'

He put his gloved finger to her mouth. 'Let us not talk of that today. But be reassured, I have checked with Nyanya, and none of the children have inherited their mother's intolerance to fish, so if they want to sample a coulibiac then they may.'

That he had had the foresight to check was astonishing, Allison thought as Aleksei directed Catiche to turn left over the canal. Then there were the little coin purses. But most astonishing of all was the fact that Aleksei had dreamed up the expedition in the first place.

The market was a long, low building rather like a very large stable, painted terracotta and white. Inside, the space was cavernous, with rows and rows of stalls set out around a huge fountain. The children, quite overawed, huddled close to Aleksei and Allison, their eyes wide with wonder. As her own most likely were, for though she was accustomed to the Covent Garden market, there was almost nothing at all familiar in the wares on display, save the flowers, which spilled out in large buckets in the space closest to the fountain.

One half of the market was given over to basic foodstuffs. Vendors of the same foods

were grouped together. There were greengro-
cers in one corner. Along the back wall were
all the fish stalls and the butchers, where the
various cuts were set out like a work of art,
black and white sausages strung out between
the shelves like bunting. Next came cheeses,
milk and curds. The breads at the bakers' stalls
came in all shapes and sizes, sold whole or by
weight. There were rye breads and black breads,
soft white floury breads, and crispy, long breads
plaited into complex shapes. The smells were
mouth-watering. To the children's delight, one
baker offered them sugar-coated sticks of hot
fried dough, which they took, too awed to say
thank you, until prompted by Aleksei.

The baker bowed low to Nikki, who returned
the bow, making the man laugh. From a sweetmeat stall, a woman approached bearing a tray
of twisted barley sugars, begging Aleksei for
permission to approach. 'Only one piece each,'
he cautioned them, slipping some coins unob-
trusively into the woman's hand.

A little crowd formed around the children,
with offers of pies and pastries, sweetmeats
and fruits from competing stallholders, but
while Nikki happily helped himself, smiling
and laughing in Russian, Catiche was looking

very uncomfortable as people milled around them, desperate for a glimpse of the aristocratic visitors. And Elena—where was Elena?

Casting around in a panic, Allison saw her talking animatedly to a young peasant girl. Allison gestured that they should join them, which the awe-struck girl reluctantly did. 'This is Tatyana,' Elena informed her. 'Her papa has the best sweetmeat stall in the market, may I go and see it?'

'Indeed you may,' Aleksei said, 'and take Catiche and Nikki with you. But be sure to pay if you wish to sample anything.' He smiled down to Tatyana, addressing her in Russian. The little girl looked intimidated at first, but then she smiled, nodded, and seemed, to Allison's amusement, to grow in stature.

'What on earth did you say to her?' she asked, as the four children headed off, with Tatyana firmly in charge.

'I told her that I relied upon her to look after them and to meet us at the fountain in half an hour.'

'You think they will be safe on their own?'

'I forget that you don't speak Russian, and wouldn't have heard Nikki boasting that he was Duke Derevenko, and that I am his uncle, the fiercest soldier in the Tsar's army,' Aleksei replied wryly. 'Everyone knows who they are now, and no one would dare harm a hair on their privileged heads. The only threat to them will be a sore stomach from eating too much food. Talking of which…'

The hot-food stalls lined the central aisle of the market. There were large pies, sweet and savoury, called *pirog*, small ones called *pirozhki* filled with potatoes and meat, and *vatrushka* pastries filled with cheese. *Knish* was a dumpling made of potato, and *syrniki* pancakes were stuffed with jam. There were endless varieties of cabbage soups and stews, and almost as many dishes featuring pickled cucumbers.

'I can't eat another crumb,' Allison said finally, refusing the tiny blini pancake which Aleksei offered her, 'I think I might burst.'

He had sampled far more than she, careful to spread their custom as widely as possible, exchanging relaxed banter in Russian with the stallholders. It was the first time she had had the opportunity to watch him like this, and she could easily imagine how he would have been with his men. Though he was perfectly at ease, there was an invisible line between him and the stallholders, drawn out of respect mingled with awe, the product not only of Aleksei's demeanour, but of his family name.

At the Winter Palace all those weeks ago, and later at Peterhof, she had taken for granted that he not only held his own but stood out among his class. Here at the food market, she had for the first time a taste of the fame which power fuelled. Aleksei might think of himself as first and foremost a soldier. When he said that he loathed the pomp and circumstance of his brother's rank, she believed him. But he was still of that rank. And that rank was miles above her own lowly station.

The children returned to the fountain with empty purses and full stomachs. 'When I am big, I am going to have a market stall and sell sweetmeats,' Nikki announced, and for once neither of his sisters reminded him that he was a duke.

Catiche had bought prettily wrapped sweetmeats for Nyanya, while Elena's gift was for Ortipo. Having, to their delight and astonishment, obtained Aleksei's permission to bring the famous bulldog on an expedition to meet their new friend Tatyana in the park a few days hence, they were subdued on the way home, though profuse in their thanks for the adventure, when they arrived back at the palace. 'Even though Papa would never have permitted us to set foot in such a place, I am glad you did, Uncle Aleksei,' Catiche said. 'You were right, it was fun.'

Watching them charge up the stairs in search of their nanny, Allison surrendered to the melancholy which had settled on her at the market. She began to walk away in the direction of her dispensary, but Aleksei followed her.

'What is wrong?'

'Seeing the reaction to the children at the market reminded me that they are only one step removed from royalty. As are you, Your Illustrious Highness.' A lump rose in her throat. 'I'm sorry. It simply struck me forcibly, how very different we are, that is all.'

'It is precisely because you are so very different from anyone I've ever known that I like you so much.'

'You do?'

He caught her in his arms. 'How can you doubt it?'

Her heart kicked up a beat. She forgot all about their different social stations, and remembered only how they merged and morphed, one into the other, when they kissed. And when they made love.

'Only two nights ago,' Aleksei said, as if he read her thoughts. 'So much has happened. And, no,' he added hastily, 'I do not want to revisit it or think about it.' He pulled her closer. 'Do you know what I have found to be the perfect way to stop thinking?'

Allison twined her arms around his neck. 'No, but I hope you might have stumbled on the same solution as me.' She kissed him.

'Identical,' he said, kissing her back, a deep, hungry kiss that unlike yesterday's kisses would not be sated simply with more kisses.

'Will you come to me tonight in my quarters?'

Aleksei exhaled sharply. 'Are you sure?'

'Certain. She kissed him again, just to make sure he knew that she was.

Allison waited in her sitting room, where she had taken her dinner alone, for Aleksei had another engagement. The confidence with which she had issued the invitation had turned to fluttering nerves as she waited, still in her day dress, but with her hair down. But when he arrived, knocking softly on the door, the nerves dissipated instantly, for he pulled her into his arms and kissed her deeply, and Allison stopped thinking.

The first time they made love, it had been an urgent satisfying of a hunger. The second time, they had made a banquet of each other. This time it was different again. Their touch was more confident. Their kisses measured out the pace, from the slow fire which had been smouldering since their kisses this morning, to the stoking of that fire as they touched each other, as their clothes dropped to the floor, as they sucked and licked and stroked and cupped, hurtling toward the urgent need for completion.

Naked, in front of the sitting-room fire, they knelt facing each other, still kissing, their breathing ragged. When he slipped his hand between her legs, stroking into her, she took his shaft in her hand, stroking too. He fell back on to the rug, taking her with him. When she leaned over to kiss him, her breasts brushed his chest and he shuddered, so she did it again, relishing the shivering, delicious, dragging response in her nipples. But it was not enough.

She needed him inside her. She had to have him inside her. As she took him in, his thick, hard, satin length, she tightened around him, watching her arousal reflected on his face, feeling him thicken. She sat back, pushing him higher, and he groaned, cupping her bottom with his hands, though she needed no encouragement to move, to lift herself, to thrust. She tightened around him, wanting to savour that twisting, throbbing, tension that preceded her climax. But she could not stop, did not want to stop. Harder, faster, she moved, lost in a rhythm that was theirs, only theirs, until she was thrown, out of control, could hear herself crying out her pleasure, pulsing around him, barely aware that he had lifted her free to spend himself, falling against the breadth of his chest with a sob, and finding his mouth for one last, deeply satisfied kiss.

But later, after they had lain communing silently in front of the fire for hours, lying alone in her bed, the hazy, floaty aftermath burst like a bubble, leaving Allison anxious. There had been so few words, because they had needed none. Their touch had been so sure, for lovers who barely knew each other. How many more days did they have together? How many nights? How many more times would they make love?

Not enough, that much was certain. Not nearly enough.

The future beckoned. The future she had come here longing to grasp was within her reach now. She wanted it. She did want it. But just—just not yet.

Aleksei watched the children at play in the garden from Michael's study the next day. Grigory had just stopped by, en route to Finland once more, at the Tsar's behest. Aleksei had no problem in keeping silent on the matter of Elizaveta, having a very strong desire to draw a veil over the whole affair. If Grigory was in blissful ignorance of his sister's perfidy, let the poor man remain so. There was nothing to be gained by shattering his illusions.

'I will be gone for a considerable period,' Grigory had informed him. 'As for you, dear boy, it is time you stopped burying your head in the sand and accepted what you must have known in your heart from the moment the contents of Michael's will were made known to you. Your army career is over. Your future lies here, with those children.'

Grigory had left with a jaunty wave, leaving Aleksei silently fuming. How dare the man dictate his life. How dare he presume to know what was best for Aleksei. And for his wards. Dammit, how dare he!

Over and over again, he'd asked himself why Michael had excluded Felix from his will. It occurred to him then, that the more salient question was why he had written Aleksei in? It didn't matter why Michael didn't want Felix, what mattered was that he wanted Aleksei.

Deep down, he realised with a sinking feeling, he must have known this. It explained why he had been so reluctant to agree with Allison when she'd pointed out that he was now free to do what he'd planned to do all along, and reverse Michael's decision.

Wearily, Aleksei put his cup down, leaned his head back on the wing chair, and closed his eyes, trying desperately to talk himself out of this most unwelcome insight. Felix was the perfect guardian. He knew the ways of the court, the ways of the city, the ways of tradition. Felix would ensure that the girls made excellent marriages. He'd ensure that Nikki made a conscientious duke. He would ensure that the Derevenko dynasty continued as it always had, using its sons and daughters to spread its influence, increase its wealth. Exactly what Michael wanted.

Until he changed his will.

He jumped to his feet, cursing. Michael was under no illusions about Aleksei's views on the subject of dynasty and power and influence. But on the other hand, he also knew that Aleksei had a very strong sense of duty. Michael would expect Aleksei to see that things were done as Michael wished them to be done. He would not expect Aleksei to change things. Would he?

Outside, the children were screaming with laughter at Ortipo, who had once again jumped into the fountain after a stick. Aleksei smiled as the dog clambered out, shaking water all over a delighted Nikki. He would miss them, but it wasn't as if he'd never see them again, once they were in Felix's care. He could visit them. Send them presents from whatever part of the world he ended up in, doing whatever he ended up doing.

Which would be what, precisely? Was Grigory right? Was his future here in St Petersburg with those children?

No! He had come to care for them, he couldn't deny it, but to make them the centre of his life? No, it was not what he wanted. He would resent them in the end. He would blame them for the sacrifices he'd made on their account. None of them would be happy. Not the children. Certainly not Aleksei. And not the wife he'd be obliged to take in order to complete the picture-perfect family. If he'd wanted a wife and family, he'd have married and had children of his own. But he'd never wanted either. He was married to his career. Just like Allison.

She was not in the garden, Nyanya was supervising them. Aleksei checked his watch. She would be holding her dispensary for the servants.

It struck me forcibly, in the market, how very different we are.

She was right. They were from radically different worlds. And soon she would return to hers. That odd feeling returned, a tightening in his chest, that was becoming familiar each time he thought of her leaving.

Whatever it was it would pass quickly enough once she was half a world away. Aleksei nodded to himself, reassured. Yes, it would pass.

It was Catiche's idea to ask her uncle to accompany them to the children's ball two days later, and Uncle Aleksei had surprised both his niece and his niece's governess by accepting with alacrity.

He arrived in the schoolroom to collect them wearing his uniform. In order to distract herself from a bout of lustful staring, Allison made a twirl. 'Catiche is not quite ready yet,' she informed him, 'you know what young girls are like getting ready for a party.'

'I don't, but I am learning quickly,' he said with a wry smile.

'Pink is most definitely *not* my colour.'

Aleksei pretended to shade his eyes. 'Salmon-pink, I believe. What on earth possessed you to select it? Wasn't there mention in that letter from the Orlova woman of blue or gold? Either would have suited you very well.'

'Thank you, kind sir, and may I commend your impeccable taste. But pink was Catiche's choice, and since it is the tradition for mother and daughter to wear the same colour, then pink it must be. And actually, I take it as a compliment that she is happy for me to stand in for her mother. What I'm not clear about is the purpose of these children's balls.'

Aleksei grimaced. 'It is the custom here, a phased introduction into society which supposedly ensures a more confident debutante when the time comes to embrace court life.'

'I thought it was simply a social occasion,

a chance to make new friends,' Allison said, somewhat aghast. 'Catiche is only thirteen.'

'As a Derevenko, she will be expected to attend court in as little as a year, two at the most. Michael and Elizaveta will have been planning her successful debut from the day she was born.'

'A responsibility that falls to you now.'

'For the time being,' Aleksei said grimly. 'And as a consequence I must set my personal views aside. If she doesn't attend, she will miss out on—I don't know, connections which may prove important in the future.'

'You mean she will miss out on—oh, I don't know, connections which may prove important to the future of the Derevenko dynasty,' Allison threw at him.

'That is it precisely.' Aleksei ran his fingers through his hair. 'It is unpalatable to me, but it is the truth, Allison. The Derevenko dynasty is one of the oldest and most influential in Russia. Marriage is a question of bloodline, of influence, and of suitable alliances. It is expected that Catiche play her part.'

'By making a suitable marriage, you mean.' Allison crossed her arms and glared. 'You have, by your own admission, rejected all of the great Derevenko traditions. Yet you are perfectly happy to make your nephew and nieces endure them.'

'Would you prefer that they become followers of Volkonsky? Shall I have the girls dress in peasant clothes and learn to play the balalaika? Nikki is a duke. As for Catiche and Elena, have you any idea of the size of their dowries? They will be able to command an alliance with the highest in the land. Or in England. Or any other land.'

'How fortunate for them. Save that they won't be the ones doing the commanding, will they? That will be your cousin Felix's province.'

'No. I mean, yes, it would be if I—look, it's just a ball, for the love of heaven.'

Allison narrowed her eyes. 'Have you changed your mind about Felix?'

'I have not yet made up my mind. It's not the same thing.'

He looked tired. And a little dejected. And she had been haranguing him like a fishwife. 'A very different thing,' Allison agreed. 'I'm sorry. I'm a little nervous.'

'You?'

'Yes. Believe it or not, herbalists very rarely get the opportunity to attend a ball hosted by the Empress of Russia, standing in for a duch-ess, accompanied by a count.'

'You manged to play the lady very well at the Winter Palace, and you have been living at this palace for weeks now.'

'But aside from Peterhof, I have not been abroad much in polite society.' Allison could feel the telltale colour at her throat. 'I don't want to let Catiche down.'

'Catiche obviously doesn't think that's likely, since she's asked you to stand in for her mother. And I certainly don't think it's possible, because I've never known you to let anyone down.'

Save once, she thought. The familiar sad-ness laced with guilt was still there, but it was a faint echo of what it had been.

'You have certainly not let me down, Alli-son.' Aleksei held her at arm's length to study her. 'And you know, the more I look, the more I think that salmon-pink *is* your colour.'

She chuckled. 'You once told me that you never lied. Take that back, or your unblemished reputation will be in tatters.'

'I won't take it back. I think you look quite delectable.' He closed the gap between them. 'So delectable, that I think I might have to—'

'Uncle Aleksei!'

'Catiche.' He whirled around. 'I was just admiring Miss Galbraith's dress. She tells me the colour was your choice. A most excellent one.' He made a flourishing bow. 'May I compliment you, Lady Catherine, on your attire. It is an honour to be escorting such a lovely young lady on her debut.'

Chapter Eleven

The ball was being held at the Catherine Palace at Tsarskoye Selo, the Village of the Tsar, situated in the countryside about two hours' drive from St Petersburg.

'Everyone thinks that the Catherine Palace was named for Catherine the Great,' Catiche informed them as the carriage turned on to the driveway, 'but it was actually Peter the Great who had it built for his wife, the Empress Catherine. Is that not so, Uncle Aleksei?'

'I bow to your superior knowledge, Catiche.'

'Madame Orlova's superior knowledge,' she said with a shy smile. '*Madame* knows everything about every Imperial palace in St Petersburg. This one, you must know, celebrates not only the first Empress Catherine but also the Empress Elizabeth, after whom Mama was named. If you look carefully, Miss Galbraith, you will see the initial "E" in the insignia. "E" for Elizabeth, and for Ekaterina. It is above many of the doors, Madame Orlova told me. We must look out for it.'

Their carriage joined a slow procession of others. The palace they approached was baroque in style, painted blue though with the usual abundance of gilt and gold which Allison had come to expect of every royal palace, and an abundance of statuary lining the driveway and holding sentry along the entire frontage.

'The wings are an extension to the original building,' Catiche continued, obviously keen to show off her knowledge. 'But when the Empress Elizabeth came to the throne, she decided that it was not luxurious enough, and so she employed the Italian, Count Rastrelli, to redesign the entire palace. Count Rastrelli and the Empress Elizabeth were very fond of gold. Madame Orlova said that if you took all the gold from the reception rooms it would weigh more than Papa.

'Miss Galbraith,' she continued in a very different tone as the carriage steps were let down, 'you will stay by my side, won't you?'

'Don't fret, we are both here to support you,' Aleksei said, taking her hand.

They proceeded, flanking Catiche, through countless carved and gilded doorways, through endless corridors glittering with yet more gold, before joining a snaking queue of people at the entrance to what must be the ballroom. As they edged forward as each aristocratic family was announced, Catiche became paler, her posture more rigid, and Allison, recalling her own ordeal on her first public outing at the Winter Palace, could do nothing save smile reassuringly and pray to whoever watched over society children that Catiche would come through the occasion without mishap.

As they reached the entrance to the Great Hall, Allison, who thought she had seen the most elaborate rooms St Petersburg had to offer, was struck dumb. The two longest walls seemed to consist entirely of glass. Daylight streamed through the windows, bouncing off the mirrors placed in between and off the highly polished parquet flooring, making the chamber seem as if it were made entirely of burnished gold. Lit by candlelight it would be quite dazzling.

Catiche's hand tightened on her own, and she saw they were at the head of the queue. The

Derevenko name was announced. Catiche was handed a dance card, and claimed by an immense woman wearing a terrifying headdress that must have left at least one ostrich plucked clean. There was nothing more to be done but to watch nervously as her charge made her debut into society.

'She's not happy,' Aleksei said, two hours later.

'She has danced every dance, and has not once lacked a partner.'

He sighed irritably. 'She's a Derevenko, of course she's not lacking willing partners. Look at her, though. She's putting on a brave face, but it's obvious to me that she's miserable.'

Instead, Allison studied Aleksei. 'She expected to attend this ball with her mama. It is yet another painful reminder that her parents are dead.'

'Yes. I suppose that could be it.' A Russian peasant dance had begun, involving much twirling and waving of scarves. Taking her arm, Aleksei led Allison away from the crowds to a window embrasure looking out on to the gardens. 'When Grigory called the other day, he told me that I should stop burying my head in the sand and accept my responsibilities here.'

'And what do you think of that advice?' she asked, careful to disguise her surprise.

He shrugged. 'It's logical in one sense, though I maintain that I am not best equipped to raise them in the traditional manner.'

'And if things were to change?'

Aleksei gave an exclamation of disgust. 'Reform and Russia are anathema to each other. I don't know. I could—but I'd feel trapped.' She caught a brief glimpse of his anguish, before he recovered himself. 'The children's future is not your problem, Allison.'

Nor was his future. His future without her. The knowledge she had been hiding from herself pressed at her heart. She could not, would not listen to that persistent, insistent inner voice. 'I do understand,' Allison said, trying desperately not to betray her feelings in her voice. 'I of all people understand your desire to make your life your own. A lifetime of following orders, of doing someone else's bidding. Why would you leave the army, only to tie yourself to…?'

A high-pitched scream pierced the air. 'Miss Galbraith! Miss Galbraith!'

'Catiche!' Grabbing Allison's arm, Aleksei

forced his way through the crowd. Catiche was standing with a huddle of other girls, ashen-faced but unharmed. 'Please help her, Miss Galbraith, quickly.'

A shout went up for a physician, but Allison was already beside the little girl writhing on the floor, her mother sobbing hysterically as she tried to pull the child into her arms.

'Leave her,' Allison snapped, pushing the woman away unceremoniously, for she could see the girl's skin turning blue. 'Lie her on her side. Aleksei, quickly, get me a spoon from the buffet table over there. *Madame*, has she taken a fit before?'

'A fit! My daughter has never—who are you? Get away from her. What are you doing?'

Allison took the silver spoon from Aleksei and placed it carefully in the little girl's mouth.

'Unhand the child, *madame*,' a male voice said. 'You are not qualified.'

'Miss Galbraith knows what she is doing, she is...'

'Whatever she is, or claims to be, she is not a physician. I, on the other hand am. Now get out of my way, please and let me attend to the patient.'

Allison leapt back as if she had been scalded.

'You are quite mistaken, sir,' Aleksei exclaimed, 'she is a…'

But Allison grabbed his arm, shaking her head violently. 'Leave it.'

'Merci à Dieu.' The mother fell on the doctor.

'I thank the stars I arrived in time before any further damage could be inflicted.' The doctor threw Allison a disdainful look. 'A cupping is what is required,' he said, scooping the still-writhing and unconscious child up.

The spoon clattered to the floor. 'If you are not careful…' Allison remonstrated in a shaken voice, neither the doctor nor the mother were listening.

'She might choke on her tongue,' Allison finished, staring at the little party as they hurried across the room. 'A cupping will sap what little strength she has. But what do I know.'

'Why did they do that?' Catiche asked, staring after the doctor and his entourage. 'Why didn't they let you help?'

'Because the same rules apply here as in London,' Allison answered furiously. 'Because I will always be an outsider. Nothing has changed.' She turned to Aleksei. 'Will you go and check on the little girl for me?'

'Of course,' he said. 'It's to your eternal

credit that, despite the way you have been treated, your thoughts are for the child. And I'll call for the carriage. The ball is clearly over.'

Allison was lost in a silent reverie during the carriage ride back, her fists clenching and unclenching in her lap, a myriad of emotions, none of them pleasant, sweeping over her countenance. Aleksei wanted desperately to comfort her. He wanted to vent his anger at the despicable way she had been treated. He wanted to tell her how difficult it had been to resist the temptation to punch that smug physician square on his supercilious nose, or to rail at that snob of a mother, who put status before her daughter's well-being. He wanted to hold her, to soothe away her anger. But she sat stiffly, staring sightlessly ahead, looking as if one touch would shatter her into a thousand pieces. And besides, Catiche was with them, and so he garnered as much patience as he could muster.

But the strength of her emotions puzzled him. Unpalatable as they had been, the reaction of the mother and the physician to Allison's intervention was natural enough. They didn't know Allison, and Allison had made no attempt to explain herself.

The same rules apply here as in London.
I will always be an outsider.
Nothing has changed.

She almost never spoke of her past. So much had happened since her arrival that he had forgotten his initial curiosity about her motives. Why was she here? Independence, she said. The fee she had earned would give her that, but he was sure it wasn't just about the money. Why would a woman, having worked so very hard to succeed in a man's world, walk away from it all for a temporary posting on the other side of the world?

As the carriage arrived back at the Derevenko Palace in the dusk, the huge front door flew open, and Elena and Nikki flew out, anxious for news of the ball, thankfully sweeping Catiche away with them. But when Allison, giving him the merest of nods, made to follow them up the grand staircase, Aleksei caught her arm.

'I am tired,' she said, trying to shake him off. 'I would prefer to retire alone to my chamber.'

He could let her go, but it wasn't only that he didn't want to. 'I want to help,' Aleksei said. 'Whatever it is, I want to help.'

She stopped struggling. Her mouth, which

had been pursed into a straight line, softened. 'You already have. Now it's time for me to help myself.'

He took her to the blue breakfast parlour because it was the nearest room. A footman, caught unprepared, followed them with tapers for the candles, another arrived with spills for the fire, and another, rather miraculously appeared bearing a silver salver of cakes, sherry and madeira.

The curtains were drawn against the night. The fire crackled obligingly into life. Allison, still huddled in the rose-pink evening cloak which matched her gown, sank on to one of the few comfortable chairs in the palace, a blue wingback affair with only one gold-embroidered cushion. She took the sherry he gave her, but immediately set it down on the table beside the arm of the chair, and began to strip off her long evening gloves.

'You're still angry,' Aleksei said, pulling off his own gloves and taking the seat opposite her.

'Furious.' Her smile was glittering.

'May I ask why?'

'I thought it would be different here, but nothing has changed.'

'And you will always be an outsider. You said so at the ball. What did you mean by that, Allison?'

She let her head drop back against the chair back, closing her eyes.

He sipped his sherry. It was, like most of Michael's cellar save the champagne, of surprisingly poor quality. His brother's abstemious palate must have been tortuous to his dinner guests. Allison was rubbing her temples. Any minute now, she'd pull out a hairpin. There it was. Now she'd start to fashion it...

'What are you smiling at?'

Aleksei nodded at the bent pin. 'You must get through a great deal of those.'

'Fortunately none of them are pearl-or diamond-tipped.'

He watched her as she made her customary circle of her hairpin, frowning down at it, clearly wanting time to marshal her thoughts, happy to give her the time, now that she was here with him. She never wore jewellery. Only the locket which her grandmother gave her, and which contained the key to her herb chest. She wore no rings. No bracelets. No other adornments at all. He'd assumed, foolishly, he supposed, that it was because she preferred not to.

It hadn't occurred to him that it might simply be that she didn't possess anything else. The pink gown she wore had been a gift from Catiche. She had worn one of Elizaveta's gowns to the Winter Palace only at the dresser's insistence, she'd admitted to him. Doubtless Elizaveta had countless other unworn gowns Allison could have worn, but she had not chosen to.

He was so accustomed to his wealth, spent so little of it himself, that he never thought about it. But Allison had not that luxury. 'Why are you here?' he asked, losing patience, startling her into dropping her hairpin. 'I mean why did you come to St Petersburg? Don't tell me it was for the money, because I know you, Allison, you are not an avaricious person. It is what you intend to do with it that really matters.'

Her brows shot up in surprise. 'I am still not exactly sure what it is I'm going to do, though today—yes, today has certainly decided what it is I won't be doing.' She reached for her sherry, took a sip, wrinkled her nose and put it back. 'A salutary lesson, that is what today was. I intend to learn from it.'

'And do you intend to share your lesson with me?' He leaned forward to touch her knee. 'I would like you to. I'd like to understand. To help you.'

Her lip trembled. 'You have. You've done so much. I told you, it's time for me to help myself now.'

'Then tell me how you propose to do that.'

Allison sat up, unfastened her cloak and reached for the sherry glass, suddenly feeling the need for some fortification. 'When The Procurer sought me out, I had all but given up. She is the strangest woman, Aleksei. She knew what had happened to me, but she did not offer me sympathy or false hope. What she offered me was a second chance, and what she made me realise is that I deserve it. Only I've not known until today what form that might take. I've been thinking only that I'd move somewhere else, some other city than London, and start again. But today made me realise that would be simply stepping back into another form of bondage. I know that's an exaggeration, but—well, you know what I mean, don't you?'

'You mean I would be doing the same by choosing to quit the army only to dance to my brother's tune—or the Derevenko family tune?'

'I would not have put it quite so—but, yes, I suppose it is the same thing.' Allison chewed on her lower lip. 'If I wish to be successful again, it would once again be on the terms of the society I served. Which requires a spotless reputation, and a care for never overstepping the mark. Displaying due deference to the eminent physicians and apothecaries who must know better than me, not daring to question their practices, and most certainly never challenging them. That's how it was before, Aleksei. And I thought it was a price worth paying, because I was doing what I loved, I was easing suffering, I was curing sickness.'

'What changed?'

The familiar nausea assailed her, but she ignored it. 'Everything. A child died and I allowed myself to take the blame, but I know now that it wasn't my fault. Mother Nature was determined to claim the child, and nothing I did, or the physician did, would have made any difference.'

'I'm so sorry.'

'You must have felt the same feeling of helplessness countless times, in battle.'

He leaned over to take her hand. Her fingers were icy compared to his. She allowed herself the comfort of his touch for a fleeting moment, but then she slipped free from his clasp. 'I've never spoken of it. But I think it's time. If you care to listen?'

He nodded. And so she braced herself to speak. She had relived that fateful night on so many occasions, in her dreams and in her waking nightmares, yet she had never once articulated her feelings, never once described events in words. It was dreadful and it was draining and it was difficult, but as she explained the unfolding drama to Aleksei, the little boy's symptoms, the various remedies she had tried, a certain calm took over.

'I would not allow myself to believe the outcome would be fatal,' she said. 'He was not the first patient I had lost, but on previous occasions the cause was clear, I knew the sickness, knew the odds. With this little one, there was no explanation for the fever, no reason that I could determine for my herbal remedies to fail, because they had always worked in similar cases before. I did increase the dose beyond what I would usually administer to such a small child, I did do that, Aleksei, and I did tell his mother that I was doing so. When he did not improve but worsened, I could not believe that it was because of my herbs—but I have to accept that it might have been.'

She drew a shaky breath. Aleksei said nothing, waiting for her to continue, his blue eyes intently focused on her. 'In the end, they summoned an eminent physician. Dr Anthony Merchmont.' She could not repress a shudder. 'A renowned expert in childhood illnesses. When he first arrived I was at my wits' end and I was—I was actually relieved to see him. The little boy was dying, and in such pain, I thought—I so foolishly thought—that we would be united in trying to ease his suffering, if not in curing him.'

Her lip curled as she remembered the way the physician had looked down his nose at her, had commanded her to leave. 'It was the boy's mother who insisted I remain. She trusted me— at that point, she still trusted me.' It was so very painful to recall the woman's face when she believed that Allison had betrayed her.

The climax to the tragic tale was quickly told. 'Dr Merchmont did only what any other physician would have done for a fever. He cupped blood. He applied blisters.' And the child had screamed and screamed as the heated glass was placed on his back, and she had tried to intervene, because it was obvious by then that the harsh treatment was draining what little strength the child had left. 'He died in his mother's arms as dawn was breaking. I have never witnessed such raw grief.'

There was no blocking this memory. The silence, the stillness of the shock, the utter disbelief. And then the screaming. Allison wrapped her arms around herself. 'He was five years old, only a year older than Nikki. Two days before, he was in perfect health, and now he was lying there, like a—a wax doll, and his mother could not believe he was gone. I could not believe it myself. I still find it…' A sob racked her body, and she tightened her grip on herself, motioning Aleksei away. 'Let me finish. I have not yet described the aftermath.'

Now anger fizzed again inside her. 'He—Dr Merchmont—his first reaction was to absolve himself completely of any blame. He was called in too late, he said. By this time his lordship— the child's father was in the sickroom, so angry, looking for fault—and who can blame him for that, but…' Allison clenched her fists. 'There was so much shouting, and all the while the child, the poor little boy was lying there, his mother cradling him in her arms and rocking him, as if he were simply asleep.'

She paused, took several deep breaths. 'I

don't know, I can't recall precisely how—it must have been her, or the maid who disclosed the fact that I had increased the dose of my herbal potion. The poor woman, she did not intend to point the finger at me, but she was hysterical and I—well, it was true, I *had* increased the dose.'

Aleksei swore viciously. 'So this Merchmont fellow seized the opportunity to pin the blame on you, even though it might have been his intervention which hastened the boy's death?'

He was incredulous and, Allison now realised, rightly so. 'It was easy enough to do,' she said, tight-lipped, 'and I made it easier for him, for I didn't defend myself. How could I, when I thought—when it was possible that I had contributed in some way?'

'Allison, you don't really believe that? Had you ever made such a miscalculation before?'

The very same question The Procurer had posed. 'No, I had not, and I am as sure as I can be that what I did was not harmful.'

'Then why didn't you defend yourself?'

'Because by the time I had recovered from the shock of what had happened, it was far too late.' She told him then, in clipped tones, of the orchestrated campaign waged against her. Of the slanderous things which had been said of her. The lies. And the defilement of her reputation.

Aleksei listened, anger and resentment at her treatment burning in his eyes. 'What did you do?'

He expected her to have acted. It was flattering. And mortifying. What a poor wee soul she had been. 'Nothing,' Allison confessed. 'And by doing nothing, I tacitly admitted my guilt.'

Aleksei caught her hands in a painfully tight grip. 'I am not surprised. You are one of the strongest, bravest, most confident women I have ever met, but even you must have faltered under such an onslaught as you have described.'

'The Procurer said I should have fought back.'

'That is like suggesting that a last soldier standing should continue to fight a futile rearguard action. You retreated. You licked your wounds. You regrouped. And here you are, living to fight another day.'

She couldn't help but smile. 'Thank you, your faith in me is most flattering.'

'It is well founded, not flattering. What happened to you would have destroyed most other people—men as well as women. The incident this afternoon at the ball, it must have brought it all back.'

'Yes, but it also made me think about the future. In society, whether it is in London or St Petersburg, I will always be an outsider because my sex prevents me from becoming part of the medical establishment, even if I desired it, which I don't. It shouldn't matter that I am a woman, and one moreover whose appearance gives the illusion that I'm free with my favours, but it does. So I'm not going to practise in society any more, and it's thanks to you, in part that I've realised I don't want to.'

'What on earth have I done to help you come to such a conclusion?'

'You've allowed me to set up my dispensary, of course.' Allison sat up, fired with enthusiasm. 'The people I've been treating don't care who I am or what I look like. They care only that I can ease their suffering. Unlike that little girl at the ball, they have no physician on hand to attend them. These are the people I want to treat, Aleksei. These are the people who need me most, the people I can make the biggest difference to. These are my kind of people, good-hearted, hard-working ordinary people. And when I leave here, the fee I have earned provides me with the means to do that.'

Aleksei looked satisfyingly confounded. 'A dispensary? Is that what you mean?'

Allison beamed. 'Not for society, but for the people society depends upon. I can't save every child, but I can help those who have no access to any other help. You see, they won't care, the physicians and the apothecaries, that I am not a member of their societies and guilds, for they don't care about the people I will treat, the people who cannot pay. So they won't hound me, I doubt they will even acknowledge my existence, because I will not be a threat to their livelihood or a challenge to their position.'

'Though they won't be able to ignore you, for you will shine a light on their shortcomings.'

'Oh, no, now you really do flatter me. Truly, Aleksei, as far as these men are concerned, the poor are unworthy of their attention. My services will be free for those who cannot pay, and for those who can afford a small contribution—oh, but I've not thought through the details. I plan to train an assistant too—you see, that was also your idea. What do you think?'

'I think you will be a great success wherever you go. I think it is a truly wonderful idea.' He pulled her to her feet, wrapping his arms around her. 'And I think you are wonderful.'

'Then perhaps we should start a mutual admiration society, for I think you are wonderful too.' She reached up to brush the white-blond kink in his hair. 'Are you really contemplating remaining here in St Petersburg with the children?'

'I have no option but to consider it,' he said wearily.

'Aleksei, you've lurched, as you said yourself, from battle to babysitting without a moment to consider the future. Do not make any rash decisions or promises you might come to regret. I don't know why it hasn't struck me until now, but there are some similarities between your case and my mother's. I told you that she left me with my grandmother when she married? Well, what I didn't tell you is that she promised to come back for me when she was settled. There were a few visits, always with the promise that the next time she'd take me with her. Then the visits were replaced by letters, saying the same. And then finally very occasional letters, containing no promises at all.'

'I'm so sorry, Allison. That must have been hard to take.'

'Horrible, when I was wee. It would have been much better for her to have been honest from the start. A clean break would have been very painful, but I'd not have had to endure years of hoping in vain for the impossible. I think she knew in her heart that it would be a mistake for the pair of us. Her husband wanted no part of me, while my grandmother brought me up as if I were her own child. So as it turns out, it was better for both of us that we parted. Do you see?'

'I do, though I'm afraid I can't be as generous as you regarding your mother's behaviour.'

'Then you don't see, because what I meant was it would have been wrong for her to sacrifice her happiness for mine. I wouldn't have been happy anyway, and once I was old enough to realise what she'd done, I'd have had guilt to contend with too.'

'Allison. I do see. I promise you, I understand what you're saying, though I seem to remember a time not so long ago, when you advocated my staying.'

'At Peterhof. I remember. I was wrong.'

'Maybe you were. Maybe not. It is my conscience at stake, not your mother's, and I think—oh, you know, I don't know what I'm saying. I don't know what I think at the moment.' He kissed her brow. 'Save that it's not your problem.'

'No.' A lump rose in her throat. 'I wish I could help you more.'

'You have, more than you can know.' He kissed her brow again. 'Now it's time, in your own words, for me to help myself, and to let you get on with helping yourself.'

A tear trickled down her cheek. She made no attempt to catch it. 'You think it's time for me to head back to England?'

'Allison.' He pulled her tight against his chest, hugging her so close she could hear his heart beating even through the thick wool of his uniform coat. 'I think Grigory was right, it's time I stopped burying my head in the sand. Not about the children, but about you.'

He let her go, holding her at arm's length. 'From the moment you walked into my life, I wanted you. I've never met anyone like you, nor am likely to again. I know it won't last because it can't, for all sorts of reasons, not least the fact that you've a perfect future back in England mapped out for yourself, but the thing is, the longer it goes on, the more likely we are to get hurt. Or at least I am. I can't speak for you.'

'Aleksei, you know you can.' Another tear trickled down her cheek. Her throat was clogged. 'It's one of the things about us, it has been from the start, hasn't it, this—this unspoken connection between us. You know I want you every bit as much as you want me. When we make love...'

He swore under his breath. 'Don't say any more.' He swallowed hard. 'It's time for me to stop procrastinating. Whatever that means, it is not your concern. And as for the children, they will miss you greatly, though not as much, I suspect as you will miss them. Your work is done here, Allison, and I've no right to keep you with me simply because I'm not ready to let you go yet.'

Yet. Not yet, but soon. They had no future together. She knew that. She was a herbalist and part-time governess. He was a count. She could shed her tears over that fact, and leave him with that watery memory, or she could make the most of what very little time they had left now, and create sweeter memories to sustain them in the lifetime spent apart that lay ahead of them.

Allison brushed her cheeks dry. She smiled mistily up at him. She twined her arms around him. 'You're right. I wish I could say otherwise, but I can't. Though you're wrong about one thing, Aleksei. You don't have to let me go. Not quite yet. Make love to me,' she said, and then she kissed him.

Chapter Twelve

It was still very early. The sky was overcast, a lowering grey that promised that particularly unpleasant drizzly soft rain that wasn't quite rain, but soaked you anyway. Allison, having spent a torrid night tossing and turning, made her way quickly out to the fernery, her favourite of the succession houses, in search of solitude before resuming her governess duties.

Sitting down under the now familiar statue of Aphrodite, she unbuttoned her cloak and massaged her throbbing temples. To call yesterday a bit of a day, as Seanmhair would have, was a serious understatement. The first revelation had been born of the indignity of her being slapped down at the children's ball. From the pain of her confession to Aleksei, had come catharsis and then a liberating hope, a bright new vision for her future that the herbalist in her couldn't wait to embrace. It was as if all her life she had been preparing for this, lending meaning even to the role she had played in her own downfall, and the scandal she'd had to weather as a result.

So many ideas, so many plans would be fighting for room in her head, were it not for the second, even more momentous revelation emerging from yesterday. She was in love with Aleksei.

Not so much a revelation really, more like a secret that had been suppressed. Of course she was in love with him. Now she'd admitted it, it was impossible to imagine she could ever have been anything else. The attraction had been irresistible from the start. She'd never felt so drawn to a man, never desired any man the way she wanted him. But it wasn't only that. He understood her. He knew what mattered to her and what didn't, because he understood in a way she'd thought no man ever could, how much a part of her were her skills. Her need to heal. Her need to try to ease any sort of pain or suffering, whether it was the minor ailments of the Derevenko servants, or the heartache of his wards. He encouraged her. Even more importantly, she was certain he would never try to change her, never expect her to sacrifice her life for his. She'd always thought that there could be no room in her heart or her life for anything other than her vocation, but how wrong she had been. For the right man, for this man, there was a veritable palace in her heart.

The right man, but Aleksei was wrong in every other respect. If circumstances had been different—oh, so very different—then how blissfully happy they could be. He'd admitted he cared, last night, and that had been the most difficult thing for her to deal with. Her poor aching heart longed to declare itself, but she would not cause him the pain of having to reject her, as he must.

Think of it! She forced herself to do so, yet again, in the hope of extinguishing hope completely. She was as low-born as it was possible to be, with no idea who her father was, only the one certainty, that he had never been married to her mother. Aleksei was as high-born as it was possible to be, second in line to the most powerful and wealthiest dukedom in Russia. Even promiscuous St Petersburg society, which accepted without a blink of an eye, Count Derevenko taking a nonentity of a governess as his mistress, would not tolerate him taking her as his wife. She would be shunned, which she cared not for, save that it would hurt Aleksei, though not as much as the pain she would bear when society ostracised the pair of them. No, she was born on the wrong side of the blanket, and she would be on the wrong side of the fence for Aleksei for ever.

So it was just as well, really, that she had no inclination to switch sides. Just as well that her calling would keep her on the side of the poor and the needy. Just as well she would soon have the means to bring her precious, newborn plans to fruition. It would be a soothing balm as she tried very hard to forget all about her precious, newborn love.

With this melancholy thought she roused herself. What she must not do was permit Aleksei to guess the depth of her feelings for him. She was not gone from St Petersburg yet. There were still days and nights, like last night, to savour. Memories to squirrel away to sustain her in the solitary future which was her destiny. Fastening her cloak against the rain which was now battering hard against the glass of the succession house, she hurried along the soaking paths to the garden room.

'Miss Galbraith! At last. Where have you

been?' Catiche's face was tear-streaked. 'We've been looking for you everywhere. Please hurry. It is Ortipo.'

The silly creature had eaten some poisoned bait put down by the gamekeeper to control vermin. Allison had managed to force him to take a small dose of *ipecacuanha*, dried golden root from her herb chest, with revoltingly spectacular though very effective results. The children's much-loved pet lay snoring loudly in his furlined basket now, with Elena, Nikki and Catiche hovering over him, leaving Allison to seek out Aleksei in his study, clutching the present a grateful Catiche had presented her with.

'Allison. You look very serious.'

He was in his shirt sleeves, his black coat draped over the chair behind the desk where he had been sitting, neat stacks of papers, letters and journals spread before him. He looked tired, the grooves around his mouth, the fan of lines at the corner of his eyes more accentuated. Had he lain awake all night too?

She walked into his outstretched arms, resting her cheek on his chest, drinking in the essence of him for a long, aching moment, before disengaging herself. 'I'm sorry to disturb you but I have something very important to show you.'

He shrugged. 'I was working on the plans for the modernisation of Nikki's estates. We are thinking of trialling them on one of the smaller manors first. I have in mind appointing one of my ex-comrades to oversee matters. It is an important but rather dry task, so I am glad of the distraction. What is that you have there?' She handed him the volume of Culpeper's *English Physician*. 'One of your herbal texts?' Aleksei said, frowning over the ornate frontispiece.

'No, Catiche just gave me it as a thank you for saving Ortipo.'

She went on to explain the morning's events. 'Where on earth would she come by such a thing?' Aleksei asked when she had finished.

She braced herself. 'I'm afraid that it was yet another keepsake that Catiche "liberated" from her mother's bedchamber.'

It took a few seconds for her meaning to dawn on him, but when it did, Aleksei let slip the weighty tome, catching it just in time before it dropped to the floor before sinking on to the window seat, looking quite astounded. 'This was in Elizaveta's room?' He stared at the book, holding it now as if it was about to explode in his face. 'Is it in there, Wolf's Bane?'

And when Allison opened the text at the relevant page, he paled. 'Proof positive that my brother was murdered by his own wife, and with malice aforethought too. My wards' mother was a cold-blooded murderess.' Shock and anger turned his Baltic-blue eyes to ice. 'The children, they must never, ever—dear God, they must never have so much as an inkling of this.'

'Of course not!'

He stared down at the page for long minutes, dark thoughts flitting across his countenance. When finally he closed the pages, his face was set and extremely grim. 'So, I have the definitive answer I sought after all. The timing is most serendipitous.'

He did not sound in the least happy. Allison's heart sank. 'What do you mean?'

His reply made it feel as if her heart was breaking. 'I had word from the docks this morning. There is a ship sailing for England in four days, and there won't be another for some time. With your permission I will reserve the best cabin possible for you.'

'Four days?'

Aleksei covered her hands with his again. 'We agreed last night...'

'I am not—I know we did. It is just that it is so soon.'

'Winter can set in very quickly here. It would be prudent to travel while you can.'

Winter, when the canals and rivers froze. Aleksei would take the children out on one of the sleighs. Though *that* sleigh was unlikely to be used. She must not think of *that* sleigh. 'Then it makes sense,' Allison said, unable to disguise the tears which clogged her throat. 'Will I tell the children?'

'I will tell them. I will write to Madame Orlova, asking her to resume her post forthwith.'

'That is—that is very efficient.'

'Allison.'

He sounded as wretched as she felt. No, not quite as wretched, for while he had put a rein on his feelings, hers had bolted away with her. She loved him so much. Too much to hurt him.

'You're right,' she said, relieved to find that she had command of her voice again. 'The sooner the better. Best not to prolong—you're right, Aleksei, it's what we agreed to last night.' She managed to pin a smile to her face. 'I have plans to make, many plans. A dispensary to open. Oh, and one to close. There is so little time, I don't think...'

'Leave that with me. You are irreplaceable but I'm sure I'll find a competent substitute to carry on your fine work.'

'You flatter me. No one is indispensable. I'm sure there are skilled herbalists out there.'

'Perhaps, but they will not be you.'

She should be pleased he valued her so highly. She was pleased, she was, and it was very foolish indeed of her to feel hurt. Anna Orlova would take her place in the schoolroom. Some other herbalist would take her place in the dispensary. She could live with that. But would Aleksei also substitute someone else for her in his bed? She was much less sanguine about that prospect. Would he take another mistress, or would he start his search for a suitable wife, just as soon as her ship sailed? A woman of breeding suitable to bear the Derevenko name, an aunt for the Derevenko heirs, a mother to Aleksei's own children.

A tear trickled down her cheek. She brushed it away angrily. 'It seems you have everything well in hand.'

'Allison, you must not be thinking...'

But she shook her head. The dam of her

feelings was threatening to break and she was desperate to escape to the sanctuary of her bedchamber and burrow under the sheets. 'I'm not thinking anything. Save that I meant it, I am pleased that you have contingency plans and I shall not be missed too much.'

'You know that's not true.'

But she brushed him aside. 'I need to—the children—their lessons—my dispensary—I need to go and do—I need to go.' From somewhere deep inside her, she summoned a brittle smile. 'One last thing. Promise me you will not be too hard on Catiche, Aleksei. About the text, I mean. She is no thief. She is more like a magpie, stockpiling memories in the form of keepsakes. Like the miniatures.'

Aleksei stood unmoving in the centre of the room, staring at the door Allison had closed softly behind her, forcing himself to ignore the impulse to run after her, the urgent need to pull her into his arms, to kiss her, to soothe her, to dry her tears. What was the point? A fleeting comfort that was all it would achieve. And the danger of doing what he had promised he would not do, and beg her to stay till spring. Because she would love St Petersburg in the snow. Because then there would be time for her to properly train up someone to take over the dispensary. Because she could ensure that Madame Orlova continued with the children's new, physically active regime, while resuming their lessons. Good, practical reasons. But trivial compared to the real reason. He desperately wanted her to stay for him. Selfish? Yes. Irrefutably true? Absolutely!

And yet he did resist, though it took almost all of his self-control. He forced himself to sit back behind the desk, staring at the astounding, incontrovertible evidence that Elizaveta had murdered Michael. That a Derevenko duchess had murdered a Derevenko duke. In any other St Petersburg family, it would not be so shocking. The history of the Imperial family was littered with heinous crimes. But his family name was beyond reproach. There had never been any scandal attached to the Derevenko name.

He still struggled to believe that Elizaveta had taken a lover. What kind of a man would dare to bed her? Who was he? Where might he find the answer to that question? Why in a magpie's nest of course!

He jumped to his feet and was halfway across the room before pulled himself up short, recalling Allison's warning. Catiche must not be made to feel she had done any wrong. He would tell her that he wanted to get to know her mother better through her keepsakes—yes, that was it, and dammit, it was the truth too! There was a chance, just the tiniest chance, that Catiche unwittingly held the answer to the final question.

It was late afternoon when Aleksei sent for Allison. He was in his study, in formal dress, motioning her to take the chair on the opposite side of the desk. 'What is it? What has happened?'

He handed her a cup of sweetened tea and sat down. 'You would not believe—I still cannot believe it myself.' Drinking his own brew in one gulp, he set down the plain china cup. 'After you left, I got to wondering what else Catiche had appropriated from her mother's rooms. Do not worry,' he added hastily, 'I promise you, I did not accuse her of anything save missing her mama. Which she does, just as you told me, much more than I had realised.'

'Your relationship with your own mother was so very different, Aleksei.'

'As was yours, yet you understood. I have much to learn.'

'So you have decided…'

'I am beginning to think that I have no option. Hear me out. You will understand why soon enough. Amongst other trinkets, a handkerchief, a bottle of scent, a few buttons, Catiche had this in her little collection of memorabilia.'

He pushed a leather-bound scrapbook towards her. Inside there were sketches of the children, cuttings of their hair, ribbons, little childish notes, all pasted into the pages with annotations in French, in what Allison assumed must be Elizaveta's handwriting. If ever any doubt had been cast on the extent of the Duchess's love for her children, this touching testimony would put her feelings beyond question. 'No wonder that Catiche took this,' Allison said. 'It is right that she should have it, to share with Elena and Nikki.'

'I agree. But the book does not only contain keepsakes of her children,' Aleksei said, looking very grim. 'If you turn to the last page.'

She did as he bid her. Another lock of hair was pasted there, dark blond, and much coarser than the others, and beside it, what looked like a name, though unlike the rest of the book, the script looked to be Russian. 'What does it mean?'

'*Vezuchiy,*' Aleksei said. 'It means lucky.'

Allison frowned. 'You mean this lock of hair was meant to bring luck? It did not come from one of the children. In fact it looks like yours, though why Elizaveta…'

'Michael's hair was the same colour. It is a trait in the male line of my family.'

'I'm not sure where this is leading.'

'I have a male relative with similar colouring.'

'Your cousin Felix? But why—?' She broke off, staring at Aleksei in horror. 'Felix. It is from the Latin, isn't it? It means…'

'Lucky,' Aleksei said with a pronounced sneer. 'And well named! It is extremely lucky for Felix that I did not call him out when I confronted him earlier this afternoon.'

'Aleksei, you did not hurt him?' Allison said urgently.

'There was no need. The pain was self-inflicted and he is a broken man. I doubt he will ever recover.' He took the keepsake book from her, closing it over. 'Felix is not a murderer, Allison, but he was, inadvertently, the cause of my brother's death. I will explain, but for once, I feel the need to fortify myself with something stronger than tea.' He took the stopper from the decanter which was set on the desk, with two glasses. 'Will you join me in a cognac? You need not fear, it is the proper French vintage, not gut-rot from Michael's cellar.'

'Thank you. Since you seem to think I will require it, then I will.' She took the heavy crystal glass, holding it in readiness, watching with a sense of dread as Aleksei, who seemed to be almost as abstemious as his brother had been reputed to be, swallowed a large measure, and immediately poured himself another. Her mind was wanting to race ahead, but she forced herself to stay calm, for it was clear that was what Aleksei needed most from her.

'Where to start?' he said, twisting his glass around and around on the desk.

She articulated the terrible, shockingly obvious conclusion, to save him the pain of saying it aloud. 'Felix was Elizaveta's lover?'

'My first cousin! The man Michael would have entrusted with the care of his children. The change of the will is explained now. It proves that Michael must have known about their treachery, though my cousin...' His jaw clenched. 'The man whom I used to call my cousin, Felix Golytsin, believed Michael was oblivious. He ended it, he tells me, precisely because he was terrified that Michael might find out. The night before my brother died, Golytsin told Elizaveta that their affaire was madness, that it could not continue. The guilt was eating him up, he said. Though I suspect he was more concerned about saving his scrawny neck.'

'So on the night she was absent from the palace, Elizaveta had been with her lover, just as Anna Orlova suspected and we concluded. He summarily ended the liaison, which would explain her highly distressed state of mind the next day.'

'She did not recognise her mistress,' Aleksei said. 'you remember, that's what the Orlova woman said, and Golytsin said the same. Elizaveta was like a madwoman, he said, talking wildly about them eloping and taking the children with them, and when he pointed out that the outcome would be to destroy all their lives, she simply wouldn't listen. He went to Peterhof, he says, to give her time to come to her senses, to realise that there was no future for them, to accept it was over. I've never seen a man so broken or so consumed by guilt. There is no doubt I think, no matter how wrong it was, that he loved her. Her death added to the remorse he felt, for cuckolding my brother, his nearest relative.' Aleksei thumped the desk with his fist, but with a supreme effort regained his self-control.

'Do you think he suspects foul play?' Allison enquired tentatively.

'He concedes that Michael must have found out somehow, there is no other explanation for the change of will. As to whether he suspects Elizaveta took Michael's life—no, I don't think so. He confessed that he had considered the possibility that she had taken her own after Michael's apoplexy, a case of severe guilt and repentance, but like me, he dismissed the notion. Whatever else Elizaveta was, she loved her children. They had already lost their father…they would need their mother more than ever.'

Allison set down her untouched drink, letting her hand lie on the keepsake book. 'So when she murdered Michael, she was not thinking that she was taking their father from them.'

'No. She was deluding herself into thinking that Golytsin would take Michael's place.'

'And her death—it seems it was an accident after all.'

'It seems so, just as you surmised.' Aleksei

finished his cognac. 'One thing we need not fear, is that Golytsin will talk. My discovery of the affaire was the final straw for him. He intends to resign all his positions at court and retire to the countryside. I can think of no better punishment for a man whose life centred around the Imperial court, than to be exiled from it because of his own actions. It's ironic, isn't it? I knew that such a murder must have had the strongest of motive. I knew that custody of my wards was the strongest of all motives. But I never guessed that love rather than money or power could be at the root of it. A warped kind of love it was, but there is no denying that is what it was all the same.'

'Oh, Aleksei, I don't know what to say.'

He leaned across the desk to clasp her hand. 'You don't have to, Allison, I know your thoughts without you having to speak them.'

That is one of the many things that I love about you. Dear heavens, she sincerely hoped he could not read her every thought.

He stood up, pulling her to her feet to wrap his arms around her. 'It has been, as your grandmother would say, a bit of a day.'

She hugged him tightly. 'You must be exhausted.'

'I'm certainly tired of thinking.'

'We have established a remedy for that. Why don't we meet tonight and I can administer the cure?'

'Light every candle,' Allison said some hours later, turning the key in the lock of the State Bedchamber. 'I want to see you in all your glory.' To see him, to etch the memory in her mind, and to imprint herself on him. She wanted to demonstrate her love for him by truly making love to him. She wanted to show him what she could never allow herself to say.

Light flickered from every sconce, every candlestick in the huge chamber, reflecting the rich gold and blue hues of the furnishings in the gilded mirrors. As she stepped into Aleksei's arms, Allison could see their entwined figures reflected too, his dark-blond head, her auburn, bending towards each other, and then their lips met, and she forgot about their reflection, and concentrated on the reality.

Their lips clung, their kisses not yet passionate but the kisses of two people seeking to banish the world, to forget themselves, to find succour in each other. Sweet kisses that went on and on and on, making her head spin, making her body pliant, bending and shaping itself into him. Her hands fluttered over the short, rough hair at the back of his head, down to the breadth of his shoulders, the length of his back, to rest on the firm slope of his buttocks. How she loved this man. How very much she loved him.

He tangled his fingers in her hair, scattering pins, combing through her curls as they cascaded free. His hands caressed her, flattening over her back, the dip of her waist, the curve of her bottom, back up to her breasts. And all the time their lips clung. Deep kisses. Licking kisses. Soft kisses. And then kisses that became darker. Their breath became shallow. Desire leapt inside her, a sudden flame, an aching tension, but when Aleksei began to unfasten her gown, she stopped him.

'Wait. You first.' She smiled up at him, a smile that was deliberately teasing, sinful, confident of her effect, rewarded with an answering, dark gleam in his eyes.

He cast off his coat, and at her behest, his breeches, boots and waistcoat too. Allison shivered in anticipation as she untied his stock, leaving only his shirt to cover his modesty. But only just. She slid her hands under the soft fabric to cup the taut muscles of his buttocks, pulling him against her, arching herself into the hard length of his erection, then kissing him again. A different kiss. A heated kiss, that he responded to with heat, but she slowed him, leading him through the strange little gate that guarded the bed, easing him on to it, standing between his legs. More kisses. The hardness of him against her belly, through her gown, was the sweetest ache.

'Your shirt,' she said, watching him, letting her desire show blatantly on her face as he lifted it, watching the ripple of his muscles, belly and chest, as he raised it over his head, then watching, simply staring for a long moment as he sat before her naked, while she was fully dressed. Even this was shockingly arousing.

He waited, sensing that that was what she wanted. No need to tell him. Another one of the things she loved about him. He waited while she removed her gown, slowly peeling it down her body, enjoying the way he watched her, registering the sharp intake of his breath as it slid to the ground. She turned around, and he unlaced her corsets, kissing her neck, his hands smoothing over the fullness of her breasts, circling her nipples through her chemise, making her moan, arch backwards against him.

And then she turned, pushing him back on the bed, discarding her chemise, now dressed only in her stockings and garters, to straddle him. More kisses. His mouth. His eyes. His mouth. She could never have enough of his mouth. Then his throat. His chest. His nipples. Did he like to have her do what he did to her? Sucking. Licking. Circling. Undoubtedly.

More kisses. Slowly easing herself down his body, licking and kissing her way from the dip of his rib cage to the rippling muscles of his belly, then back again, shuddering as her nipples grazed his skin, aware all the time of his bright blue gaze fixed on her, waiting, watching, taking his cue from her, stoking her confidence and her desire. She loved him so much. So very much.

She hesitated only briefly as she came to the soft line of dark-blond hair arrowing down from his navel. Kisses. She remembered the shocking delight of the kisses he had given her, and though her only clue was to echo that, her desire to make tonight unique, and to know all of him, gave her the confidence to continue. Sliding down from the bed between his legs, she felt the shock of his response in the way he said her name, and feared she had made a mistake. 'Did I—don't you want me to?'

'I want only what you want. You don't have to…'

'Oh, but I want to,' she said, sure now, very sure. 'I want to.'

Kisses. The sleek muscles of his thighs. Then between. Kisses. And touch. Trailing fingers, making him contract, the lightest of kisses, making him shudder, and then her tongue, licking, eliciting a deep, feral groan. Kisses, along the satiny length of him, and then deeper kisses, daring to do what she had never dreamed of, aroused by his pulsing, throbbing arousal to more, until he cried out, begging her to stop because he didn't want it to be over, not yet. And because she didn't want it ever to end, she did stop, kissing her way back up his body to meet his mouth once more.

Their passion had never been like this. Not so feverish. Not so all-consuming. And not so desperate, as if there was a clock ticking down the hours. How she loved him. She loved him. She loved him. Hands and mouths clinging, skin to skin. When he slid his hands between her legs to stroke her, she ignited, tipping into a climax that shook her to her core, and still they kissed.

But she wanted more now, urging him, crying out with surprised delight when he wrapped her leg over his, still lying side by side, and slid into her, pulling her tight around him.

Different *frissons*, as he began to rock against her, inside her, a gentle, slow, pulsing movement that set her pulsing too once more, her muscles clenching around him. She watched her own arousal reflected on his face, in the dilation of his pupils, in the slashes of colour on his cheeks, the way his eyes finally fluttered closed, and the thickening inside her, the deep, guttural moan of his that she had come to know presaged his own climax. She clung, lost to the consequences, digging her fingers into the muscles of his back, her heel on his buttock, she clung as he pulsed, rocked, and with a deep shudder and a cry his release took him, but not before he pulled himself free.

Honourable to the very last, she thought, kissing his chest, twining herself back around him. She kissed him again, burrowing her face in his chest, where it seemed to her she could smell the very essence of him.

Chapter Thirteen

It was very late. Aleksei stared out of his bed-chamber window at the dark garden. Tonight, they had made love again in the State Bedchamber they had claimed for their own, as they had for the last three nights. Their passion had an increasingly desperate edge to it, an intensity that left him feeling stripped bare, raw, and strangely complete. He had never before surrendered himself so absolutely in this way, never lost himself so utterly. He'd never felt like this before and never imagined that he could feel like this. It was as if their lovemaking merged more than their bodies.

Though they never spoke of it. There was no need to, he'd thought. Until three nights ago. Day one of the countdown to her departure. It had been different that night. Allison had been different. Not only what she'd done—by all the stars, what she had done!—but—he couldn't explain it.

Aleksei frowned out at the darkness. It wasn't only the intensity, it was the intimacy. He'd never felt so close to anyone, while making love and in the aftermath. He wanted to hold her, so close there was no space between them, so close that their skin stuck like glue, but Allison—afterwards, it was as if she withdrew from him. Though he liked to believe he could read her every thought, there were obviously some she kept from him.

He leant his forehead against the cold window frame. Dammit, wasn't it simple enough? They had agreed, hadn't they, that they were already in too deep! It was why she was leaving sooner rather than later. Their affaire had always been just that, an affaire. He would miss her like the devil, wouldn't he? So it was safe to assume she would miss him. He knew that, of course he did, though he couldn't bear the thought of causing her pain. He'd do anything to spare her hurt, no matter the cost to himself. It was why he was letting her go, when what he wanted…

Aleksei cursed furiously and fluently in Rus-

sian. What he wanted was entirely irrelevant.
Duty, that was what had always driven him,
though fortunately for him, it had coincided
with his love of the army. Now his duty lay
here, with his wards. It was what his brother
had wanted, and since he'd done with the army,
and unlike Allison, had no other future mapped
out, then his duty was what he would do. Even
though it meant giving up…

Once again, he swore long and viciously. No
point in thinking such things. No point in imagining a place where his and Allison's worlds
could collide because such a place did not exist.
If it did, though, if there was, what a glorious
place it would be. And oh, how he ached with
the wanting of it.

Cursing again, unable to imagine sleeping,
Aleksei quit his chamber, heading as he had
done so many times in the past, for the boathouse, and the rowing boat, and the peaceful
solitude of St Petersburg at night. His St Petersburg. The rhythmic splash of his oars working hard against the flow calmed him. It was a
cold, crisp autumn night, presaging the arrival
of winter, earlier than usual. Above him the sky
was a canopy of stars. He'd never have an opportunity now, to row Allison all the way up

river, to show her the magical view of St Petersburg, like an island rising out of the mist. They would never race through the snow in his troika. They would never glide along the frozen canals on skates. He loved her so much. So very, very much.

Overwhelmed, Aleksei pulled the oars in, throwing his head back to stare up at the stars. His heart felt too big for his chest. He felt sick and elated and defeated and at the same time oddly free. He loved her. '*Zvezda moya*, Allison. *Lyubov moya*.'

My star. My love. From the first moment she'd walked into the room, he had felt it, that tether pulling them together, unlike anything he'd ever known before. Unlike anything he'd ever know again.

He loved her. Every muscle ached with the urge to run to her, to sweep her into his arms and to kiss her, and to say the words over and over and over. And that's when he finally understood. The way she seemed to retreat from him after their lovemaking. The way she had refused, when he'd asked her, to stay with him, to spend the night in his arms. If they made love right now, he'd tell her. If he woke with her in his arms, he'd tell her. He wouldn't be able to resist. But she had. Because she loved him. Because she didn't want to burden him with her love. Because she would do anything to spare him pain. As he would her.

The rowing boat was drifting back downstream with the tide, but Aleksei dropped his head into his hands, heedless of the movement. He loved her, and she loved him, and it was impossible. One more day, one more night, and she would leave. She would leave Catiche and Elena and Nikki. She would leave the Derevenko Palace and the dispensary she had created. She would leave St Petersburg. And she would leave him behind. For ever.

The children were distraught, and making no attempt to hide it. They had come to him yesterday, a little delegation led by Nikki, with a list they had drawn up of all the reasons why Allison should stay. How different they were, all three of them, despite their sorrow, glowing with health and confidence and wearing their hearts on their sleeves. Gone were the formal manners, that disconcerting way they'd had of looking at him, displaying not quite fear, but something approximating it in the early days. He saw that now. And he saw too that it had been his fault. With no idea how to behave, he had treated them exactly as they'd treated them—with awe, a touch of fear, as if they were alien beings, not simply grieving children.

Allison had seen that from the start. With nothing but her instincts to guide her, she'd seen that what they needed was affection, and though they hadn't made it easy for her, she had persisted. And won them over. Elena and Nikki were forever seeking cuddles from her, and even Catiche, he'd noticed, though she would not make the first move, clung to her governess when a comforting hug was offered. In the last few days, since he had announced the date of Allison's departure, they'd been clinging a great deal more. He'd better make damned sure the Orlova woman overcame her natural reserve and gave them the affection they needed and deserved.

The servants would miss her too, despite the fact they'd been reassured that the dispensary would close only temporarily. Like the children, they had petitioned him to allow Allison to remain. As if it was his decision that she was leaving. As if she did not have a life of her own, thousands of miles away, waiting on her to claim it.

She said she was looking forward to it, and

he believed her. She talked so enthusiastically of her plans, he did not doubt her. But he wondered now, were her feelings mixed? Could she want the impossible, as he did, to embrace both her vocation and their love? Because she did love him. He knew it, was as certain of it as he was now of his love for her.

Aleksei groaned aloud. It was so unfair! So damned unfair! Why must love be the price they paid, she for her vocation, he to do his duty? Though while he was confessing to the stars, why not admit that he no longer saw the children as a burden? Why not admit that he had come to care for them—yes, even to love them! Why not admit that this made it even more impossible, because if he were to stay here as their guardian, to raise them as Michael would have wanted, how much of himself would he be sacrificing, in addition to his heart?

If he gave up everything for the children, sculpting himself to fit the St Petersburg traditions so revered by Michael, he would be miserable, and he would, though it pained him to admit it, come to resent his charges. He would be happy with Allison, of that there was no doubt. He could sacrifice the children instead of himself, leave St Petersburg to live her life with her, in whatever city she chose to settle. But how long before guilt ate away at his happiness? How long before their perfect love became tainted by that guilt? His heart told him it could be done, but his conscience told him the price would be paid not only by himself, but by Allison too.

Though if she felt as he did, if she loved as he did, wouldn't she be paying a bigger price in leaving him? His heart began to race. If she loved him as he did her, wasn't there a part of her that would also be deeply unhappy? Like him, she had always been wed to her vocation. But if she was like him, if they really were cut from the same cloth, could she find room in her life for both?

Like the rowing boat, his mind was slowly turning in circles. Aleksei picked up the oars. There was one thing, one shining truth in all of this, and that was his love for her. If her love for him was the same, then they would find a way. He had no idea how, but they had to find a way to make a life together. They simply had to.

His Illustrious Highness, Natalya informed Allison as she delivered her morning coffee, requested her presence in the Square Room as soon as possible. It was her last day at the palace. The children were planning some event to commemorate it, Allison knew. She only hoped she could keep her composure. Anna Orlova would arrive today to replace her. Later this morning, Allison would hold her last dispensary. She had prepared a list for herself, of patients she must discuss ongoing treatment with and of the stock of everyday remedies she would leave behind. Not that she needed such a list, but it had been something to occupy her in the sleepless nights.

Aleksei probably wanted to put a formal end to their contract. That would be why he'd chosen the Square Room. There was the question of her fee, and perhaps he'd want her to deliver a letter to The Procurer. So that tonight, when they met in the State Bedchamber for the last time, all their business would have been concluded. They would make love for the last time. And then first thing tomorrow…

Tears seeped from her eyes. She tried to wipe them away before Natalya spied them, but it was too late. The maid handed her a white kerchief, her own eyes suspiciously damp. 'I've become—I will miss the children,' Allison sniffed, 'that is all.'

'Of course,' Natalya agreed, 'that must be it.'

By the time she reached the door she was, she persuaded herself, quite composed, and by the time she entered the Square Chamber, she was determined to remain so.

Unlike Aleksei, who looked as if he had not slept, and whose hand shook as he handed her a cup of tea. 'What is wrong?'

For a moment he simply stared at her, shaking his head. Then he laughed, a harsh, painful sound. 'Everything.'

She set her cup down. 'Aleksei?'

'No.' He squeezed her fingers, but then gently pushed her away. 'Sit down. I need to—I can't speak when you—please, sit down. I need to talk to you.'

She felt sick with a sense of foreboding. He was leaving today, she thought. He was leaving her to say her goodbyes without him. They did not have one more night. Last night had been their last. Every fibre of her being protested. She opened her mouth to speak, to beg, then closed it again. If this was what he wanted, if this was the easiest way for him, then she would find a way to cope. Allison sat down on a sofa, reaching for her teacup.

'I can't let you go.'

Her dainty Sèvres china smashed to the floor. 'What?'

Aleksei stood as if rooted to the spot. 'Not without telling you. I can't let you go without telling you.'

'What?' Her sick stomach was joined by a racing heart. 'Telling me what, Aleksei?'

His fists clenched an unclenched. 'No, that's the wrong way around. I thought I had it straight.'

Shaking his head when she made to speak, he headed automatically for the samovar, though he made no attempt to make himself tea and indeed, Allison noticed, there were already two full cups set down on the side table. With extreme difficulty, she restrained the urge to jump to her feet and to demand once more that he explain himself. He needed time to order his thoughts. So she took one of the untouched cups of tea and sipped it, noticing abstractedly how much she had come to enjoy the drink, even Aleksei's sugarless version of it, and she pretended to study the carpet, watching through her lashes as he paced from the samovar to the back of the Square Room and back again. Twice. Three times. Then he came to a halt and squared his shoulders, and Allison braced herself.

'Last night,' Aleksei said, sitting carefully down opposite her, 'it was last night I finally realised. I should have known, I suppose it was perfectly obvious if I'd asked myself, but I didn't, not until last night. I went out on the river,' he added, as if that explained it all. 'After we—after you retired to bed. I couldn't sleep.'

'Nor I.'

'No.' He touched her knee. 'I thought not.'

'There is so little time left,' she said.

He nodded. 'Exactly.' A fleeting smile. 'That's one of the things that made me see sense. Not the time, or lack of it, I mean that we think the same. I don't have to explain myself.'

'Not normally. But at the moment I'm failing dismally in understanding you.'

He laughed. 'Bear with me. It is all—you see, I don't have answers.'

'Then tell me the questions, Aleksei.'

'Yes, that is a good way to start.' He sighed. 'Some are obvious enough. Should I honour Michael's wishes and remain the children's guardian?'

'I think we know the answer to that,' Allison said softly.

'Yes. I think you knew before I did that it was what I would choose in the end. Even Grigory realised that.'

'It is a choice then? It is not simply your sense of duty which compels you?'

'You are thinking of your mother. I thought of her too. It is duty, it would be a lie to say otherwise, but it is also a choice. It is what I want.'

'Because you are an honourable man,' Allison said sadly. Hadn't she known that from the first? Though her heart ached for him, and what his honour would cost him. 'Aleksei, are you sure? It will mean living the life here in St Petersburg which you have never chosen to do. More than that, you have always rejected the city completely.'

'I know. Which brings me to the next question. Must it be so? Don't look so surprised, you are the one who has always questioned…'

'But you never have. You have always said that Michael would expect…'

'Michael is dead.' Aleksei drank down the remaining, cold cup of tea. 'The only thing I know from his will is that he wanted me to take care of his children. What I know from you, and from the children, is that he loved them. And what I know from Catiche—because I have asked her. After the ball, I spoke to her, Allison. What I know is that they know no other life. It is a cossetted and privileged life. It is one which is the envy of most. But they have no concept of any other life. You saw them at the food market. They won't choose any other life because they have nothing to compare it with.' He laughed. 'I can see from your face that I have astonished you.'

'In a good way, I promise. In a very good way. What are you proposing, then?'

'I have no idea. That is one of the many things which I hope we can—but it's not the most important, Allison.'

We? Had she misheard. She must not hope. To hope would be folly. Besides, it was not only the children who...

'It's not only the children,' Aleksei said, joining her on the sofa and taking her hands in his. 'It is you, and what you are destined to be, what you must do, or you will be miserable.'

She smiled crookedly at him. 'You have always understood that about me.'

'And admired you for it. And known I would never seek to dissuade you.'

'No. Any more than I would change you, and

your sense of honour.' So this really was good-bye, after all.

'I would not change you, but I wonder if there is a way for you to fulfil your destiny here, rather than elsewhere?'

'I—you want me to stay? Here, in St Petersburg? You want me to—to keep the dispensary at the palace open? Is that it?'

There was a light in his eyes she didn't recognise. His hands tightened on hers. 'That wouldn't be enough for you.'

'No, not in the long run, but...'

'I can't ask you to give up your dream, Allison, but I am asking you if you might find a way to make your dream come true here?' He broke off once more, cursing under his breath. 'You know, I think after all that I did start this conversation with the most important thing, only I put it the wrong way. It is not that I can't let you go, *lyubov moya*, because I will, if it is what you want. But I don't want to let you go. Because I love you.'

Her heart leapt. No, she must have misheard. 'What did you call me?'

'*Lyubov moya*. My love.'

'You love me.' She closed her eyes. This was a dream. She opened them again. There was no such thing as love light shining. That could not be what she was seeing.

'I love you with all my heart. And unlike you, I knew from the moment I admitted it to myself that I wouldn't be able to keep it a secret.'

'You love me.' She was feeling dazed. Dazzled. Were her eyes shining like his? 'What do you mean, keep it a secret? How did you guess? When did you guess?'

'Am I right?'

'Of course you're right. When did you…?'

But her words were smothered, as he swept her into his arms and kissed her. Kissed her in a way that left her in no doubt. She wrapped her arms around his neck and kissed him back, in exactly the same way. It was a very long, heartfelt kiss. When they finally drew apart, it was to smile at each other in a way that could only be described as besotted.

'You love me,' Allison said, no longer a question but an astonished, delightful statement of the truth.

'And you love me,' Aleksei said, sounding just as vehement as she did.

So much so that they laughed. And then they kissed. And then they kissed again. And it was a long while before they stopped kissing, their breaths ragged.

'But, Aleksei,' Allison said gently, as reality reared its unwelcome head, 'I still don't understand what you're suggesting.'

'I have no idea, my darling. Last night I was in despair, trying to find a solution that would make everyone happy, but there is none. There is only one truth. If we love each other, then we will be happier together than apart. So we will have to find a way of being together.'

She laughed. 'You make it sound easy.'

'No.' He took her hands, kissing her knuckles. 'It won't be easy. There will be sacrifice on both our parts. I must remain in St Petersburg for at least part of the year, in Russia on Nikki's various estates for most of it, which would require you to give up your country. Neither of us will be as free as we would wish, we will be forced to compromise, there will be times when we are forced to follow other people's rules. But because we will not follow all those rules, there is bound to be upset and pain. It won't be easy. But if you will stay with me and the children, if you will consent to be my wife…'

'No.' The stars fell from Allison's eyes. 'I'm sorry, Aleksei, I cannot marry you.'

His face too fell, quite ludicrously. 'You told me that you never would. You told me that your vocation came first, and I understand that. I am not asking you to give it up, nor even suggesting that we add to the family we will have…'

'It's not that. It's not that I don't want to marry you, my love.' She brushed the rebellious kink of his hair back, kissing him briefly on the lips. 'It's not that I won't marry you, it's that I can't. There is more than enough room in my heart for my work and for you. But if you married me, my darling, my precious darling, it would ruin you, and it would be the blight on the Derevenko name that you have worked so hard to prevent.'

'No!' He leapt to his feet, a pulse beating in his throat, looking so angry that she flinched. 'You cannot imagine that I would care about your name, about your—your lineage…'

'Aleksei, that is precisely the point. I have no name. I have no lineage. I am not even of legitimate birth.' She got to her feet, taking his hands, giving him a little shake to force him to meet her eyes. 'And you do care. Look at the lengths you have gone to, to protect your family name. Think of the scandal, if you married a complete nonentity, and think of how much more scandal there would be if my origins—or lack of them—were discovered. They tolerate me as your mistress, but as your wife—no.'

'But I don't want you to be my mistress, Allison. I'm an honourable man. You've just told me you wouldn't change that. I honour you, I honour our love, I want to honour it in public, and I won't have it demeaned. If you have no objection to being my wife...'

'It's impossible,' she said wretchedly. 'Society would shun us.'

He did not deny this. Instead, he poured himself another cup of tea, frowning heavily, drinking it in one draught as usual. 'What if you could establish a status here, on your own terms. Not in society, but as part of society, accepted by society, would you marry me then?'

She sipped from her own cup. 'I cannot change my heritage.'

'But you could forge a new one,' Aleksei said eagerly. 'One that made the old one irrelevant.'

'How?'

'I don't know. Set your dispensary up here in the city—there must be at least as many needy citizens in St Petersburg as London. Take on apprentices, involve some of our society ladies as patronesses. There is nothing this hypocritical court likes so much as being seen to support a good cause, provided they don't have to get their hands dirty.'

Allison stared at him in astonishment. 'Are you teasing me?'

'No. Yes. No. Do you think it's a good idea? Could you do it?'

'I think it is genius. I think it could be done, if...' She bit her lip, but now was not the time for holding back. 'Aleksei, what about you? You need a purpose too.'

'Oh, I shall transform Nikki's estates for him.'

'That is already in hand, you told me.'

'Yes, but only on a very small scale so far. Nikki, my love, has some very, very large estates.'

'Big enough to need dispensaries for the servants?'

He gave a shout of laughter. 'Big enough to need some huge dispensaries.'

'So you won't be spending all your time in St Petersburg?'

'No, but I am not proposing to travel alone. We will all go. It will be good for Nikki, young as he is, to understand exactly what it is he's going to inherit.'

Allison sighed. 'You make it all sound so—so easy. And so wonderful. Do you think it can work?'

Aleksei shrugged, laughed, shook his head, smiled. 'I wish I could promise you it will, but we don't lie to each other, do we? I think we would be mad not to try. Now will you marry me?'

She was so very tempted. But it was such a huge risk, and there were so many other uncertainties. 'A year,' Allison said. 'In a year's time, if we are happy here, truly happy, and we can see a future that will keep us all happy, then ask me again.'

Aleksei checked his watch. 'Fair enough. A year exactly from today. I will expect you here, in the Square Room, with a yes on your lips.'

'Provided we are…'

'Allison, do you doubt that we will be happy?'

'No. But I doubt…'

'Have faith, my darling, because you are destined to be Countess Derevenko.'

The way he looked at her made her believe they could do anything together. The way he looked at her made her heart leap, made her pulses flutter, made her want to cast all her doubts aside and say that she would marry him now, become that impossible-to-imagine creature, the Countess Derevenko. But she couldn't. She needed proof that they could find a way to be happy, and though he might not realise it, he needed it too. 'A year,' she said, wrapping her arms around his waist. 'It is a great deal to achieve in a year.'

'And a very long time to wait before I can call you my wife.'

He smiled down at her, tucking an escaped curl behind her ear. 'My heart says damn the consequences and marry the woman now. My head tells me that there are too many uncertainties for us to follow our hearts just yet. We think the same, you see. That is why I know it will work.'

'I love you so much, Aleksei.' She smiled up at him. 'You know I'm not suggesting that we—that we discontinue our—our—I mean I'm not suggesting that we refrain, for a year...'

He gave a shout of laughter. 'Miss Galbraith, are you propositioning me?'

She pursed her lips, pretending to consider this. 'Count Derevenko, I do believe I am.'

Epilogue

$\underline{\mathcal{CON2O}}$

St Petersburg—December 1816

Allison gazed at her reflection in the long mirror. Her hair was in one of Natalya's deceptively simple coiffures, elegantly high on her head, with artful curls permitted to fall seemingly at random. Diamonds glittered in the myriad of hairpins—her one concession, save for the gown, to her new status.

Natalya had offered pearls as a compromise to Allison's usual plain pins, but pearls, Seanmhair had always claimed, were for tears, if worn at a wedding. Allison was determined there would be no tears. Not even happy ones.

She touched her locket. What on earth would her grandmother make of today's events? Ordinary is for life's passengers, hadn't she always said? Allison smiled to herself. She couldn't think of anything more extraordinary than the fact that she was about to become a countess. As long as she didn't get too big for her boots in the process, she reckoned Seanmhair would approve.

Unlike some of St Petersburg's society. There were many who had come round to acceptance, to recognise Allison's honorary status earned by dint of her reputation as a pioneer and crusader for the provision of medical care for ordinary Russians. The poor called her a saint. The court was cynical enough to bask in reflected glory by endorsing her. She and Aleksei had not attempted to make St Petersburg their own, but they had succeeded in making their own St Petersburg.

Though none of society, accepting or no, would be here today. Only the children, the Derevenko household, and Grigory Fyodorovski would attend. Which, when you counted all the household mind you, amounted to a great many pairs of eyes. But they would all be sympathetic and they would all highly approve.

Allison gave a final twirl in front of the mirror. Her gown of cream silk had long sleeves and a high collar with an overdress of specially woven cream lace as fine as a spider's web. Tiny flowers of gold thread were embroidered on the cuffs and hem. There was a cream, fur-lined cloak to match, and a huge fur muff too, to keep her warm on the journey they would make later. Under her gown, the spider's web lace trimmed her chemise and her garters. Silk undergarments, which rustled seductively as she walked, and which she knew Aleksei would take great delight in discovering and uncovering.

A blush stole over her cheeks. Her eyes in the mirror lit up. Aleksei. *'Lyubov moy,'* she whispered. My love.

Mindful of Natalya's dire warnings about crushing her gown, Allison rustled over to the window. Outside the garden was white, a velvet-soft carpet of snow. Aleksei had proposed in the Square Room precisely a year after he had promised he would, and precisely a year after she had promised a response, she had said yes.

Such a year it had been. A year of sacrifice and compromise, just as they had known it would be, but one of such joy and happiness too. To be loved, unequivocally loved, was the most liberating feeling. To have someone always on your side, to have someone you could rely on always to tell you the truth, to tell you when you were right and when you were wrong, to counsel you on when to concede and when to stand strong, knowing that first and foremost they had your best interests at heart. Well, that had not been such an easy lesson to learn for either of them, now she thought of it. They were both so accustomed to making all their own decisions, taking advice as interference. They had disagreed. But slowly, as the months passed, the disagreements became discussions.

They had not achieved everything, but they had made a start on all of it. Small dispensaries at five of Nikki's transformed estates, as well as the main dispensary in the city, with an apprentice in each working under Allison's supervision. It meant Aleksei had been away from St Petersburg a great deal, but sometimes she went with him, sometimes the children too. And when they did not, his homecomings were worth the time spent apart.

She had three active and four reluctant patronesses for her dispensaries. When Allison's name was mentioned at court, Grigory said, it was with a mixture of awe and astonishment. She knew, because she asked him, and he was a man who lied abysmally, that there was gossip. But it was, he assured her, more of a jealous nature than a disdainful one. For once her ancestry was in her favour. The Scots were commanding Russia's navy, building the ships they sailed in, and Allison was one of a long line of Scots in the medical profession here in the city. She was part of a benign invasion, Grigory informed her with one of his hearty guffaws, the Scots' latest weapon, in their plan to capture Mother Russia, by capturing the heart of one of the country's most eligible bachelors.

Grigory was incorrigible, but he had been a staunch supporter from the start, proving himself first and foremost a loving uncle, for he could see what others cared not to, that the union would be what was best for his nieces and nephew. Allison was hopeful that he would be proved right. Anna Orlova had been joined by extra tutors, in an attempt to counterbalance the governess's highly inflated opinion of her charges' heritage. History of all sorts other than the Derevenko one, was now taught to the children. The girls attended one of the bigger schools one day a week, and in the spring, Nikki would be permitted to attend military academy for a term. There would be no lessons in estate management until he was able to decide for himself that was what he wanted, Aleksei said. Choices, that was what he wanted for all of them. It was early days to speculate about what choices they might make. And besides, she had a great many other things to think about right now.

Such as her wedding. She turned away from the window to survey her bedchamber, which she would leave for the last time today. The Count and Countess Derevenko had a new suite, in a different, distant part of the palace. But they would not be occupying it tonight. A soft rap on the door, and Natalya arrived, telling her to hurry. It was time. She wouldn't want to keep His Illustrious Highness waiting.

'No, but I know he will wait,' Allison said, giving the maid a hug. 'Wish me luck.'

Natalya pinned the wispy laced veil to her hair. 'You won't need it.'

The Derevenko private chapel was clad entirely in marble. White and black in the form of the Derevenko crest on the floor. The walls, the high-arched ceiling, and the supporting pilasters were white, throwing into stark relief the stunning Byzantine images which adorned the ornate altar. But Allison had eyes only for the man waiting there for her. Aleksei wore blue and gold. A blue coat with gold buttons. A gold waistcoat. Blue pantaloons. Long black highly polished boots. Plain attire for a count. But this Count, Allison thought as she gazed at him down the short aisle of the Derevenko chapel, could have worn rags and still taken her breath away. He smiled, and her fluttering nerves vanished. She smiled back. A few short steps, and she would be his and he would be hers. Count and Countess, plain Mr and Mrs, she didn't care a whit.

'Ready?' she asked of her escorts.

Nikki nodded solemnly, taking up one side of the heavy gold casket which contained the rings. Catiche hurriedly grabbed the other, as it almost slipped from his grasp. They had been arguing for weeks over who was to have the privilege, and Aleksei had decreed that they decide for themselves. Where was Elena, though—was she sulking after being excluded? A yelp betrayed her arrival. Allison saw her own laughter reflected in Aleksei's eyes, as she appeared with the bulldog on a silk leash. 'Ortipo is a member of the family too,' Elena said. 'It is my duty to make sure he behaves himself impeccably.'

'And a very important duty it is too,' Allison said, nodding solemnly. For the first—and most likely the only—time in her life, she found herself extremely grateful for the bulldog's presence.

It was a short, but emotional ceremony. The new Count and Countess Derevenko remained only for a brief champagne toast leaving their guests to celebrate the long-awaited nuptials by feasting and dancing, while the couple left to celebrate in their own way, alone. Aleksei drove them from the palace in his troika. It was twilight, the stars only just beginning to come out as they sped across the snow. Allison tucked into his side, watched breathlessly as he handled the three horses with seeming ease, the cold air stinging her cheeks, the glow inside her making her oblivious of the rapidly falling temperature.

The troika turned up a long carriage way, gliding to a halt in front of a house built to resemble a Chinese pagoda. 'What is this place?' Allison asked.

'Ours,' he answered. 'Do you like it?'

'It is ridiculous. It is beautiful. I love it. Is it really ours?'

'I thought we needed a retreat. Somewhere no one—not even the children—are permitted.'

'I can't wait to explore it.'

'Later, my Countess.' He leapt down from the carriage, pulling the furs aside, helping her down to the front step, where a carpet had been set out, the door waited ajar, and a groom appeared from nowhere to lead the horses away.

'Aleksei.' She looked up at him, a smile trembling on her lips. 'I love you so much. I can't quite believe that we are married.'

He kissed her then, his lips icy from the journey. 'Nor can I. I think we need proof, don't you?'

'Yes.' Ridiculous to be nervous, this was Aleksei, but she was none the less. 'Is it silly to say that it feels like the first time?'

He kissed her again, pulling her tightly up against him. 'It is the first time. Now I am truly yours, and you are truly mine. For always.'

'Always.' She reached up to smooth the rebellious kink in his hair. 'It is a family trait, this little question mark,' she said. 'Your brother's hair was the same. And Nikki's too. I wonder…' She bit her lip on the question she had been asking herself for months, but it felt—yes, it felt right to raise it on this most auspicious day. 'Aleksei, it is not that we need anything else to make our love perfect, but…'

'*Lyubov moya.*' A smile dawned on him—one she had never seen before. 'Are you telling me that you would like us to have a child of our own?'

She nodded. 'I've been thinking—wanting…'

'Why did you not say?'

'You've been thinking the same?'

He nodded. 'But you said that you had never…'

'And you said you had never…'

'Not until I met you.'

Tears filled her eyes. Tears of joy. But she was not having tears on her wedding day. Allison blinked them away furiously. 'I love you, Aleksei.'

'And I love you, Your Illustrious Highness.' Aleksei grinned at the shock on her face. He scooped her up into his arms, holding her high against his chest. 'Let me show you just how much.'

* * * * *

Historical Note

I've never visited St Petersburg, but after all the reading I've done researching this book I feel as if I have. If you're interested in knowing more about the history of this hotbed of plotting and poison, intrigue, factions, sexual shenanigans and perversities, then I'd highly recommend Simon Sebag Montefiore's wonderful book, *The Romanovs*.

I have taken some liberties with real-life historical characters in my story.

I couldn't resist having Princess Katya Bagration—otherwise known as The Naked Angel, or The White Pussycat—visit the Winter Palace. In fact she was still in Vienna at the time, celebrating world peace post-Waterloo with her various lovers.

As to General Arakcheev—I have no idea

whether I've captured the essence of his personality. I confess I imagined him as a much more bloodthirsty version of another famous military man I've given a walk-on part in several of my books, his contemporary the Duke of Wellington.

And the ballroom in the Winter Palace, which became known as the Nicholas Hall, was actually completed some time after Allison and Aleksei made their debut there.

Tom Atkinson's book, *Napier's History of Herbal Healing, Ancient and Modern,* gave me an insight into the world of herbalism at the time when Allison practised. In this book I came across Albert Coffin, herbalist and entrepreneur. 'Coffinism', as it became known, borrowed its model from Albert Coffin's mentor, the American Samuel Thomson. It was effectively a franchise of herbal dispensaries called *Friendly Botanico-Medical Societies*, established in poor industrial areas in the early part of the nineteenth century, and is obviously the inspiration for Allison and Aleksei's dispensary chain.

Though I've located the fictional Derevenko Palace on the site of the Mariinski Palace, the interiors are a mish-mash of rooms from other

Imperial palaces around the city. And as for the ducal barge—it's actually *Gloriana*, the barge built for the ceremonial journey down the Thames made by Queen Elizabeth II on her Diamond Jubilee.

As ever, there's a wealth of research and reading I haven't mentioned, but which I'd be more than happy to chat about on Facebook or Twitter or by email.

Any mistakes or historical inaccuracies in this story are entirely my own.

MILLS & BOON

Coming next month

IN THRALL TO THE
ENEMY COMMANDER
Greta Gilbert

'It is true that I am low,' she began, 'and that I was purchased by the Queen as her slave. As such, I am bound to protect her. But that is not why I do it.'

'Why do you do it, then?' he asked, but she ignored his question.

'You speak of logic. Well, logic tells me not to believe you, for you are a Roman and I have never known a Roman I could trust.'

'You are a woman for certain, for you are ruled by humours and whims,' he growled, aware that his own humours were mixing quite dangerously.

A wave hit the side of the boat, causing it to tilt. To steady herself, she placed her hand over his, igniting an invisible spark.

She glared at him before snapping her hand away and stepping backwards. 'Good Clodius—though I know that is not your name—I would ask that you please not insult my intelligence.'

Her sunny words seemed to grow in their menace. 'I may not be as big as you, or as smart as you, or as sly as you, but believe me when I tell you that I know how to handle Roman men.' She flung her braid behind her as if brandishing a whip. 'If you do anything to endanger the Queen, or our quest to restore her rightful reign, or if your deception results in harm to either the Queen or either of her handmaids, you will be very sorry.'

Her audacity was stunning. No woman had ever spoken to him in such a way.

He refused to give her the satisfaction of revealing his discomposure, however, so he placidly resumed his efforts at the oars, taking care to stay in rhythm.

Still, his troops were in retreat; they had lost the battle. His unlikely adversary had utilised all the tricks of rhetoric, along with the full force of her personality, to enrage him, then confuse him, and then finally to leave him speechless.

Nor was she yet finished. As the great yellow globe shone out over the shimmering sea, he felt her warm breath in his ear. 'Just remember that I have my eye on you, Roman.'

He turned his head and there were her lips, so near to his, near enough to touch.

And in that moment, despite everything, he wanted nothing more in the world than to kiss them.

Continue reading
**IN THRALL TO THE
ENEMY COMMANDER
Greta Gilbert**

Available next month
www.millsandboon.co.uk

LET'S TALK

Romance

For exclusive extracts, competitions
and special offers, find us online:

- **f** facebook.com/millsandboon
- **⊙** @millsandboonuk
- **𝕏** @millsandboon

Or get in touch on 0844 844 1351*

For all the latest titles coming soon, visit
millsandboon.co.uk/nextmonth